RUNNING SCARED

MICHÁEL SELMER

Snowy Range Press

Laramie, Wyoming

Running Scared
Published by Snowy Range Press
PRINT HISTORY
Snowy Range Press edition/ March, 2012

Cover Art:
Damon Za

ISBN: 0984768122
ISBN-13: 978-0-9847681-2-7
Library of Congress Control Number - 2012902014

PRINTED IN THE UNITED STATES OF AMERICA

ERIN!
DON'T LOOK BACK!
Mark Lehner 4-4-16

Dedication

To my Dailymile friends
and to everyone who accepts the challenge to "get out the door" and run.

Contents

Author's Notes

Running is an important part of who I am. It helped me grow from sickly youth into healthy adulthood. My wife and I met because of running and running helped put all four of our children through college. Completing the 2010 Race Across the Sky, a 100-mile endurance event in Leadville, Colorado, gave me the courage to achieve another impossible dream ... write my first novel and become a published author.

It is only natural that I draw inspiration from something that I love. Since my writing is heavily influenced by the likes of Stephen King and Dean Koontz, it is also only natural that the resulting stories have a dark or supernatural twist.

Programmed (originally titled "Keep Running") was written after my wife and I took our first vacation in the Rocky Mountains. As I was driving north from Denver on Interstate 25, the expansive vistas of Colorado and Wyoming awakened an urge in me to stop the car and take off running toward the glittering mountain peaks in the distance.

The Money Clip came to me while out on a run during an unusually warm day in January of 2009 and was inspired by my wife, who really did carry home from various runs all of the things mentioned in that story ... and more.

I enjoy running at night, in part because it is sometimes spooky. In the dark, sounds and shadows make it easy for a person with imagination to get that creepy feeling of being stalked. The Ghost Runners may make you question whether it really is imagination.

Runner's High was written in the mid-90's and was the product of a particularly intense dream I had of a brightly colored tropical bird leading me through a snowstorm.

Road and trail racing are among the fastest growing recreational sports in the world. Although most participants compete only against the clock or their own limitations, there are a few whose hyper-competitive nature lead them astray. I wanted to write a crime story about a character who went too far in order to stay on top and *Driven* was the result.

Ultramarathoners are a breed apart. Although I've done Leadville and other races over the marathon distance, I don't (yet) consider myself one. *Cowboy Joe* was originally going to be an exploration into the psyche of an ultramarathoner. Somewhere in the process it morphed into more of a *Twilight Zone* romance. I had a blast writing it.

As I began to assemble stories for this collection, I realized that most of the ones I had written had fast, athletic main characters. Sheila's Marathon Year was the result of creating a non-athletic character, giving her an impossible challenge, and letting her lead me. Sheila kept me company on many of my runs as I was recovering from the Top of Utah Marathon in the fall of 2011. She was an entertaining companion and I hope you enjoy her story.

A common theme running—you had to see that one coming!—through all of these stories is that a person can accomplish remarkable, and sometimes frightening things when sufficiently motivated. For some, trying to achieve the impossible is part of our nature; for others, it takes a little push. Either way, sometimes we need to remember to keep our hand on the throttle.

Acknowledgments

My sincere thanks to Diane Alexander for her exemplary work in copy-editing this work. Thanks also to my many friends who read and helped improve the final product. I had once thought to list them all here, but that list would have added too many pages and I'm sure I would have missed someone. You know who you are and you have my heartfelt gratitude.

Most importantly, thanks to my wife and children—the youngest will soon turn twenty-eight, but they are all still my children—for taking time out of their hyper-busy schedules to encourage and support my dream.

SHEILA'S
MARATHON YEAR

Prologue—At the Finish

Her shoe slammed into a raised lip of asphalt at the edge of the manhole cover. Like the deep, throbbing vibrations of a massive church bell, a cruel tag-team of pain and fatigue began to climb through her body, drumming on every bone, tendon and muscle. Quivering with exhaustion, Sheila began a slow-motion fall to the pavement, crumbling to her hands and knees.

The tall, dark-haired woman wasn't stunned by the fall, quite the opposite. The sudden arrival of the road in her face served to shake her from a half-conscious daze, driven into her by long miles and an ever-expanding weariness. Her first lucid thoughts were: How did I end up here? Was it all for nothing?

Five million steps. Walking steps. Jogging steps. Running steps. She had endured a full year of training; fighting the heat, rain, wind, cold, snow... and the crippling instability of a divided mind.

Now she was back where she started—on her knees, beaten—she didn't know where she was, where she was going, or how much farther she had to go.

And the day had started so well ...

MILE 0.25

A Crushing Weight

The sun was still hiding below the horizon, unwilling to rise and chase the chill from the air—but the goose bumps on Sheila's arms weren't caused by the cold. A morning fog still clung to the ground, keeping the world shrouded in mystery. That fragile veil would lift as the spring sun burned off the mist; she was less than confident that the mystery that had ruled her life for the last year would be so easily stripped away.

Today, all that she had experienced, everything that she had learned about herself, forgotten about herself ... everything that she had *changed* about herself, would be challenged.

The pack on her shoulders and the water belt around her waist told her that she wasn't coming back. Today was the day she would cross the point of no return.

Sheila placed a Nike Pegasus-clad foot on top of the trashcan and tightened her shoelaces—for the third time. It wasn't that her shoes were loose on her feet; she was stalling, hoping ...

... hoping that Audra would come. Audra had been there for her at the beginning; it didn't feel right that she wasn't here at the end. Sheila remembered when her closest friend, her *only* friend, had walked into her life ...

᳭

The top of the rusted trash can squealed and collapsed under her three hundred eighty-three pounds. Sheila held her breath and cringed. The metal sides were still sturdy, though, so she didn't end up in a heap on the ground. Despite the noise and the late hour, there were no barking dogs or complaints from the neighbors; the trailers nearby were abandoned. In fact, the Sunnyside Meadows Mobile Home Park was all but vacant. A desperate few would probably stay until the bull-dozers came and demolished their sprawling red-neck ghetto to make room for the new Turnpike Industrial Center. It was still a year off, but the smart rats had jumped ship early.

As her enormous body settled and spread over her impromptu stool, Sheila wondered what had possessed her to be sitting on a trashcan in the middle of this low-rent ghost town.

Then she noticed a few things: an ache behind her shoulders, the stinging welts on her back, painful bruises on her butt ... and the drying tears on her face. She'd felt like this often in recent years.

Bert had been beating on her again.

Yeah, I goddam sure did, ya deserved every stripe of that belt... stupid, ugly cow!

Sheila put her hands over her ears and moaned. Her stringy brown hair covered a broad, bloated face as the marks of fresh tear-drops joined a variety of stains on her tent-sized Famous Dave's sweatshirt. Even though Bert hadn't followed her out of the trailer, the bastard still managed to reach her with his brutal words. What had happened before she stumbled down the road was just a dull, gray blur. But his voice in her head was sharp and caustic.

You're worthless, Sheila.

So, why she was out here was solved. The can gave out a metallic whine as Sheila leaned over, stared at the ground beneath her feet, and tried to think.

The next question was... how? How had she come to be a quarter-mile from her own decaying single-wide? Sheila could not remember. She never walked anywhere. Walmart was the only place she shopped because they had plenty of those fat-man carts for her to motor around in. Little kids sometimes stared at the sight of her body as it sagged around the little scooter. Bigger kids even laughed and pointed when the cheap things broke down under her and she was forced to ask an associate to fetch another. But getting around the store any other way was inconceivable.

Walking this far should have been impossible.

"Maybe not," she said to the cool spring night, "my feet feel like I been walkin' on 'em all day. Could be, I'm stronger than I thought."

The words were no sooner out of her mouth than Sheila wished she could snatch them back; Bert got mad at her when he heard her talking to herself and now came the scritch, scritch, scritch of approaching steps on the dirty asphalt. The perpetually jittery woman ducked her head automatically before she saw, in the weak half-light, that it wasn't Bert's size ten Carolinas coming up the road, but a pair of white leather walking shoes. New and unmarked, they joined the cracked and twisted license plate frame —*I'm not tailgating/I'M DRAFTING*— the smashed can of Rock Star, a Clark Bar wrapper, and assorted cigarette butts in the patch of dirt between her own pink slip-on shoes and the edge of the asphalt.

Sheila took her hands off her ears and hid her dirty, tear-streaked face and her crooked, twice-broken nose.

"Are you all right?" The woman's voice was as soft as her shadow, cast by a distant streetlight.

Sheila didn't look up. "I'm fine," she croaked, revealing in the tone and the bent of her head that, despite the words, no, she wasn't really fine at all.

"Anything I can do to help?"

Sheila shook her head and was immediately embarrassed as she saw, from between her fingers, the locks of her unkempt, greasy hair sway back and forth in front of her bowed eyes. She could imagine how appalling she must look.

There was a moment of uncomfortable silence during which Sheila could hear a rat scurrying about in a nearby dumpster. Though she waited nervously for the white shoes to move on, they didn't.

"I like walking in the evening," the woman said in a relaxed and unhurried manner that indicated that, unlike Sheila, White Shoes wasn't at all uncomfortable. "The early spring air smells like hope to me; new things coming to life, old things reaching once again for a second chance. And it is always nice to get away from the Lord of the Manor, if you know what I mean."

Sheila almost choked on the laugh that clawed free of her throat. A picture had popped into her mind, one of Bert with his feet on the coffee table, dressed in his standard camouflage boxers and tattered brown bathrobe, which was split open to reveal his pale, scrawny chest; there was a Rolling Rock in one hand and a Winston in the other; his head lolled to the side, a glazed look on his hard face.

The Lord of the Manor, indeed.

"My name's Audra, by the way." Sheila was certain that a hand was being extended, but she didn't look up to find out.

"Sheila," she whispered in reply.

"Well, Sheila. It's nice to have met you. I wasn't sure there was anyone else still living in this place." "This place" was clearly meant to encompass the words pigsty, hellhole and other epithets from the lowest rung of descriptive phrases. "I've started walking almost every night; I really need to start getting in shape, so I can get out of here. Maybe you'd come out and keep me company on occasion?" Audra only waited a moment before she spun on the soles of her white shoes and started walking away.

"You really should," she tossed over her shoulder, "because you *are* stronger than you think."

Sheila snuck a peek as Audra walked powerfully up the road. She looked tall and confident in her dark blue sweat suit. Although she could only see her profile, Sheila could tell Audra had dark hair and a strong, straight nose; the nose made her a little envious. Bert had broken her nose again four years ago and it hadn't healed straight.

But a friend would be nice, Sheila thought. It was hard for her to determine whether this was a new emotion that was coming to life for the first time, or an old one rising from the ashes of a burnt-out existence; but she thought that the unfamiliar feeling in her heart was *hope*.

"Maybe I am getting stronger," Sheila said softly to herself, "at least I can try to *get* stronger."

Ya better be strong enough to get back in here and bring me another beer, you worthless piece of shit.

The trash can wobbled as she pushed back onto her swollen feet. Her legs, and the rest of her enormous body, wobbled too. Newfound hope weakened as she turned toward their ramshackle trailer that was more like a prison than a home. As she slowly shuffled toward it, hope dropped away, and the world became dull and gray once more.

∽

Sheila re-tied her shoe one last time. But it was obvious Audra wasn't coming. She hadn't seen her friend since the run after the blizzard. That was also the last day she could remember hearing voices. If it weren't for the fact that she was only conscious of her actions while she was out on the road, Sheila might have thought she had run free of the strange mental condition which ruled her world.

As spring had worked its way free from the clutches of winter, Sheila had discovered strength in the solitude of her daily runs. It wasn't a strength that relied on cruel words to drive her, or encouraging ones to prop her up. It was not a strength that used someone else to pull her through, but the fortitude she had inside, to face challenges head on.

Now she knew she could handle the long run ahead on her own; even if she didn't know where it would take her. She only knew it was taking her away from here, never to return. And so Sheila turned and faced the road, took the first step ... and another ... and then another.

"Goodbye, Audra." she whispered, and broke into a run.

MILE 1.0

The Threshold to Oblivion

Crab apples and wild cherries shaded the narrow asphalt road. After years of neglect, the road was ugly; the black surface was rutted and cracked, lined by rusty barbed-wire stretched between the trees and rotting posts alongside. Weeds pressed in from the litter-strewn shoulders and squeezed through tiny fissures in the asphalt. But it had become a bright, crisp spring day, with pink and white petals flittering through the dappled shadows, filling the pot-holes and cracks. It felt as though nature was holding a confetti parade in her honor.

Energized, Sheila let her feet carry her swiftly away from what had served as a poor excuse for a home during these last fifteen years. A swirl of pastel colors followed in her wake. The nervous excitement which was entwined with every thought and every breath pushed her faster than was prudent ... but she was powerless to resist.

The strength she felt was in stark contrast to the struggles her first short walks had been.

෬ೕ

There was no ringing or buzzing, but the metal trash can seemed to function like an alarm clock all the same. Sheila felt like she had awoken and walked out of a dark dream that left no images behind. But night had only recently arrived; a fading smudge of red on the western horizon was proof.

Her clearest memory was of the first time she had sat on that can and caved in the lid. But there were other memories, more recent, of waking at this same spot with hope in her heart. From here she would start her slow walk along the trailer park road. Often Audra walked beside her; sometimes she walked alone. How many times had she struggled down this road? She had no idea. Five? Ten? Twenty?

Too many times, you dumb bitch. What a waste of time!

She flinched, but only a little, and hoped that Audra hadn't noticed. They had joked about Sheila's propensity for talking to herself, but what Audra didn't know was that Sheila was often responding to a voice in her head. Neither had she told her friend about her memory problem, or about her husband problem, although Audra already seemed to know enough about that.

On that first day she'd only made it a quarter-mile before she almost had a heart attack. After resting on that dented trash can at the end of the lane, Sheila had walked back ... to what? No matter how hard she tried, she couldn't hold onto or retrieve any conscious thought once she crossed the mystical threshold that the trash can seemed to mark. Often during her runs she would try to picture what was going on in the rest of her life. She was losing weight fast. Did that mean she had turned away from the gallon buckets of Turkey Hill ice cream, the Krispy Kreme donuts, and the Golden Corral all-you-can-eat buffet? Was she eating her veggies now? Drinking skim milk? Did she do yoga on the kitchen floor while she watched Dr. Oz? Every day she felt healthier, but it was all so hard to imagine. These short, painful walks could not possibly be the only reason that the pounds were melting away.

What she didn't have to imagine was Bert in the background trying to drag her down.

Drag you down? How could I drag a mud-puddle down? Can a buzzing fly drag down a steaming pile of dogshit? Chugga, chugga, choo choo!

Sheila was starting to get used to Bert's constant heckling during her walks. In a way, his cruel words helped to keep her moving. Each time, she got a little farther away from that acid tongue. This time, she walked by the peeling wooden sign that welcomed visitors to "Beautiful Sunnyside Meadows."

"Who wouldn't want to keep goin'," she said, and gestured over her shoulder, "when that's all there is to go back to?" In her mind "that" included a range of negatives; this trashy development, the run-down trailer, Bert, his belt, and his endless cruelty.

"You can bet that's what I'm planning," Audra said. "One day, I'm going down that road and never coming back."

Only the crickets, and the moths flying around the bare bulb above the sign, were around to hear them. The road stretched into the dark woods, and beyond. Yes, indeed; it just kept on going.

Right now, just the thought of what it would take to follow that freedom road, exhausted her. But someday she would be able to do that... keep going. Now *that* was a dream worth fighting for.

Pipe dream! Nuttin' but a fuckin' pipe dream. I know you'll never make it out of here. You know it, too.

Sheila frowned. Good ole Bert. He had always been there to make sure her dreams couldn't come true; making sure that she didn't *have* any dreams; only nightmares.

I'm hungry. Get that fat ass of yours back here and make me some dinner!

"What choice do I have?" she whispered.

"Did you say something?" Audra asked.

No choice at all, balloon-butt. None a-tall.

"This is as far as I can make it tonight," Sheila said. "I'm getting stronger, though. I'll make it farther tomorrow night."

Audra smiled, "I know you will, girl."

MILE 2.5

Too Many Voices

And she had—gotten stronger… gone farther.

Sheila laughed, amused at the confidence she was feeling and certain that confidence would wane as the miles went by. Some of the motivation that had pushed her a year ago was gone for good, and Sheila was glad of it. But she was counting on the stubbornness that had helped her survive those dark, early days to see her through the long miles ahead.

❧

Hell woman, you gotta be as dumb as a bucket of cow manure. When you gonna give this shit up?

"Never!" Sheila screamed. Her voice was swallowed by the damp night air. She was hungry, sweaty and exhausted. But Bert's voice made her growl, put her head down, and push herself into a faster shuffle-walk.

Atta girl, Sheila. You are awesome.

She jumped and glanced back down the road, expecting to see Audra running out of the darkness behind her. The long, gloomy stretch of asphalt looked empty all the way back to the light at the trailer park entrance. But she was sure a woman had spoken to her, someone who sounded friendly and supportive; there was something familiar about the voice, but she couldn't think why. Sheila's eyes tried to penetrate the dark woods on each side of the road, but her effort was halfhearted; no one was there urging her on, and she knew it.

"I'm not sure I'm ready for another voice inside my head."

Everyone needs a little encouragement now and then.

"Audra does a pretty good job of that."

Audra can't be with you all the time.

That was true. When Audra was on the road beside her, the walks were always better. She felt stronger and more confident when she had her friend at her side. It helped her to forget that the rest of her life was a blank space; an empty box with no pictures or mementos from her existence when she wasn't walking the road.

It was weird, what her life had become; the only time she felt awake was when she was out in the night, putting one foot in front of the other on the dark asphalt. She couldn't pull up memories of anything else she did during the day; brushing her hair, fixing dinner, bringing Bert his beers, even shopping at Walmart. It was like the rest of her life was a nightmare and all of it was erased from her mind each time she strolled by that trash can. It freaked her out a little, and she wondered if she might be losing her mind.

Got news for ya doll… that train done left the station! Chugga, chugga, choo choo!

"Leave me alone, Bert."

Her goal was still a good distance off, but she could see it now, and worked to move a little faster. Sweat had long ago soaked her Simply Smashin' t-shirt. It was a triple-XL that had barely fit her when Bert had bought it for her at the demolition derby up in Allentown last summer. As expected, he'd gotten drunk and spewed a colorful concoction of nachos, beer and hotdogs all over her blouse—the t-shirt was a grudging replacement. "You are simply smashin'," he'd laughed. "Every time you sit down, your fat butt smashes whatever it lands on."

Now, the black cotton tee wasn't tight at all. The many folds and wrinkles in the cloth were clear evidence of the progress she had made. And she was working for more.

You can do it, Sheila. I'm so proud of you.

"Well, I guess I like your voice better than Bert's," Sheila said. "One more mile. That mobile tower is only a mile away. I can walk a little when I make it that far."

What fucking difference does another mile make? You're still a lard butt!

Through the darkness, she could see light from a farmhouse on top of another hill far ahead. Sheila knew that, some evening soon, she'd be able to make it that far. Every day she was going farther, even if distinguishing one day from the next was hard, the way things were. The nights were getting warmer, so she was sure that it had been more than a month since she'd started walking, maybe two. She'd had to take in all her clothes, even if she couldn't remember doing it. And her legs had gotten a little slimmer … and much stronger.

"I'm even jogging a little now and then."

Yeah, a reg'lar Speedy Gonzales you are. That squish you just heard was a slug you been followin'… for a FUCKING HOUR!

As she jogged along, Sheila looked down at her cheap canvas deck shoes; they were better that the pink slip-ons that she'd worn until she lost enough weight to be able to tie her own shoes. The pink shoes were history and now the canvas ones were filthy and falling apart, too. She was afraid the soles were about to wear right through, and hoped that the slippery feeling under her left big toe was another popped blister … and not the slug.

"It'd be nice to have a new pair of shoes." Sheila thought saying it out loud might help her think of it next time she was at the store, assuming she ever went to the store during the cut-off part of her life that existed in the oblivion on the other side of the trash can.

One of these days, she was going to have to start her walks during daylight hours. Nights were getting shorter, and waiting until dark to start her walk meant she was real late getting back to the trailer. She was certain it pissed Bert off, not being around evenings to bring him his beers; though she couldn't really recall whether he had hit her lately.

You betch yer ass I'm gonna whip ya tonight, you tub-a-blubber. That's right, I'm gonna whale on my whale for damn sure!

Sheila stopped and put her hand on her knees as the red beacon of the mobile tower flashed over her head. It wasn't Bert, or his threats, that had stopped her. She'd come two and a half miles! The longest yet! Standing up, she gazed longingly at the farmhouse in the distance, and then she turned away. It was long walk back.

Though she was walking back toward a life that was empty, the road still beckoned. She couldn't run a step farther tonight. But someday ….

MILE 4.0

An Uneven Split

The sun was fully risen as she sped down CR 17 past familiar landmarks that she would never see again; signposts and mailboxes that represented challenging milestones in her training. Soon she was striding north on Mount Vernon Road, among the dark brown, freshly-plowed fields that would soon sprout corn, barley, or potatoes. Like a curator presenting a landscape retrospective, her mind displayed a slideshow of the fields in full bloom, green and thriving under a warm sun; and again during autumn as the Amish in broad-brimmed straw hats led sturdy plow horses by the halter while the strong beasts pulled a gleaming, green John Deere harvester. Finally, she saw a brief image of the moonlit fields resting beneath a blanket of white, waiting for the cycle to begin again.

༅

"Audra, I'm not sure if what I'm seeing is real," Sheila said. She was surprised that she was able to jog and still have enough breath for a conversation.

You got that right. All that fat bouncin' down the road is *hard to believe.*

"Well, thank you," Audra smiled as she laid on the sarcasm with gusto. "I always wanted to be a figment of someone's imagination."

"I don't mean you," Sheila said, "I mean everything … all of this." She gestured to a landscape that seemed touched my magic.

In every direction, a hazy, dreamlike quality touched the land. The asphalt miles passing beneath their feet glimmered under a pregnant moon that trailed behind them as if it were a balloon on a string, tied to their shoulders. Their moon-shadows slanted across the road ahead and set a challenging pace through a muted landscape populated by the gray ghosts of telephone poles, silos, and skittish deer.

"It is kinda spooky, but I'm pretty sure this isn't the Twilight Zone, if that's what you're saying."

"God, Audra! I'm not talking about *this* this; I'm not talking about tonight. I'm talking about everything; me ... my feet slapping on the road. Hell, I'm talking about the road itself, and the world that road is leading me through."

"I'm sorry, Sheila. It still isn't clear to me what you mean. I don't know how I can be real if you, and everything you see, isn't." The silence that followed was broken only by the patter of their shoes on the pavement and the occasional rustle of deer through the waist-high corn along the road.

Sheila knew that something was seriously wrong with her, but it felt like the time she spent running, either with or without Audra, might be the only part of her life that was right. How would she know, since this was the only part of her life that she could remember? Sheila was afraid that letting Audra in on all her dark secrets could ruin that; it might drive her friend away.

But she couldn't bear the burden alone anymore.

She told Audra everything; Bert's haranguing rants inside her head, the mysterious female voice that balanced his negativity, and the fact that her mind blocked every memory of her existence except that which took place while she was "on the road."

"Audra, I'm not sure how much longer I can take this. Bert may be right," Sheila said, "maybe I'm insane. Maybe I'm strapped to a bed at Philhaven and this is all a delusion... the only way I can escape."

Audra ran in front, put her hands on Sheila's shoulders and stopped her. Then she stomped her foot on the road. "This road is real, Sheila." She pointed over Sheila's shoulder. "That bright moon lighting your way, it is *real.*" Audra hugged her friend and whispered in her ear. "*You* are real. I know this to be true."

"You know? How could you know?"

"Because I've seen you when you weren't on this road; I've sat at your kitchen table and shared a cup of coffee ..."

Sheila pushed Audra away. "Christ! I knew it! I'm a schizo or somethin'."

Audra took Sheila's hand and looked intently into her eyes. "The person I see here and the one I've shared coffee with may have different memories, they may be working on their problems differently, but they are the same person ... and both are very real."

" 'They'... 'both'?" Sheila shook her head. "That doesn't sound like 'sane' to me. OK, maybe I'm not hallucinating, maybe I'm not locked up ... but I oughta be."

"Don't even think that, Sheila. If you were using this split memory of yours to avoid doing something about the bad things in your life, I'd agree. But you're not avoiding the bad things, you're working on them. You are very brave woman and I think what you are experiencing is the way that your mind is dealing with the problems you have ... very real problems."

"So, what you're telling me is that I'm crazy, but it's OK because I've got a good reason to be?"

"Most crazy people think they're sane. The fact that you don't..." Audra laughed and started on up the road, pulling on Sheila's hand. "Come on, why don't we finish this run before the sun comes up again?"

As they made their way through the rest of the run, Audra convinced Sheila, to some degree, that what was happening to her might be a good thing. It wasn't like there were many options available to her anyway. Whether she wanted it to or not, the situation existed and she would have to continue to deal with it. There was one consistent positive that was hard for her to ignore. No matter how tired she was, no matter how her joints or muscles might hurt and no matter how loud Bert's complaints got, all of her runs had two things in common.

They started with a feeling of hope, and ended with a feeling of accomplishment.

MILE 5.5

Blind Trust

Sheila moved smoothly along the dirt shoulder as she neared the end of Mount Vernon Road. The five and a half miles she'd covered had been easy, over roads that she knew so well she could run them blindfolded. In many ways, blindfolded was the way she felt right now, even if her eyes were open. These easy miles had allowed her mind to wander. Inevitably, it had wandered to the question: Where am I going?

The driveway ahead led to an Amish farmstead; neat, organized, industrious; it was like hundreds more packed into this fertile slice of Southeastern Pennsylvania. From high above, the area looked like an earth tone, patchwork quilt put together by a bevy of grandmas who'd had a few too many glasses of sherry.

There were a dozen similar driveways that she'd already passed for the last time without stirring any memories, or at least any important ones, but the driveway ahead was special. For much of the past year, she'd felt like a leaf tossed about on a rushing stream, without a choice about her final destination.

But, at this driveway, she'd made a choice.

༄

Sheila woke with a start. The hot sun was still up, and cast her shadow across the trash can. She had become used to the brief disorientation she felt at the start of her runs, like a subject who was suddenly alert after a hypnotist had snapped his fingers. But it was daylight still; she'd never come to under a full sun. And the shadow she was staring at didn't match up with the image she had of herself. It was big ...

Christ! Woman, are you blind? That shadow is huge, monstrous...

"Shut up, Bert."

But it wasn't round anymore. And she felt different, too. The rolls of fat under her arm were almost gone. There was less jiggle in her walk. Her feet weren't sore.

Damn, you really are dense. Yer feet ain't sore 'cause you just got started on your fucking-waste-of-time walk!

"I'm not just walkin', I'm joggin' now ... most of the time." She looked down at her feet. The white Danskin sneakers had been a help; they were easier on her tootsies than her beat-up deck shoes had been. A long string of memories filled her thoughts; dozens and dozens of walks and runs that she had completed. That those were the only memories she had worried her a little, but she chose to look on the bright side. Sure, maybe Bert was waiting with his belt. Maybe a cruel, bitter life was all she had. But at least she had found a way to block all that out. Right now, she felt strong, happy ... self-reliant.

Sheila reached out, patted the trash can affectionately, and started down the road.

The sun had set by the time she was heading up the long hill toward the farmhouse. She'd been distracted by the changing colors of the sky. From pink to orange, then red and purple, the enchanting beauty of the sunset had allowed her to ignore the heat and endure the hard work her body was doing.

But now, darkness was closing in. Her legs, legs that had maintained a jog all the way here, were aching in ways that were new. She stopped and took a deep breath, enjoying the feel of the moist night air as it filled her lungs. Five miles! It seemed such an impossible distance. And yet, she'd made it this far.

Yeah, shit-for-brains. And now ya gotta make it all the way back and bring me another fucking beer!

"Get it yourself," she said. "I'll be a while yet."

An idea came to her, a new one, but one that she thought may have been floating around her subconscious for weeks. She could keep going, turn into that driveway ahead, run up to the farmhouse, and ask for their help.

Great idea, Sheila. Run on up there; knock on that door, all sweaty and stinky and out of breath. Outside of your fucking ignorant joggin', you have no idea in hell what you been doin' these last four months. You talk to yourself, you hear voices and you haul that load of blubber up and down this road every fuckin' day. The first call those folks will make is to Philhaven. You'll be in the loony-bin where you belong before the sweat dries on that gargantuan ass of yours.

"Go to hell, Bert."

No, doll. Hell is where you get locked up, tied to a bed and stuck full of needles. It's all yours, babe. Fuck, now that I think of it, maybe you're already there. Maybe that fucked-up mind of yours snapped a long time ago and you're strapped down in the loony-bin, RIGHT NOW!

Sheila shivered at the thought, a thought that dogged her mind.

Go ahead. Your brain is ninety-percent cow manure and ten-percent dog shit, but maybe you've come up with the first good idea of your entire sorry-ass life. So, go ahead ... do it.

Her abusive husband was five miles behind her, back at their patched and battered trailer. But his words; needle words, knife words, his hateful machete words ... those kept up with her pretty damn good.

It was his charming grin that had attracted her when she was a shy, overweight junior and he was an outcast high school senior. That grin had reminded her of Quaid, that actor from her favorite movie, *The Big Easy*... not Randy, the skinnier one... Dennis. And the year they were married, Bert looked dashing and dangerous, a lot like Doc Holliday, another Quaid role.

You won't do it. You're a chicken-shit, gutless, fat whore.

Bert turned out to be dangerous all right, even when he wasn't swinging his belt. Once again, he had managed to bring tears. She pushed the heels of her hands into her eyes to force them away.

"No more!" she said, and staggered toward the driveway.

No, Sheila dear. Don't do it.

Sheila stopped as if she had hit the proverbial wall, and fell to her knees.

"Why?" She looked up at the stars and cried. "Why? Why? Why?" This was the voice that was supposed to help her, encourage her. Instead, it would send her back to endure another day.

It's what Bert wants you to do. You don't know what might happen ... it could break you. And that isn't part of the plan.

"There's a plan? What plan?" Falling onto her forearms, she whispered to the asphalt, *What god damn plan?* Her head dropped against the pavement that was still warm from the daylong sun. "My life is this; walking, jogging, running ... day after day after day. The remainder is so horrible that I bury it where I'll never see it again. What kind of plan is that?"

You are on a path, Sheila. It is taking you where you need to go. Trust yourself.

"Trust myself? How?" She sat back on her heels and her eyes returned to the heavens. "How can I follow a path when I don't know where it's going?"

One step at a time, dear. One day at a time.

In the end, she'd made her painful way home, into the oblivion that waited beyond the trash can.

⌒

So much time had passed since that day, and she still didn't know where that path was leading. But she was powering along it no matter where it might take her.

MILE 7.0

Good Bad Memories

Sheila cruised along the shoulder of Springhead Road, trying to shake the memories of doubt and despair that had plagued her during those early months. Then a powerful tide of emotion hit her as she approached Cambridge Road and imagined a pretty, white, fox terrier, one with distinctive black markings. Tears welled in her eyes as the phantom kept pace with her.

᠃

By mid-summer, Sheila had learned of every loose dog from CR 17 to the foot of Welsh Mountain; the ones that were all bark and the couple that had a little bite in them. It was the Fourth of July weekend when the terrier, mostly white but with one black ear and black socks in the rear, ran up to her as she turned on to Cambridge. She was startled and a little nervous, but he didn't bark or growl and he trotted along behind her like it was his duty. As days passed, she became so fond of him that she named him Rocky. Like a personal K-9 bodyguard, he would tag along at her heels for the entire length of Cambridge Road, tongue wagging out of a wide, happy, doggy grin all the way. Occasionally he would race off, chasing a rabbit or a squirrel, but before long he would be back at her side, panting … and grinning wider than ever. At Kauffroth Road, the limit of Rocky's patrol area was reached; there he would stop and catch his breath, waiting by the intersection so that he could follow her all the way back Cambridge on the return trip.

Kauffroth is a road that drops one-hundred and ninety feet for the one mile of its existence between Gault and Cambridge. Yeah, you're right, if you're going from Cambridge to Gault, it goes up the same amount, getting you ready for the serious climbs on the way up Welsh Mountain. On the southern end, it crosses and then follows a stream that, while not exactly a rushing, scenic masterpiece of nature, was prettier than the drainage ditch by the trailer park; it gave Sheila a warm, wholesome feeling.

That downhill mile always felt good to Sheila, in part because she knew Rocky was waiting. One of her vivid memories, one that stayed sharp regardless of how many days went by, was of a gorgeous fall day. It must have been early November; all the leaves were off the trees, but there was a serious Indian summer going on, the kind that had people pulling their summer clothes back out of the storage box, the kind of day that gives you hope winter might never come. She was on her way back down Kauffroth feeling better than she'd ever felt on a run; the "I traded shoes with Mercury and, woman, these winged suckas can *fly!*" kind of good feeling that a runner who sticks with it gets to experience every now and again.

On this "I am invincible" day, she was motoring down the road, nearing Seldomridge, sweat dribbling off her forehead, and she spotted Rocky in his usual spot, not far from the intersection with Cambridge, under the tree next to the stream, waiting patiently for the trip home. On a hot day like it was, he'd usually be lying in the shade, soaking wet from a dip in the stream ... but he looked dry. Once she crossed the road, he'd usually sit up... but he didn't. As she approached the tree, he was always on his feet, tail a-waggin'... but not this time. He still hadn't moved by the time Sheila was even with the tree, so she stopped and called him, "C'mon Rock lets go, time to head home."

It was already in her throat when she called him, but seeing him not move was what caused a dry, painful swallow that made her notice the lump. That hard piece of *godpleaseno* got heavier and fell into her stomach as she walked across the dusty shoulder of the road, into the grass, and got near enough to see how still Rocky was, how terribly still—and heavy— *everything* was. Then that hard piece of *godpleaseno* did something strange ... it got bigger and heavier, and smaller and lighter, all at the same time.

Everything inside Sheila got hard and heavy, while *godpleaseno* turned into a desperate, whispered no... *no... no... nononono.*

The memory was a little wet and blurry here. Soon, Sheila was using a stick to dig in the black, loamy soil next to the tree; sweat and tears were pouring off her face like she was a human serenity fountain; except there was no serenity to be found that day. A mud-puddle was forming between her legs when she noticed that Audra must have run by and seen her because now her friend was kneeling next to the shallow hole with her own stick, helping to make it deeper.

That one memory took the place of all her deeply buried bad memories; it pushed them out so completely, even the best hypnotist in the world could not recover them. All in all, the memory of Rocky wasn't too terrible as bad memories go, although she also remembered dreading her run the next day. Audra was there and that helped, especially when she got to the start of Cambridge and Rocky wasn't there. It was cold that day; the Indian summer had broken overnight and the long-sleeve cotton shirt Sheila wore was soon gross with snot and tears. Without Audra to lead her, a teary-eyed Sheila might never have reached the end of Cambridge and Rocky's shallow, unmarked grave.

Only it wasn't an unmarked grave anymore. It had a white cross on top that said "Rocky," and the small patch of dirt was covered by river rocks, colorful stones gathered from the stream where Rocky had spent so many hot afternoons drinking and splashing. She didn't bother asking Audra who had placed the cross; she had a pretty good idea already.

Sheila didn't know how her memories of Rocky had done what they did. She only knew that his memory, though heavy and sad, had left her somehow ... liberated. It was a good kind of hurt, a healthy one; the kind that held no shame, no fear; a feeling rooted in love. Unlike the kind of hurt that came from abuse, this bittersweet feeling was one she knew would heal over time and eventually be more sweet than bitter.

❦

When she reached Kauffroth her breathing became ragged, smothered by feelings that leapt uncontrolled from her heart to her throat. The cross where Rocky was buried stood sentry over a riot of color. The gravesite was piled high with fresh flowers ... and there was a small, hand-printed sign in front of it that stated simply "Go, Sheila."

"Goodbye, Rocky." The emotions clogging her throat made the words hard to say, but she managed all the same. "Thank you, Audra." Though she may have known better, Sheila chose to believe that her friend had placed the flowers and the sign.

She was glad for the rising grade of Kauffroth Road; it helped her concentrate on a quick arm swing and a short, efficient stride on the hill. Soon, the tears were dry and she was focused again on the many miles that remained.

MILE 8.0

Dog Day Afternoon

Sheila drank when she was thirsty and forced down a gel when she felt her fuel reserves lagging. The top of Gault Road, on the heavily wooded southern flank of Welsh Mountain, was still a hard, climbing mile ahead. As clear as the *Deer Crossing* and *Hidden Entrance Ahead* signs, the first indications of fatigue appeared. Her breath became more labored, there was a tightness building in her shoulders, and her hamstrings made whispered complaints about the unending upward route. These signs announced that the bill for her early, extravagant memory-and-emotion-fueled pace was going to come due sooner rather than later.

Since passing the low point of the run on Mount Vernon five miles earlier, Sheila had climbed over five hundred feet. Her fresh legs had hardly noticed at first, eagerly enjoying, along with the rest of her body, the thrill of this ultimate adventure into the unknown. Now they were noticing. When she hit a steep, almost unrunnable slope, she chose to save her stubbornness for later in the run and slowed to a walk.

Sheila didn't let the walking shake her confidence. She was moving well, swinging her arms loosely, and building toward a second wind, using toughness that had taken her a long time to develop. It hadn't always been this easy.

❧

Air the consistency of corn syrup hung around her; thick, sticky, heavy, hardly moving; all the things that she was feeling about herself. In the west, a storm front was gathering. The sky to her right was a bright blue; on the left, clouds changed from white, to gray, and on to an ugly black and grayish-green toward the horizon. These had swallowed the sun and, soon, would start moving her way.

"August," Sheila said, "it has to be almost the end of August." Without a memory of anything outside of her running, it was difficult to keep track of the months, much less days.

Corn, every bit as high as an elephant's eye, lined both sides of the road. The silks hadn't begun to dry out, so it wasn't quite harvest time, but it would be soon. A good way ahead, atop a hill off to the right, stood a red barn. High on the gambrel, a hex sign caught what remained of the fading sunlight, telling the world that this was a Pennsylvania Dutch farmstead, not Amish.

The stunning power of her surroundings wasn't enough to lift Sheila's spirits. She definitely did *not* have a feelin' that everything was going her way. Her summer runs had been torture. How bad must the rest of her life be, that her mind would block all of it, but not this? Every day she had driven herself farther, despite the heat. The pounds had melted off of her like butter. But, there was a price she was now paying.

Yeah, the Susquehanna has a three-inch layer of fat on it just because of the run-off from your fucking sweat.

And, of course, Bert was always there to pick at any scabs.

Her legs felt like concrete; they throbbed with every step. So what if she was one hundred and twenty pounds lighter? The remaining two hundred sixty-three were still a heavy load.

Ya think? It's fuckin' hopeless and you know it.

Sheila stumbled to the side of the road and sat on the guardrail.

"It is hopeless." A car drove by as she was agreeing with Bert, and she could feel the driver's stare. *There's that crazy fat woman again, honey, talkin' to herself.* She pictured him talking to his wife, who sat in the passenger seat knitting booties for their first grandkid. *Do you think we should call someone?* And Honey would reply, *No dear, it's none of our business. Now keep your eye on the road.*

Sheila would have preferred to continue running under the anonymity of nighttime, but covering so much distance took her hours and hours. Audra still joined her on occasion, but Sheila missed her friend during the many runs she did alone. Part of her still wondered what Bert thought of all this. She didn't think there had been any fresh welts on her back in quite a while.

Don't worry, lard-butt. Your day of reckoning is on the way; might get here sooner than your pea-brain would guess.

Ignoring the Bert voice in her head had become second nature, but every once in a while, he still made her cringe.

It will get easier, Sheila.

"Where have you been? I'm dyin' out here, you know? That supportive voice in her head had been missing for a while.

I'm always around when you need me. What you are feeling is natural. Dead legs… it happens to all runners at one time or another.

"Gee, thanks. I feel so much better." Sheila dropped her head between her knees; every speck of energy and motivation was gone. "I don't know whose path, exactly, I'm supposed to be following, but I'm ready to find a freakin' shorter one."

There isn't a shorter path, Sheila … or a longer path. There is just your path; no other.

"Great, I'm stuck with a dime-store Yoda in my head."

Whining didn't get you started. And whining won't move you any further along.

"Yeah, well, I'm hot … I'm tired … I'm thirsty, and I'm sitting on a guardrail surrounded by a gazillion acres of corn, and I'm hungry enough to eat it all, right off the stalk. Excuse me for not feeling like Suzy Sunshine."

Then maybe this is it.

"This is what? Will you please stop being so damn cryptic?"

This is the tipping point; the line in the sand; your moment of truth.

"Oh, for crying out loud! Enough with the platitudes."

Get up, Sheila.

"I don't feel like it. I want to sit here until I die … which might be any minute, as much as I hurt." Sheila heard a rustle in the corn behind her. "W-Why should I get up?"

All you have to do is get your butt off that guardrail and things will get better... I promise.

"*You* promise? I don't even know who *you* are." The sky got darker, and now there was a louder rustle from the field of corn across the road.

I'm the one who knows what you've been through. I'm the one who believes in you, Sheila. I'm the one who knows you're strong enough to finish what you've started; brave enough to break the hold that Bert has on your mind, and woman enough to make it in the world that is waiting at the end of this road!

Now, GET UP!

Her legs protested, but Sheila pushed herself off the guardrail all the same. As she stumbled toward the road, a gust of wind hit her in the back. It was cool and refreshing, and it gave her the push she needed to put one foot in front of the other. As the wind strengthened, the fields of corn on both sides of the road bowed and applauded while Sheila continued along her path, one step at a time.

When a fat drop of rain was followed by a dozen more, she lifted her face to the dark clouds that were sweeping across the sky... and laughed, opening her mouth wide to catch the water that came pouring from the heavens.

ᔐ

Between the swaying treetops high above her head Sheila could see a cloudless sky; no rain would refresh her today. The glittering patches of sunlight breaking through the canopy did an enchanting dance on the road. As she skipped from light to shadow, to light again, a satisfied smile broke across her face. She'd come through a tough year and wore the confidence of a survivor lightly on her shoulders.

MILE 9.0

High and Low

The short bit of walking had extended into a somewhat longer stretch than Sheila had planned; but the walking, an electrolyte pill and another gel had revived her almost as thoroughly as that long-ago downpour.

"Time to get moving," Sheila was still talking to herself, but at least she wasn't having conversations with voices in her head anymore. The crest of the road was in sight and she was running again, remembering the first time she had experienced a runner's high.

∽

The air tickled her nose and painted a pink glow upon her cheeks; it also brought the promise of snow. Leaves fell in drifts from the trees lining the road, eager to join their brethren that were whirling and dancing a reel around Sheila's feet.

A strange feeling had taken a hold on her during the long climb that she had almost completed. It was an experience she could not remember ever having before in her thirty-three years. At a time when she had expected to be nearly spent and struggling to reach the top of the hill, instead she was ... exhilarated ... energized ...

"Yes! Yes! Yes!" she yelled as she leapt over the crest of Welsh Mountain; never in her life had she felt so alive.

That's because you are fucking insane! Do you seriously believe that all of this is real? Jesus H Christ, a three-hundred-and-forty-three pound woman doesn't run ten miles.

"I'm not that woman anymore."

So says the stupid bitch who can't tell me what she had for breakfast this mornin'... who can't even fucking remember GETTING OUT OF BED this mornin'! Runnin' on this damn road is the only thing your screwed-up brain can remember.

"Go away, Bert."

Chugga, chugga, bitch. I'm never goin' away. Now run your fat ass back here and get me another beer.

Sheila turned back toward home, trudging morosely down the hill; the late fall afternoon suddenly felt cold and dead, instead of refreshing and alive.

Don't listen to him, Sheila.

"What if he's right?" she whispered.

Look down, girl.

She didn't know where they had come from, but she wore slick-looking New Balance running shoes on her feet. The pink Under Armour Coldgear top she was wearing wasn't something she could have ever dreamed she might someday wear. A pair of black tights encased legs that weren't fat ... a long way from slim maybe, but nothing like the legs she had started with eight long months before.

Yeah, Sheila-the-Hutt! What a disgusting sight that was! Chugga, chugga!

"Shut up, Bert!" *Shut up, Bert.* Sheila laughed as the inner voice echoed in her head.

What you are seeing is real, Sheila; no matter what Bert says, you are changing your life.

Her stride lengthened as she ran down from the mountain and that positive feeling snuck back in. Like an elaborate puzzle, a geometric patchwork of plowed fields was laid out before her. Her life was like that, a puzzle, no matter how she looked at it. Whether she would ever fit the pieces together was far from certain, and Sheila had no clue what her life would look like if she did.

But, still, she was moving forward. One step at a time was how she had started and one step at a time was how she kept going; each stride more confident than the last; Bert hadn't stopped her yet.

∽

This time, she didn't leap over the crest, but she did move strongly down the other side with her strength recovered and spirits lifted. It felt good to be running away from … Sheila was no longer sure what she was running away from. She decided to look at it as running toward something; hoping it was a life far better than what she had left behind.

MILE 10.5

A Blank Slate

A lot of downhill miles were ahead of her, so Sheila was running easy, enjoying the shade and cool breeze while trying not to let the steep hill carry her away. She was a little nervous, not because of the long distance still to go, but because soon she would be running beyond her memories. Her world was comprised of the long expanse of asphalt that stretched from here back to the trashcan. What lay behind— or ahead— was a mystery. Near the bottom of the hill she spotted a field that looked as if it was spotted with snow. It brought back more memories. Already she was nearing the farthest point she had ever run with Audra. It seemed so long ago.

❧

"You could do it, Sheila." Audra shouted above the noise. "Every day you're doing a little bit more."

Over their heads, the barren trees rattled and moaned, whipped by the biting gusts of the approaching cold front. She and Audra were splashing down the west side of Welsh Mountain. Once the weak winter sun set, the temperature would drop rapidly and the rivulets of the melting snow, fanned across the road by the wind, would freeze. Sheila thought that tomorrow they would be better off wearing skates than running shoes.

Audra had spent the last three miles trying to convince her that a new and better life was waiting at the end of this long strange road; she just had to keep running. As the temperature fell, Sheila was thinking less about running and more about thawing out in front of the wood stove back at the trailer.

Not that she would actually get to enjoy it— well, maybe she would enjoy it— she just wouldn't *remember* any of it.

"Think about it, Sheila."

"How do I do that, Audra? How do I even consider a new life?" Sheila pointed to the bottom of the hill at a barren, muddy field, strewn with broken stalks; the remains of a bountiful harvest. "See that patch of ground? I remember that from yesterday. It's where I turned around and headed back ... back to a dinner I don't remember eating; back to an abusive husband I cower from even in my thoughts, even though the memory of his face is fading. Soon I'll turn around again and return to a bed on which, night after night after night, I sleep without knowing when I went to bed or when I woke up. But I remember that ugly field.

"Tell me how to think about a new life when the one I have is nothing but a blank slate?"

"A lot of people would love to start over with a blank slate. Take the field; who knows what wonderful things might grow there in the spring? Beauty will return; in that muddy field ... and in your life. You just need the courage to start over."

Sheila slipped on fallen leaves at the side of the road; a wet reminder of an autumn she remembered only as a backdrop for her daily run. Audra's words had her stumbling mentally as well. Starting over is what she wanted, but this wasn't exactly how she pictured it. In the time before her breakdown, when she was sobbing into her pillow after another of Bert's beatings, she pictured running off with his coffee can of money and his pick-up, and driving all the way to Mexico. His features might be slowly dissolving in the bizarre vacuum that had replaced her mind, but how he treated her, she would never forget. That he was back there waiting was just another reality that hindered every attempt she made to consider her future.

"You know that's what I want, Audra." Sheila's words were barely audible over nature's wind-driven bluster. "Leaving Bert and finding a new life is what allows me to hold onto the little bit of sanity I still have; but starting over scares me. How does a person who can't plan for tomorrow, who doesn't even know the most basic facts of her existence ..."

They had passed the field and reached that day's turnaround point. Sheila stopped and put her hands on her knees and turned her head to look up at Audra; fear was in her eyes.

"How does someone like me face that? ... or accomplish anything?"

Sheila felt Audra's hands on her shoulders. She was pulled to a stand and turned to face her friend.

"You aren't alone in this, Sheila, you know that." Audra said.

"Sometimes it doesn't feel like I'm 'in this' at all," Sheila replied, her fear turning to scorn. "TP Sheila sits back at that crappy kitchen table making decisions about my life that I don't even know about." Her alter-ego had become "Trailer-park Sheila" in Sheila's mind. Sometimes she even referred to herself in the third person as "Runner Sheila."

Bitterness crept into her voice. "You two want me to just take off ... leave ... without having the slightest idea of where I'm going or how I can expect to live once I get there. Who's to say my Swiss cheese mind won't keep me split like this for the rest of my life!"

Sweat was beginning to cool on her body, bringing a chill that was exacerbated by the wind. It didn't cool her anger. Sheila shoved past Audra and began walking toward home.

"Runner Sheila would someday like to sit back, put her feet up and become 'Chill out and watch a movie Sheila', even if it's only for an evening. Can you promise I'll get that chance?"

She heard her friend shuffle up beside her.

"I don't know what the future holds for you, Sheila. I only know that a brutal past is what drove your mind to the point where it had to create a way to escape the pain." Sheila felt Audra take her hand and give it a reassuring squeeze. "Have faith that both 'Sheilas' are working on getting you out of here ... and be glad that you don't need to deal with the rest of your life."

❦

"The rest of her life" was facing her now. Sheila ran by the field that had once been ugly and barren. It was now planted in field peas; bright white blossoms were sprinkled generously across acres of lush green.

Audra had been right about beauty returning. It had bloomed again in the field. But Sheila didn't know what the future held for her; whether beauty would again grace her life was still a mystery. And Audra wasn't here to guide or encourage her anymore.

MILE 12.0

The Man and the Mirror

In her mind, Sheila saw a landscape much whiter than the field of peas she was passing—a cold white expanse of snow that was the coldest she could remember. That deep blanket of white was where she had seen Audra for the last time.

❧

Sunnyside Meadows Mobile Home Park had never looked so good, although there was no sun, or meadow, to be seen. As she awoke at her spot by the trash can, Sheila thought that it looked like a sheet of white linen had been dropped over the entire dreary landscape.

A hand-shoveled path through the waist-high snow led from her front door to where she stood; the shovel that had likely dug the route was leaning against the partially uncovered can. She couldn't recall putting it there, or using it to dig the narrow path that looked as if it continued down the road and out of the trailer park.

While she waited for Audra, Sheila searched her memory.

The last thing stored there was an icy memento of a wind-blown struggle through a dusting of white that stung her face. There were many cold and snowy runs that preceded that one. But, of course, she couldn't even remember jogging to the trash can this morning ... and the only reason she knew it was morning was because the sun was still in the eastern half of the sky.

You don't know what time it is, what day it is, what month it is... hell, you'd probably have to guess about what year your hopeless, fat ass is stuck in. What a fucking retard! Look around you! This place is empty; dontcha think if someone 'sides us was livin' here, the road a been plowed? What do you think all that means? Does the word loony-tunes mean anythin' to ya?

Sheila looked back at the trailer. A tiny thread of smoke drifted from the chimney of their woodstove. Then she did a three-sixty; there was no sign of life anywhere.

Admit it, Squirrelly Sheila, you're out here looking for the nuts you buried last fall. Now quit all this foolishness, get back in here, and bring me another beer. Chugga, chugga!

Just then, an Amtrak train came barreling around the bend. The sight of it caught her by surprise.

"The blanket of snow must have dampened the sound," Her words were like solid things, condensing in the air and floating away. Sheila shivered, despite the down mittens, hand-knit wool hat, and warm layers of clothing she was wearing. She crossed her arms and stared as the cars rolled by; the raised embankment made it seem as if they were passing directly above the trailer.

Something about the speeding train was scraping at a dark place in her mind; a place where memories were buried, the falling-with-no-bottom-in-sight, squeeze-your-eyes-shut-and-pray-they-go-away kind ... and these memories had nothing to do with running. It frightened her to think about what they might reveal.

I'll be revealin' my belt across your backside, that's what oughta be scarin' ya. I want my Rolling Rock now! Chugga, chugga, choo choo!

"Damn you, Bert! I'm thinkin' here!"

Ha! That'd be a first.

Sheila shook her head and stomped her foot in frustration. What had been hidden back there, deep in her subconscious, was important. No way was she returning to the oblivion that the trailer offered. Besides, she had a lot of miles ahead of her.

"Get your own friggin' beer, Bert."

With a determined scowl, she turned away from the trailer and saw Audra jogging toward her.

"I see you've been talkin' back to your husband again." her friend said with a sad smile. "You really should tell off that little prick right to his face."

"Audra, you know I'm not ready for that."

"Yet," Audra said, "you aren't ready ... yet."

Sheila nodded and they started to run, and talked about the blizzard. It was a rolling three miles from her trailer to CR 17, the closest road that the county pretended to maintain. For some of those three miles the snow wasn't waist high ... it was higher. Drifts shoulder-high covered the road on the lee side of even the smallest rise.

By the time she'd reached the start of the dead-end road that led to the trailer park, Sheila was awestruck; a path had been shoveled down to the asphalt for every inch of those three miles. She couldn't imagine the strength and effort ... the sheer, obsessive determination that would have been required to clear so much snow.

"Did you do all of this?" she asked.

"Don't look at me," Audra said. "That was your snow shovel leaning against the trash can. I guess that selective memory of yours has been at it again, huh?"

"It would've taken days." Arching her back and shrugging her shoulders, she felt muscles moving in places where she'd never had them before. Sore muscles, to be sure, but strength was in them nonetheless.

Plenty of muscle between your ears, you dumb snow hippo.

She climbed up the pile of plowed snow between the path and the intersection; from there she looked back along a canyon through the snow that could have only gotten there one way. Sheila protested against her own conclusion. In her mind, the one-step-at-a-time accomplishment that she had achieved over the past ten months was a Lincoln Log cabin compared to the Taj Mahal triumph that the path represented. "I couldn't have done this."

"But you've lost one hundred and sixty pounds in ten months," Audra said, as Sheila watched her friend climb over the pile and down to the two-lane road. "You're running eighty miles a week. Before you finish your run today, you'll have gone twenty-four miles. Why don't you believe that you are capable of this?"

"I ... because ..."

Because she's so shit flat-out crazy, she's fixed up her own custom-made strait-jacket. It keeps her doin' the same fuckin' thing, day after day. I mean, give me a fuckin' break! If yer gonna have a goddam hysterical delusion, a shit-for-bricks break with reality, at least make it interesting! Throw in some purple dinosaurs and goofy crap like that. She's so far off the edge, she don't realize she ain't never goin' nowhere!

"I'm not cra ..."

"Oh ... why don't you just shove it, Bert?" Audra said. "Sheila's come a long way and she's going places that you never could ... and never will."

Sheila looked back at Audra, then back toward the long, empty canyon in the snow that led three miles back to her trailer. No Bert was standing there. Of course, he wouldn't be, his voice was only in her head. When she looked back at Audra, Sheila's brow was furrowed and confusion filled her eyes.

"How can ...? What's going on...?"

Philhaven is where she's headed and I ain't goin' near that place, that's for damn sure. That lazy bitch can't do nothin' right but eat; can't even bring me a fuckin' beer anymore.

"She's done more work in the last two days than you've done in the last year."

"I don't understand what's going on," Sheila said. She turned back toward the vacant path, sat down on the pile of snow and covered her ears. It didn't matter to Sheila whether they were inside or outside of her head, the arguing voices were giving her a headache.

That ugly pile of shit probably scared the snow away.

"You're nothin' but a mean, abusive asshole, Bert."

And Sheila is John Nash in a wig and a fat suit.

"She's got courage, Bert. More than you'll ever have. You'll never hit her with that belt again, that's for certain."

Oh, yeah? How you think she's gonna stop me?

"I've got a news flash, you skinny excuse for ..."

"I can't take it anymore. Stop it ... both of you," Sheila moaned. "Stop it, stop it ... STOP IT!" Her scream rolled through the narrow, white canyon and across the frozen landscape. Dizzy and winded, she tumbled down the pile of snow to the path and rolled to a stop on her back. Silence, with the help of the tranquil blue sky framed by walls of snow, eventually helped her calm down and get her breath back.

Over the past ten months, time had become a relative thing for Sheila, so she wasn't aware of how long she had been lying there on the cold asphalt. When a passing jet drew a fuzzy white line across the canvas of blue, Sheila blinked. Through the frigid air, the sapphire heavens above looked as if they had substance. She removed her glove and reached up; her eyes were wide with wonder and her mouth formed a perfect "O" when the tip of her finger touched the sky and started a ripple that spread across the blue and erased the white line ...

And just like that she was six years old ... and looking down on the sky.

"That's where mirrors come from," said Everett Bedloe.

Father and daughter were standing on a high bluff above a lake whose water looked like it had been poured out of a can of Dutch Boy paint labeled "impossibly-perfect sky blue."

"Nuh, uh," six-year-old Sheila Bedloe said, "you're pullin' my leg, Daddy." She membered that her mommy told her never to believe anything Daddy said 'cause pullin' legs was the only thing he was good at. Sheila tried to catch that memry and stuff it back where the sun don't shine, but it was too late and the other bad memries jumped right out of the box, too; cause you know, once a girl gets started with that damn shit, she never stops. And the memries that jumped out don't like the sun, so everything went black, but black was good, better than red, the *mommy had another accident* red, a really bad one and *we have to leave right now, goddamit.*

"Sheila!" The gangly young girl flinched, and then felt her father's firm hand on her shoulder, cause a girl needs a firm hand, you know. She had no idea where they were, only that they had been drivin' forever and a day and she was glad Daddy finally decided to "stretch the crick out of his back." He made her do her business in a stinky potty-in-a-shack since he didn't want to stop where there was people, 'cause people is nosy and besides, they ain't no damn good around these parts.

Then the impossibly-perfect blue lake reminded her where she was and she looked up at her daddy. Everett Bedloe was smiling through a Fu Manchu moustache that looked out of place on his narrow face, but it served to cover his harelip. He was holding his hands in the air. "See, I'm not pullin' your leg. That there is Mirror Lake and all the mirrors in the world come from right here."

"I wanna see it then," Sheila said. Her father just pointed. "Up close," she added. Then she held her breath, 'cause it almost felt like a argament and Daddy don't like those. But Daddy said fine lets go, so she let her breath out real quiet so Daddy wouldn't notice she'd been holding it. And they scrabbled down the side of the bluff on loose scrabbly stuff that was a little scary and Sheila was glad for once that Daddy did have a firm hand and he let her hold it so she wouldn't have an accident like Mommy and crack her noggin. It was scary even holdin' Daddy's hand and he laughed and said girl you look like you shit your pants, but Sheila shook her no 'cause she knew shit in her pants would probably mean he'd let her have one, one she really didn't want 'cause it would likely be upside her head; although most anywhere Daddy would let her have one was some place she didn't want it.

Then, whew! They were down and they walked hand-in-hand to the shore and out on a nice, flat piece of rock where Sheila could walk right to the edge and not get her shoes wet 'cause Daddy hated that fuckin' wet tinny-shoe smell.

"There's your mirror," he said, and he was right. Sheila could see the blue sky at her feet and a little white cloud and could even lean over and see herself ... and Daddy holding her hand. But the mirror looked a little wobbly so she let go of his hand and knelt down to look closer. She reached out her finger and touched the mirror; it was wet like she thought, and little waves made everything blurry.

"YOU BROKE THE MIRROR!" Daddy yelled and Sheila covered her head, waiting for Daddy to let her have another one; but then Daddy proved that, yep, he was good at pullin' legs, 'cause he just laughed again, "That'll be seven years bad luck." But Sheila knew he was good at more than pullin' legs ... he was also good at lettin' her have one, sometimes two, or even seven; so she was slow at taking her arms off her head, and when she looked back at the lake, the little waves were gone and there was somebody else staring back at her, a woman who looked strong and friendly. She didn't look quite like Mommy, but almost. Then somebody that didn't look quite like Daddy came up behind her; he looked scary and mean and he had something even meaner-looking in his hands. Sheila screamed and fell on her back and looked up ...

... and the memory floated away, like each cottony ball of vapor she exhaled.

"Audra," Sheila said to the blue sky, her breath drifting up to add yet another little cloud to the picture. "I just had the strangest vision. Can I just lie here and think about it for a minute? Or maybe lie here all day and not think anything ... not think about whether I'm sane or not. I know we've got our run to do, but then what? Where is all this leading?" She noticed the hard asphalt under her head, and that her ears were cold. A twist to the left let her see the stocking cap that had fallen to the ground beside her. She grabbed it, snugged it over her head and then stared some more at the sky.

A distant, rough, scraping sound disturbed her reverie and then grew quickly louder. Sheila sat up and scrambled away in time to avoid the avalanche of dirty snow thrown up by the yellow tractor that flashed by the end of the path. The grinding roar faded as quickly as it had come.

When silence prevailed once more, Sheila called out. "Audra?" Her friend didn't respond, so Sheila stood and looked back toward the road, which she couldn't see because of the even higher pile of hard, icy mayhem that the plow had shoved into her little canyon. "Audra?"

Slipping and sliding, she scuttled over the mini-mountain of ice and into the road. To the right, red tail lights and a cloud of white marked the plow as it disappeared around a far turn. The road was empty to the left. All around was a wonderland of frosted fields glistening in the sunshine; a thin row of bushes and trees marked the border between one Amish farm and another; some were bowed, some flattened by their burden of white. In the distance, red barns, white silos and gray stone farmhouses added color to the panoramic view; a view that didn't include a single sign of Audra.

Bert didn't jump in with some cruel dig about the crazy fit she'd thrown driving Audra away, but Sheila thought of it herself anyway.

"She just got tired of waiting," she said. Sheila kept her chin up, but inside she was disappointed that her friend hadn't hung around; the miles ahead would be lonely.

Two hours later, she made a loop at Springville Road and headed back up Gault toward the top of Welsh Mountain. Twelve down, twelve to go. Once she'd conquered the next two uphill miles, the remainder of the familiar route would roll downhill.

She hadn't come across Audra on the way out, but the run had been enjoyable nonetheless. The roads were less busy than usual since schools and most businesses were closed because of the deep snowfall. They were the same roads she covered on every run she did, passing the same woods and fields, farms and houses; except that, under a blanket of white, they all seemed new. The best that winter had to offer was on display. And, to top it all off, her voices had been as silent as the snow-covered landscape.

MILE 13.1

No Turning Back

Long before she would have expected it, Sheila was approaching the point of no return. It wasn't a barrier really, not even a mental one. Neither was it a place for her to make a choice. Sheila didn't know it, but she had made her choices a year ago, and committed to them in the most irreversible way. She also didn't know how little of her old life—how little of her old *self*—was left.

Every step beyond that point in the road would be new. Each turn in the road would lead her along a path that was unfamiliar, toward a destination— and a future—which was completely unknown.

✺

A swallow of water washed the gel down; she wiped her lips on the back of her hand and stared down the road. This was as far as she would go today. Sheila could see it clearly, at least in her mind's eye. It was only a short distance ahead, that spot in the road; no, not a spot really, more of an invisible line. She wouldn't go there, not on this run; because if she went there, and crossed that line, there would be no going back. How she knew this was just another mystery, but she knew it all the same. So she turned around. By the time she returned to the trashcan, twenty-six miles would be behind her— that was enough for today.

But no going back is what she wanted, she'd been hoping for "no going back" since she'd taken her first step in that direction almost a year before.

She'd learned patience, and a lot of other things, during that year. Of course, she'd forgotten much more during that same time, but somehow she knew that forgetting was important, too.

When she'd first started walking, and then running, she had memories of things that had happened BEFORE. Before what, exactly, Sheila wasn't sure. Mashing the top of that trash can with her butt didn't seem to be a very elegant demarcation line for her memory banks. But, that's all she had. Back then she'd had short-term memories from before the trash-can mash; like dropping one of Bert's precious Rolling Rocks, and getting the belt; or doing some other damn thing, and getting the belt. And older ones, like her wedding on the day before her seventeenth birthday ("I know what I'm givin' Sheila for her birthday," a drunken Bert had loudly announced to his equally drunk friends at the reception, "and I'll be givin' it to 'er all day long!").

In the past year, all those memories had been gradually replaced. All of her new ones started and ended at the trash can. What she had now was "the road." And Sheila knew every inch of it; every ankle-turning pothole on Springhead Lane; each stretch along Mount Vernon Road that had some soft shoulder to ease the pain in her shins; all the places where old women sat staring from their front porches, and the old men, too, especially the one senile old goat who never learned, always letting out a loud wolf whistle that got cut off when his wife whacked him in the face with her newspaper. She knew the shady spots that gave relief on hot, sunny days, and the places where the wind ripped through you on the cold ones.

For almost a year now, her entire world had been narrow, winding, and covered in asphalt. It had stretched from the rusted trash can at the trailer park, to wherever the furthest point her ever-increasing running miles had reached.

Sheila wasn't sure how she knew that this was all about to change. She felt a sense of anticipation without knowing what was coming. The spring in her step was the result of more than the new shoes on her feet. The way she looked in her thigh-length compression shorts wasn't the only reason for the confidence that had been building over these last weeks. Someday was almost here, that someday when she would just keep going, running down that road and past the point of no return.

Where that road would eventually take her, Sheila was without a clue.

❧

A burst of adrenaline coursed through her veins as Sheila approached the unremarkable border. There was no difference in the road between this side and that. There was no reason that the step that would take her beyond that point would be any different than any of the million of steps that had preceded it.

No logical reason ...

... for time to slow as she passed; for the air around her to glimmer as she lifted her right knee; for the skin of her left arm to glow as she drove it forward. When she left the ground in that mid-stride fraction of a second, there was no logical reason for the road to shift beneath her, for the universe, in that singular moment, to alter the reality of her life.

And then the ball of her right foot lightly swept across the asphalt and Sheila was certain that all of those things had truly happened. She was out there ... out in the great wide open, Tom Petty might say.

Striped with the shadows of oaks and maples not yet in full bloom, the road ran straight downhill, broken only by driveways and dead-end farm lanes. For a mile or more, Sheila ran with the determination of someone whose bridges have burned behind her. Every step was new. The air itself smelled of adventure. She felt like an explorer forging into uncharted territory.

"That's enough romantic nonsense," Sheila told herself. For the past year she'd had only one thing to worry about ... going a little further each day; knowing that, at the end of the run, she would be returning to an oblivion from which she would emerge the next day to go even further. How would this run end, when she didn't return to that oblivion? Or would she finish the run and find herself waking beside the trash can once more?

Audra had once said that her split memory was a good thing, that it helped her to cope with problems that might have broken her otherwise. But what now? Sheila didn't know if that part of her life, her memory, her-*self,* was gone forever, or not.

There was one thing she knew for sure ... all she could do right now was run.

She didn't falter until an intersection came into view. Because, not only was every step new, but every junction was a choice; left, right, straight ahead? If only Audra were here to guide her. For once, Sheila wished for a voice in her head, someone to tell her which way to turn. Was there a right way and a wrong one? Was it a choice that was neither right nor wrong? She had no way to know if one direction was better than the other. A hundred similar choices waited for her down a road that looked more twisted and mysterious with each new step.

At the intersection, she stopped; waiting ... hoping ... praying for guidance.

MILE 15.5

The Road Goes Ever On

In the end, it was eeny, meeny, miny, moe that made the choice that first time. Later Sheila just went whatever way felt right. Once, she came to a T-intersection and only hesitated briefly before skipping either turn and going straight ahead along a narrow, rutted dirt lane between two fields.

Before long, she was moving through tiny farm communities with names like Green Bank and Mascot. For a while, she was passed by a stream of horse-drawn buggies as local Amish made their way to a neighbor's home for worship. The clip-clop of horseshoes on the pavement gave her plenty of notice that she was about to be passed by another passel of boys in black felt hats and girls in dark bonnets, all staring wide-eyed at the strange, running "English" woman, as their parents sat erect and proper on the front bench.

Although mostly hidden by the rolling terrain, the city of Lancaster, Pennsylvania was slowly drawing near. The clamor of cars and trucks on Old Philadelphia Pike burst upon her as she rounded a bend and was confronted and confounded by the busy highway. It was more self-preservation than decision that turned her right to follow the shoulder of the road west toward a still-unknown destination.

Stretching into the distance, the crowded, bustling road was a daunting, physical presence; a world apart from the tranquil farm roads that she had followed thus far. The smallest pebble of doubt got inside her confidence and began to wear against the skin of her determination. Steeling herself against the blistering threat, she dropped her head, focused on the uneven blacktop at her feet, and forged on down the road.

By the time she was approaching the small, touristy town of Bird-in-Hand, nineteen miles were behind her and Sheila's energy was lagging. The sense of adventure at the start of the run had fallen away miles before, battered beneath the soles of her shoes; the physical and mental high experienced earlier had drained away along with the endorphins that had fueled them. A year of training had brought her this far, but an adrenaline-driven early pace had stolen much of her endurance.

The mild hypnotic state brought on by 36,417 running strides, in combination with 19 miles of momentum, were to blame for what happened next.

On a beautiful Sunday morning such as this, hordes of people from the suburbs around Philly, Baltimore, and D.C. were visiting the "Dutch Country." It was a busy time of year for the Amish and other local craft people. On the south side of the highway, the parking lot of the Bird-in-Hand Farmer's Market was packed with colorful birdhouses, decorative wooden looms, painted wheelbarrow planters, and spinning wind vanes in a variety of imaginative designs. Booths burgeoning with a smorgasbord of foodstuffs lined the perimeter of the crowded lot.

The blended scent of handcrafted jerky, craft cheeses, homemade jams, and fresh-baked bread drifted across the road and drew Sheila's attention. Ahead of her, the shoulder of the road was filled with the cars of tourists also drawn by the rainbow of colors and mouth-watering smells.

Without thought, Sheila swerved left to avoid the vehicles; she left the shoulder and went into the road.

Squealing tires and blaring horns yanked her out of the stupor of fatigue and made her stumble further onto the highway. Metallic color flashed around her and a wicked caress of steel brushed across her thigh before her arm struck a side mirror and she was spun around on the double yellow line in the middle of the road. When her spinning ended, she found herself staring at the door of a black pickup truck that had slammed to a stop beside her.

"Stupid bitch! Watch where yer goin'!"

The angry voice chilled the sweat on her brow. Sheila's gaze rose, climbing over the "Gabby's Handyman Services" on the door to the rolled-down window above. There she saw a face that had been fading from her memory over the past year. Regardless of what happened in the oblivion beyond the trash can, her running time had been a safe haven where the reality of her husband's cruelty did not exist. Now, Bert's vicious, sneering lips were cursing at her through the driver's window.

"You ugly cow," he said. "What made you think I would ever let you get away with this?"

Sheila's hand clutched the sweat-soaked shirt above her heart as that racing organ skipped and skittered in her chest. Fear, an emotion grown rusty from neglect, squealed and began tap-dancing up her spine. For a moment it threatened to bring back the broken woman who would bend and take the punishment she was told was due her.

"Nothin' but a useless fu—"

Rage blossomed in Sheila's chest and washed the fear away. A fierce red veil clouded her vision. Like a teakettle approaching a boil, urgent, whispered noises hissed and bubbled in her throat before exploding in an incoherent, piercing scream.

When Sheila paused to catch her breath, silence filled the void as the clamor of the farm market ceased and every head within earshot turned toward the center of the highway.

It was the nervous calm before a sudden storm. Words soon filled the expectant air; vented as though lava from a long-suppressed volcano. Wide-eyed from shock, a woman waiting to cross the road covered the ears of a little girl in her pretty green Easter dress. Some faces reddened and turned away while others remained staring, transfixed by the scene.

What poured from Sheila's lips was every strangled retort that she had swallowed while Bert beat her down year after year; every angry curse that had been held back by a bitten tongue. Whispered profanities which had leaked into her tear-stained pillow during a long unhappy marriage came howling from her mouth, uncaged and fierce, clawing her throat as they claimed their freedom.

A firm hand on her shoulder and calm words in her ear brought Sheila out of a clenched-fist fury. Her eyes cleared and she saw that the frightened man in the truck no longer looked anything like her abusive husband. She stumbled as the rage that had propped her up drained away.

"Let's get you off this road," said a comforting male voice.

Sheila allowed herself to be led toward the farm market, where people were beginning to turn away, too embarrassed to remain staring as the object of their curiosity approached. The smell of fresh bread grew stronger and her mouth watered as she was settled onto a bench alongside the parking lot, Sheila found a cup of lemonade pressed against her lips. The sweet, cold liquid soothed her raw throat.

"You look like you've come a long ways."

A wide, friendly face on a balding head drifted down into the view of her lowered eyes as Sheila pondered the statement. How far she'd come was open to interpretation. The volcanic discharge just released might be considered great progress by some, while others might see it as evidence of mental instability.

"I'm Roger," the man said, "and you look like you could use a slice of my home-baked wildberry wheat bread. My stand is right behind us. You just sit tight and I'll be right back."

After such a long time on her feet, sitting was a relief despite the stiffness spreading through her muscles and the pain where her butt and hamstrings touched the hardwood slats. Sheila could already imagine the heavenly taste of the bread, washed down by more of the refreshing lemonade, as Roger talked to her about how she came to be in the middle of Old Philadelphia Pike.

The thought had hardly finished when she started to push her protesting body off the bench. It was the strong temptation to just sit there eating and talking that got her moving. Her divided mind wouldn't let her see what plans had been set in motion, or where this run would take her, but Sheila was sure that she hadn't suffered through a year of training to sit here and quit without even trying to finish. She wasn't certain how many more miles were left in her tired legs ... but she was going to find out.

MILE 26.2

Not the Finish Line
She Was Expecting

The black pavement beneath her hands and knees was real, it had to be. She pressed against the hard reality of Liberty Street, felt road grit digging into her palms and breathed a sweet sigh of relief. The brief, horrid feeling faded; the one that she had somehow been pulled back to the position she'd worked a year to escape. But this wasn't the cracked linoleum floor of her trailer's kitchen; Bert wasn't looming above her. Cars zipped by a half-dozen feet away, but she didn't feel threatened by them.

A big, wet tongue slurped across her cheek and delivered a sloppy dog kiss to her chin, lips and nose. She once loved a dog, a dog that wasn't hers, who considered being allowed to give a kiss the ultimate reward for his escort services.

"Hula, no! Bad girl!"

Sheila looked up at a smile that reminded her even more of Rocky, except this one was on the face of a frisky golden retriever.

"I'm so sorry," said the elderly man holding the leash. "Hula has never been this bad before."

"It's all right," Sheila said. "That was exactly what I needed." She pushed back on her heels and looked at the dog, which moved closer and sat in front of her.

"Whadya think, boy? Can I finish this?" She would have sworn that the dog nodded, even as the old man said that his dog was a girl, not a boy.

"Ok, then." She took a deep breath and grabbed the dog's collar. "Help me up."

The dog stood and pulled, walking backward until Sheila was on her feet.

"We'll I'll be," the old man spluttered, "She's never done that before either."

For a moment, she wavered, fighting dizziness as her exhausted body protested against being asked to move once more. When she was steady, Sheila leaned over and scratched the golden behind the ear. She accepted another kiss and whispered, "Thanks, Rocky."

What she did next—a simple thing that she'd done every day for a year—was excruciating and difficult. She focused her mind, grit her teeth … and took a step. That first painful motion was followed by another, and another.

As she made her way west on Liberty through the north end of Lancaster, her body got used to the pain and she moved slowly into a jog. She still didn't know how far she had to go, but thoughts of finishing began to cross her mind.

"I think I can, I think I can."

Sheila waited for her husband's voice to mock her. It was easy to imagine, since his coarse words had been in her ears and her mind for fifteen long years.

Fat chance, Sheila, he would say, *you ain't the Little Engine That Could… your caboose is too fucking big.* He'd demand another beer, pop the top and guzzle half the can; then he would let out a long, rumbling belch, and laugh. *Chugga, chugga.*

His words had always been cruel; vicious things used only to hurt her and keep her down. She forced herself to believe they would never be able touch her again.

"And besides, my caboose is a lot smaller than it used to be." Although, right now, her butt was killing her and each step was making her hips feel like her head did when she had a migraine. Though her body was wrapped in a blanket of pain, Sheila was smiling when she turned right at Queen Street and saw a large granite slab in the distance. The sun was shining brightly on the sign that marked the entrance to the Lancaster Amtrak station. It looked like a destination, maybe *her* destination. How would she know?

But then ... then Sheila saw a tall woman in a dark blue sweat suit standing near the sign. *It might be her,* she thought, but she wasn't sure; the sign, after all, was still almost a quarter-mile away. And then Sheila *was* sure; sure because she could hear a voice, faint, as if it was echoing through a long tunnel.

"Sheila, you did it!" Audra yelled. "Run it in, Sheila! All the way! Finish strong!"

The thrill that swept through her raised goose bumps on her arms and a fierce grin lit up her face. It hit her hard ... that powerful feeling that closes your throat and makes it feel as though your heart is bursting right through your chest. She *had* done it. Nothing in the world could stop her from getting to that finish line. Not Bert ... and not her own self-doubt. She'd left them both far behind.

The sobbing and tears which made that final straightaway a difficult, but transcendent, experience, were driven by fierce emotion whose primary component was joy.

She wasn't alone anymore.

∾

After she had finished her improbable marathon run to freedom, Audra kept her company as Sheila walked gingerly around the green lawn in front of the station, drinking Powerade and munching on a Lunabar while she allowed her legs to slowly cool down from almost seven hours of effort. Although her body was exhausted and ready for a rest, the enormity of what she had accomplished had her emotions in overdrive.

As they walked, Sheila eagerly told her friend about the experience of running a marathon; about the exuberant, adrenalin-driven early miles that had felt so easy; how even the memories of Rocky had provided emotional fuel for her engine; how the first half had felt like a review of her entire year, a trip down a broken memory lane that only showed her running, and running, and running.

She talked about the near-accident at the farm market and the explosive burst that had vented a lifetime of repressed anger. "When all that bitter vile burst out of me, I felt stronger, cleansed somehow ... but I also felt exhausted. I almost quit."

They were approaching the soaring, arched windows at the front of the station. A cloud drifted in front of the sun, bringing a chilly April breeze. A checkered taxi pulled up and dropped a man and a little girl at the curb. Sheila stared for a moment, and then crossed her arms and shivered. The fatigue that permeated her body had finally caught up with her emotion, too.

"During the second half, I was traveling through new areas on unfamiliar roads; I didn't know where I was going, or which way to turn. That lost feeling was even more like what my life has truly become." She stopped at the edge of grass and held her arms out wide. "Audra, what am I going to do? How can I exist like this? I know I can't go back; I don't want to go back. But how can I go forward with so many questions hanging over me? I want some control over my life, at least some idea of what is going to happen next."

Audra put her right arm around Sheila's shoulder. "Well, I guess this is your lucky day."

Sheila looked blankly at her friend.

"Answers, girl!" With her other hand, Audra took Sheila's arm and guided her toward the station entrance. "I'm here to give you some answers!" As they walked across the road, Audra whispered in her ear. "There are two conditions; once we go in the station, I don't want you to say a single word. Let me do all the talking ..."

"How are you going to give me answers if I can't ask you questions?"

"Hush now ... I know all the questions you want to ask. Okay?"

"Fine," Sheila said. "What's the other condition?"

Audra smiled, let go of her friend and nodded at the door. "The other condition is that you open the door and follow me to one of the benches."

"That sounds like two conditions, but all right," Sheila said as she reached for the handle. "Just so you know, after that I'm heading straight to the ladies room ... I have to pee so bad!"

Audra laughed as she walked into the historic brick train station and across the marble floors to one of the long, dark brown benches in the waiting area.

"Sorry girl, you're going to have to hold it a little while longer." She held up a finger to forestall the "but" about to escape Sheila's lips. Then she pointed at the bench. "Take your stuff off and have a seat."

Sheila removed her water belt and breathed a sigh of relief; she didn't have to pee so bad anymore with that pressure off her bladder. She stuck the belt under the seat and put her backpack beside her on the bench as she sat down. Audra sat down on the other side of the pack and pointed at it.

"Open the front pocket and take out the first envelope."

Inside the envelope were a Pennsylvania driver's permit, a social security card, and a Working Assets credit card. She'd never before had her own credit card and, as far as she knew, Sheila had never learned to drive ... but it was her picture on the license.

"Trailer park Sheila's been busy, I ..."

"SHHH!" Audra looked alarmed, and glanced toward the ticket window. Sheila followed her eyes and saw the man at the counter staring at her.

"Bu—"

"Sheila, please!" Audra reached across and put her hand atop Sheila's. "You have to trust me here. You can't say another word! Got it?"

Sheila leaned her head against the tall back of the long, dark bench in the waiting area of the Lancaster Train Station, and looked up. The glass ceiling high above her head was one of those designed to make you think there was sky above the frosted panes ... maybe. Sheila wasn't sure if it was the design, or if there really was a blue sky waiting for her beyond the clouded glass.

It was just another example of the things she didn't know. Like who she really was, and why she was in the train station to start with. Was the marathon she'd just completed only the first step of a much longer journey? Would Bert really just let her go?

Not really getting it at all, Sheila bowed her head and gave an imperceptible nod.

"Good!" The smile came back and Audra laughed easily. "And I wish you'd cut it with the Trailer Park Sheila remarks. You have no idea what she has sacrificed so that you can be sitting there."

Audra watched Sheila's head come up and knew what she wanted to say.

"Yeah, I know ... you're her and she's you. I get it. But you have to understand; it doesn't feel that way to me. Anyway, time for the next envelope."

It was from the Lancaster County Courthouse.

Audra smiled in anticipation. "C'mon! Open it!"

There were three pages inside, but it was the one on top that caught her attention, the one with an official-looking seal below a banner heading that read "Divorce Decree."

Audra watched her friend's eyes go wide and rushed to explain.

"A year ago Friday, you called the police and filed a missing persons report. You told them Bert had left on a week-long hunting trip two weeks prior and hadn't returned. As was his habit, he hadn't bothered telling you where he was going or who he was going with. Later, you filed for divorce, charging that Bert had 'committed willful and malicious desertion, and absence from the habitation of the injured and innocent spouse, without a reasonable cause, for the period of one or more years.' No one has seen hide or hair of him since. The divorce became official on Friday."

As Sheila listened, relief and satisfaction flooded through her. At last! Here was evidence of real progress; something she could put her hands on. Even if it was only a piece of paper, it was one that changed her life. A happy tear appeared at the corner of her eye.

"None of that," said Audra, "we're not done yet." After a dramatic pause, she continued, "Look inside the backpack."

Sheila unsnapped the main compartment and lifted the cover. A Walmart bag was on top.

"That is a change of clothes. There is even deodorant, powder, a brush. Take that out and look underneath."

Below the Walmart bag was a large manila envelope; the kind with red string for closing. "Just a peek," Audra said, as Sheila unwound the string. When she peeled back flap, the thick, green stacks within almost took her breath away.

"Thirty-seven thousand; it's what's left of the buy-out money you and Bert got when they closed down the trailer park. Of course, Bert never bothered telling you about it, so even if your memory wasn't Swiss cheese, this would have been a surprise. It was a lucky break that the other Sheila found it at all." Audra's mysterious smile made Sheila wonder what her friend was holding back. "For some reason, Bert didn't take it when he ran out. Another lucky break, I guess."

"Keep that in the bottom until you get to wherever you're going."

As she stuffed the Walmart bag into the backpack, Sheila looked at Audra with a question in her eyes.

"I know, I know. That's an important one. We'll get to it in a second. There are a few things I need to tell you first. But we're almost out of time, so I'll have to be fast."

"You didn't look at the license close enough. The last name on it is Wilton. It was your mother's maiden name. She was from California—Monterey probably. Sheila, the other Sheila, got your ... her ... name, legally changed. I believe that you, I mean the other Sheila, thought there might be a chance of finding your mother's family."

"I don't know when, or even if, you'll get the other Sheila's memories. I think bits and pieces will come back." Sheila couldn't hide her amusement. "Yes, I suppose, since you have a license, that it would be good if you remembered learning how to drive."

Audra gave her a quick smile; she seemed to be making an effort to keep the conversation light and positive. She reached across and put her hand on Sheila's knee. "You did so much, Sheila; you were so brave. The running was hard, I know. But what went on away from the road was much worse. It would be good if you got some of those memories back, if only to prove to yourself how much courage you have. If other memories do come back, I hope they will only be the memories from after you sat on that trash can a year ago." Audra chuckled. "I know ... part of you hates that you have a trash can as the linchpin of your life. But I hope it stays that way. You don't want to remember what went on before that moment."

Audra knew that Sheila wanted to protest, but she would have none of it.

"No, you don't. I won't answer any questions about that."

"And now, there is just one last thing. Where do you go from here?" Audra pointed at the front pocket once more.

Sheila reached in and found one last envelope.

This one held a single Amtrak ticket to Pittsburgh, with a transfer on to Chicago; only one ticket. Sheila's hand trembled as she considered what that meant.

"Once you get to Chicago, you'll have to decide where you'd like to go from there. I'm not saying it will be easy, but you have what you need to start over. You're free."

Another "but" was on her lips, only Audra was too quick.

"Don't, Sheila." She shook her head sadly and stood up. "You need to go change. And besides, I bet you *really* have to pee by now."

Sheila pushed herself off the bench. The pain in her legs was overwhelmed by the fear that the only person she knew in the whole wide world was about to exit her life again, this time for good.

"I know what you're thinking, Sheila," Audra stepped forward and hugged her and whispered in her ear, "Don't worry, you don't have to say goodbye. You'll see me again ... sooner than you think."

With the backpack slung over her shoulder, Sheila walked across the milk-white floor to the rest room. Her running shoes squeaked lightly on the marble, but the sound was amplified by the large room, and it made her feel as though everyone in the sparsely occupied station was looking at her. She wanted to look back, but she was afraid Audra would be gone already.

Her eyes stayed down as she rushed to the nearest open stall. The intense relief she experienced as she finally emptied her bladder was followed by a strong feeling of *jamais vu*; an eerie, unexpected sense that she was doing a common, everyday task for the first time. For a year it was as if Sheila had existed only when she was running. Now, simple actions like going to the bathroom, putting on deodorant, and getting dressed, felt strangely unfamiliar. Even her body didn't feel like her own. While she was running, she had been aware that she was losing weight and getting in shape, but it took dressing herself to really notice what a dramatic change had taken place.

As she left the stall, Sheila was rummaging in the backpack, looking for the hairbrush; it wasn't until she was halfway to the line of sinks and mirrors that she looked up ... and stopped ... and stared.

Sheila felt the floor beneath her tremble; a metallic growl rumbled through the station. Like a funhouse mirror, the reflection she was watching vibrated and showed two shaky images. One was familiar despite the vibration; this reflection was weak and trembling with fear, her heavy form filled the mirror; it was the Sheila from which she had run a year to escape. The other image was thinner and confident; it seemed to fight the vibration. The images merged and steadied as the incoming train ground to a halt.

Standing in the center of the room was a woman in a dark blue sweat suit. She had dark hair and a strong, straight nose. In one hand was a backpack and in the other, a hairbrush. Sheila looked down at herself and then back at the mirror, approaching slowly.

In the mirror, Audra walked steadily forward.

"It can't be!" Sheila watched as Audra's lips moved with the words. She dropped the pack and the brush in the sink, put her hands on the edge and leaned forward, disbelief on her face. Why, the last time she looked in a mirror her ... but she couldn't remember *ever* looking in a mirror. Was this *really* her face?

It couldn't be her face. Bert had broken her nose—twice— hadn't he? She couldn't recall the memory, but she was somehow certain that it had happened. Leaning closer still, she turned her face one way, and then the other. If you knew where to look, the faint white scars were visible. She'd gotten her nose fixed!

She wet some paper towels and washed her unfamiliar face; slowly she began to accept the obvious. There had never been an Audra. That strong, confident woman really was a figment of her imagination. She choked back a bitter laugh, remembering when Audra had pretended to be hurt by that accusation.

No, not a figment, Sheila thought. *Audra is part of me; more a part of me now than ever.*

Pushing away, Sheila took the brush and began pulling long strokes through her hair. As she studied her reflection, images flickered behind her eyes; most were dark and harder than the cold marble beneath her feet.

An announcement came over the PA system:

"All aboard the Amtrak Pennsylvanian, bound for Pittsburgh. The train leaves in five minutes."

Sheila turned away from images of the past and walked out of the room, imagining her future instead.

WHAT SHEILA FORGOT

On your mark ...

WHAAPP! Sheila shuddered and moaned, but she didn't scream, despite the welt making a fiery appearance on her bare back. Although she was on her hands and knees on the sticky linoleum floor, getting whipped like a dog, she wasn't thinking about how cruel Bert was, or about how much she hated him. At that moment, she was thanking her lucky stars that the unopened bottle of Rolling Rock hadn't broken when it had slipped from her hand, hit the edge of the coffee table and bounced into Bert's lap.

At the start of the evening, thirty-three bottles of her husband's favorite beer had been chilling in the galvanized tub of ice on the kitchen counter. Bert believed that the "33" on the Rolling Rock label meant that if you could consume thirty-three bottles in one sitting, you would achieve the redneck equivalent of nirvana. So, every Saturday night, while watching WWF, he would make the attempt. He'd never done better than nineteen, pretty good for a guy whose body weight was only one-sixty, even when he was soaked in beer. But he was a positive-thinking drinker who didn't stop trying.

Bert was only nine beers in when Sheila had committed the cardinal sin of beer-dropping and he hadn't been drunk enough to forget that thirty-three minus one was thirty-two. If it had broken, he wouldn't have been able to take his shot at nirvana and then he would have been really pissed.

WHAAPP! Sheila took her final stripe and crawled to the back of the trailer.

In the bedroom, a miracle occurred. A hand reached down and helped Sheila to her feet. Arms held her, gave her strength ... and led her to the closet.

Get set ...

"Sheilaya soopid fat cunt," Bert mumbled, "whaffuck y'doin'?" His wife was standing behind the T.V. in her triple-XL Famous Dave's Barbecue sweatshirt, with the sleeves rolled up to her elbows. Most of the space between the living room and their little eat-in kitchen was filled by her three hundred eighty-three pounds. The eyes in his pride and joy, the mounted head of a sixteen-point buck, seemed to be watching the scene with eagerness from behind his wife's left shoulder.

Normally, he did his best to ignore his gargantuan wife unless he needed a beer, or had to whale the tar out of her for some stupidshit thing she'd done. It was easier to ignore her with a dozen or so Rocks in his belly; he'd had fifteen, and he was still chuggin'. But the silly bitch was holding his shotgun. This brought Bert out of his drunken, boob-tube daze better than any tub of ice water had ever done. The gun looked like a toothpick in her hands ... *she's so fucking big,* he thought.

The freight train from Pittsburgh to Philly was right on schedule. It roared past and rattled the little trailer like it was being dragged over a washboard road.

"I-I-I t-t-toll y-y-ya n-n-nottta m-m-mess w-w-wid m'g-g-guns."

Well. she might be big, he thought, *that just means there's room for a few more stripes.* Trembling, not from fear, but the vibrations of the train, Bert pushed himself off the frayed, green sofa.

... BLAM!

It was another miracle! Not the fact that, despite the room shaking like they were in the middle of an earthquake, she had managed to hit him. The miracle was that, somehow Sheila had found the courage to pull the trigger.

Bert bounced back with a comical look of surprise on his alcohol-flushed face.

From ten feet away, the #6 pellets had little time for the plastic spread wad to do its job. They hit him below his neck line in a ragged three-inch-diameter circle. If he had been a rabbit, the game he most often hunted, the blast would have taken his head off. As it was, the soft metal only shredded his skin and made a bloody mess of his trachea, esophagus, and nearby muscles and arteries.

He was dead, but it would take a bit for his brain to get the tweet. Meanwhile, his heart pushed red fountains out of the ragged hole between his shoulders, and his mouth worked to deliver a final, degrading message to his wife.

Sheila didn't know that Bert had no air for his voice box to produce sound. His words still pricked, and sliced, and cut.

What a bloody, god damn mess you've made, Sheila. You are one ugly, fat, stupid cow. Look at yourself! You could feed a whole fucking country of starving cannibals. Wipe that dumb look off your face and get this shit cleaned up... I mean fucking right now! And bring me another Rock. Chugga, chugga.

Meanwhile, Sheila hammered his head into an oozing, misshapen pulp with the butt of the shotgun. After finally getting Bert to shut up for a minute, Sheila staggered to the kitchen sink. Once she'd caught her breath, she washed the blood off her face and arms, and then pulled her sleeves down. Back in the living room, she surveyed the bloody scene with a calm sense of satisfaction.

"You're welcome," she said to the buck hanging on the wall.

She walked to the door of the trailer, to the hooks on the wall next to it. Hanging there was the belt her husband had used for so many years. The long, metal-studded strip was much too big for holding up his pants; he was such a scrawny little bastard. Up until this moment, it had served one purpose only; to keep her "toein' the straight and narrow line", as he liked to say.

Flecks of pale skin, *her* skin, were still sticking to the leather of the belt. A moaning, incoherent scream worked its way from deep inside. The scream would have been easily interpreted by any of the four million women who are physically abused each year by their husbands. It translated to "Why did I let that sick asshole get away with that for so long? Hell, I should have just sat on the puny creep."

Sheila took the belt off the hook.

Don't be touchin' mah belt, or it'll be touchin' you, right hard.

Ignoring Bert's voice wasn't as difficult as she thought it might be. She walked over to where his feet flopped over the edge of the couch, and used it to strap his feet together. After cinching the belt tight, she used it and the hem of his terrycloth robe to tug him onto the floor. The blood that had pooled in his lap painted a red swath across his camouflage boxers and gathered in the folds of the robe; from there it soaked through the terry-cloth and into the carpet.

Fuck! woman, more mess to clean up. You'll pay for this, ya know... damn dearly.

Sheila dragged him out the door, around the trailer and up the gravel slope to the railroad tracks. It was a long, hard pull. When she got him up the berm and onto the tracks, she lifted her head and listened. The last Amtrak daily to Pittsburgh would be coming through soon; she knew she better hurry. Lifting her dead husband under the arms, she put him in a sitting position on the westbound track, stripped away the bathrobe, propped his body as best she could, and returned to the trailer.

A few minutes later, she was back ... carrying the deer head.

What the hell? Ya know better than ta be touchin' mah stuff!

Sheila wedged the plaque securely between her husband's legs so that the buck's long neck helped support his chest. The buck's head and his proud antlers extended well above Bert's shoulders. She grabbed his hands and jammed them, one on each side, into the rack; his fingers looked like little antler nubs.

"I knew you wouldn't want to go traveling without your buddy." She giggled and turned to go. As she made her way down the embankment, her feet slipped on the loose gravel and she went down hard on the rough stones.

Hahahaha! Who's laughing now? That had to hurt! At least that fat ass of yours cushioned the fall.

Sheila grimaced while she scooted painfully down the remainder of the slope, dragging his bathrobe behind her, and then struggled to her feet. Bent over at the waist, she closed her eyes and gritted her teeth against the agony that was now blooming from almost every part of her body. She opened her eyes when the Amtrak train blew its horn at Hendrick's Crossing, five miles away.

Bert's whipping belt lay on the ground at the bottom of the embankment. She moaned as she squatted down to pick it up, and then she walked over to the burn barrel in the back yard.

That was a perfectly good robe, bitch! What a fuckin' waste.

The flames were already dying down when Sheila came around to the front of the trailer, still carrying Bert's belt.

Make sure you hang that up by the door. I'm not done with it yet.

"Yeah, Bert, you are. Have a nice train ride."

You're wrong, bitch. I'm not going anywhere.

Icy fingers on her back made Sheila shiver, but she kept moving, down the crumbling road lined with abandoned trailer homes, and away from the tracks. Fifteen years of accumulated pain were evident in each step of her ponderous body through the trash-strewn wasteland. From Musser Junction, two miles away, the train horn blew again.

She cried out when the belt jerked in her hand and spun her around. Then she shrieked.

Bert had a hold on the other end of the belt. He looked as if he had been dipped in the blood that was now only gurgling, not spurting, from the hole in his chest. His jaw was broken and his mouth was an open, bloody maw. The left side of his head was misshapen and his left eye was hanging from its socket. But his right eye was firmly fixed on Sheila.

Gimme that belt.

"No," she screamed, grabbing hold with both hands, "you can't have it!"

Don't you back-talk me, woman! I'll whip the fucking hide off you if it takes me all night!

A low rumbling arose from the east, growing rapidly louder, and closer.

Stumbling along the road, she cried and moaned, her massive body trembling as she struggled to hold on to the belt.

Sheila kept pulling, shuffling backward away from the tracks.

The vibration started in her feet, climbing quickly up her legs and through her body. In the darkness, the bright headlight of the train appeared around the bend; for a brief moment, the beam swept across Sheila, and then she looked past Bert toward the trailer. Above and behind it on the tracks, Bert and his sixteen-point buck were aglow in the burning brightness of the onrushing train.

That won't change a fucking thing, Sheila. I'm going to beat the living hell out of you; tonight, tomorrow... and every day for the rest of your shitty, worthless life...

GIVE ME THAT FUCKING BELT!
The leather dug into the skin of her hands as Sheila set her feet and resisted. Terror gripped her and tears filled her eyes; streaking mascara bled down through the make-up, the dirt, and the blood on her face; her jaw clenched as she strained with every ounce of will she had.

Arnie cursed and slammed the button for the horn. *What is it with all the suicidal deer on the track tonight?* he wondered, *that's the third one since we left Philly.* He didn't even think of hitting the breaks, even though he did believe it was a shame to run over a beauty like that. *That's some rack on that fella! Won't be nothin' but a bloody smear on the ties once this train chews him up; right ... about ... now!*

Sheila stumbled as the belt went slack. The passenger cars of the Amtrak Pennsylvanian sped by, the interiors softly aglow. To Sheila, it felt like every person inside those cars was looking directly at her. The last fifteen minutes raced through her mind like a silent film, playing across the moving train and the shocked faces of the people inside; the blast, the blood; pounding the shotgun into Bert's brains; dragging his body up the embankment, and watching the buck's antlers shatter as the train erased any trace of her husband. Each scene drained her fear away, and replaced it with an overpowering guilt.

Then the last railcar whipped by and she covered her face with her hands.

"Oh my god!" she sobbed, "What have I done?"

A firm hand settled on her heaving shoulder. Sheila gasped, and fear staged a furious comeback.

"You did what you had to do."

She spun toward the unexpected voice, stumbling backward off the weathered asphalt. A tall, broad-shouldered woman was standing on the road, looking strong and confident. A pillar of chiseled stone would not have looked any more striking than this imposing woman. Depth of character and determination were evident in her strong face.

"You don't need to be afraid." She gave Sheila a sympathetic smile. "I'm here to help you."

"Who ... who are you?"

"Audra. My name is Audra."

The woman looked left, down the long, dark road leading out of the trailer park. Sheila followed the woman's gaze. The pot-holed passage leading away from her exploded into a raging mountain stream, rushing into the future. She existed in a stagnant, polluted backwater, poisoned by fear and self-loathing. The churning whitewater she saw ahead would flush the poison from her soul and scrub the darkness from her life. Navigating that stream would be harrowing. A year of back-breaking work awaited her, full of complex plans and daunting goals that seemed impossible to reach. It was too much for Sheila; the weak, overweight, autophobic Sheila that had accepted a lifetime of abuse. But the path this woman was showing her led to an ocean of possibilities; if, somewhere deep inside, she could find a Sheila who had the courage and strength to follow it.

"I can't do that." Sheila said, nodding her head down the road. "It's impossible."

"You *can* do it. You *must* do it. The gun has already gone off; the race has started."

"How do I even begin?"

"One step at a time. One day at a time." Audra pointed ahead, to a spot beside the road, to a rusted metal trash can. "Getting rid of that belt is the first step."

Sheila turned to the left and saw the dented old can. She lifted her hand and looked at the belt. The belt that had left layers of scars on her back, scars on her soul. It would never touch her again.

She wrenched the rusted top from the can, dropped the belt inside and replaced the lid.

When she turned back, her mind was clear ...

... and ready to start the race.

THE END

THE MONEY CLIP

The Money Clip

Now that I, Melvin Simpson, realize everything has changed for me, I have decided to write down what I have experienced during the last seven days. I am a very different person than I was last week. Since the catalyst for this transformation is resting in front of me on my cluttered desktop, next to this keyboard, I will, as an introduction, explain how it came to be in my possession. This may help me later to remember that I was once a loving, kind, and, I suppose, mostly unremarkable, middle-class husband and father. What I am now is ... well, I'll get to that later. First off, I'm going to tell you how the money clip came to be in my possession.

❧

I'm a foreman for an electrical contractor, strictly a blue-collar kinda guy—except that I run. It isn't something that most of the guys on my crew understand; they think my groundwire's a little loose. Anyway, last Wednesday I got off work early and decided to go for a ten-mile run. Of course, I hadn't run a step in almost a month, but I guess those guys are right, I'm a little crazy when it comes to my running—up and down, hot and cold. The seasons were just beginning to change from winter to spring and I was feeling the itch. I needed to get out on the road.

Even though it was almost fifty degrees, I wore Under Armour long tights since I knew my legs would be protesting before the ten miles were over and I thought the tights would help fend off some of the muscle cramps I was expecting. With a short-sleeve tech top and a fuel belt strapped around my waist, I shot out the door before common sense set in or my Sobe Adrenaline Rush wore off.

The afternoon sky was a crisp blue. It had that crystal-like quality you only get during the winter. It makes the sun seem so much brighter, even when it fails to impart much warmth to your body. I felt great starting out. It had rained heavily the previous night and washed away almost all of the ice and snow that had accumulated during a bitter cold February. The shoulders of the road where I did most of my long runs were clear, except for the occasional plow-mound of dirty, crusty ice that had started out big enough to survive the rain.

Like I said, I had planned on ten miles. The problem is, I have this obsessive/compulsive streak that is usually trouble. It sometimes benefits my running, makes me itchy if I miss a day, allows me to run long miles without getting bored. But it often leads me down the road to overuse injuries. I get a little pain, then my OCD kicks in and keeps pushing; it almost always leads to an injury that keeps me out for a long time.

When I got to the intersection at five miles, the spot where I meant to turn around, I couldn't ...

Turn around, you idiot!

Turn ...

No... noooo!

around.

Ach! What a fool!

This conversation actually took place in my head.

Instead of turning around, I made a left and kept going. I had gotten a bit warm, what with the tights and all, and I was headed for a long, shady stretch that I knew would cool me down. This stretch is a large stand of oak and ash trees that straddle the road for about a quarter mile. They are so thick that even in the winter, without their leaves, they completely block out the sun. It is an island of shade amidst on ocean of barren fields.

The cool shade did its job a little too well and when I reached the sunlight on the other side, I was glad for what little warmth it gave. I picked up the pace again, partly because I wanted to warm up and partly because I wanted to get back in time to start dinner before my wife, Katie, came home from work. At the turnaround spot for twelve miles, I was tired enough that I convinced myself to head back.

Approaching the woods again on my return trip my upper back began to get stiff. I swung my head back and forth to try to loosen up and, as I did, I was almost blinded as the sun reflected off something in a pile of ice off to the side.

I'm not that much of a scavenger when I run. Depending on my mood, I may occasionally pick up a coin lying on the road, but not always. Not like Katie. She is the queen of roadside scavengers, often coming home from her runs with some pretty amazing items. Once she carried home an eight foot long two-by-four that she thought I could use in my wood shop. She couldn't just note the location and drive back later to get it. No, she had to carry it for two miles, all the way home. Another time, she ran home hauling a ten-pound sledgehammer with a long yellow handle. I can just imagine some slimy stalker driving by, seeing her with that sledge and thinking, "Nah, she's not my type, I think I'll pass."

When I do pick something up, it's always with a *grab it and go* action; which is what I did with the sparkle I saw. As I regained my stride, I shook the cinders and ice crystals off the item in my hand. It was a strange-looking money clip with a soggy glob of bills in it. And they looked like big ones. I stuffed it in my belt and continued on my way.

My imagination fueled my run home. How much money was there? How did it end up in that pile? What was that unusual design on the clip? I was barely able to resist pulling it out to look at it again. Before I knew it, I was cruising up my driveway, amazed at how quickly the miles had passed.

A couple of years ago, I got in the habit of taking an ice bath after my long runs. It helps my tortured muscles recover so I can torture them again sooner. As I sat soaking and shivering, I took the sodden money out of the clip, pulling one bill at a time off the wad. I rinsed them in the water and spread them on a towel that I had draped over the edge of the tub.

Thirteen one hundred dollar bills, side by side. Then two Hamiltons ... I thought at first they were tens, but two extra zeros at the corners were a pretty good clue that I had found something unusual.

Looking closer, I saw "Series of 1918" to the left of Alex's profile, and I noticed that the serial numbers were consecutive. At the time, I didn't know much about collectible currency; a deficiency I've since corrected. But I did know that old things tend to be worth more.

I cut my bath short and headed for the computer. Googling "thousand dollar bill availability" I came up with the site "Collectiblecurrency.com." It showed lots of thousand dollar bills, from 1934 back to 1918. Most were worth tens of thousands of dollars. One from 1918 was worth $57,000. The only consecutive numbered ones were from 1934 and they were selling for almost $100,000.

My hand was resting on the empty money clip and the trembling started there, spread up my arm and through my entire body. I was briefly disoriented, as if my world had shifted on its axis. In the past, I'd always been the type of helpful, honest person who wouldn't hesitate to do the right thing in a circumstance such as this; now I was hesitating.

Folding the now clean and dry money, I put it back in the clip. Then I pondered the magnitude of the find I had made ... and considered my options. After checking Lostandfound.com for any mention of the money or the clip, I looked in the city paper classifieds. There was no listing in either.

At this point, I'd like to say that, when Katie came home from work, I told her about what I'd found, called the police and turned it over to them.

But I didn't. Didn't tell her. Didn't call the police.

What I did was hide the money in my shop out behind the house, put the clip in my sock drawer, call Ledo's to get pizza delivered for dinner, and wrote a classified ad:

'Found: money clip w/money. Will return to rightful owner who can describe clip and denominations of bills. Call ...'

The number was a disposable one I got online and would forward incoming calls to my cell. I suppose I could have put "Don't screw with me! I'm pretty much insane!" at the end of it... in CAPS and **BOLD**, but, in my defense, I wasn't aware at the time how really crazy I was becoming.

છ૭

That evening after dinner I went out to the shop and cleaned off the money clip. It's about two inches wide by two and a half inches high, with a lustrous, steely sheen. The back is flat and unmarked while on the front is a medallion one-quarter inch thick. There are two inset jewels in it that look like they could be diamonds. The rest of the surface of the medallion is covered with extremely fine lines, like a laser etching. If you look straight at the medallion it has the appearance of a strange watch face, with the jewels where hour hands would be if they were pointing to ten o'clock and two o'clock.

But when you look at it from the right, the face of a smiling man with bright shining eyes looks back. From the left side, the face changes. A flaw in the jewels gives them a glint of red and the smile becomes a devilish leer.

I had missed a small piece of dirt along the edge of the medallion and tried to use my thumbnail to clean it off. As I pushed and scraped, suddenly the top of the medallion slid aside, revealing a chamber beneath. A slimy white film coated the inside. I wiped it away with a tissue and saw, in a handsome script, this engraving:

"To M.S.—A Killer is Born."

That the initials are the same as mine was interesting, but I was mostly intrigued by the inscription. Was this the token of some gang of drug dealers? I now suspected that the white film might be cocaine; the devilish leer certainly looked evil; and the amount of cash in the clip sure seemed like drug money to me.

I began to think that the calls I might get in response to the lost and found ad might become very interesting.

◦◦◦

As expected, I was sore the next morning, but not enough to keep me from heading off to work. I wasn't at work long before I got the first call. Since the ad involved found money, I knew I'd get calls from people who were hoping to get lucky. But with the uniqueness of the clip and the odd currency, it would be quick and easy to weed out the liars; which is what I did that first day.

The next morning, though, I got a call that altered my whole slant on the clip. After the initial pleasantries, the guy got all emotional on me.

"It's been so long; I never thought I'd see my money clip again." He sounded ancient, like Marlon Brando in *The Godfather*, when the old Mafioso was about to kick the bucket. "Figured whoever had found it would hold on to it. You must be a man with character."

"You're pretty sure it belongs to you?" I asked.

"Of course," The old man's voice was soft, and whistled as if each word was an effort. He described the clip in perfect detail.

My heart dropped, far from relieved at having found the rightful owner. I was disappointed; more than that, I felt like something belonging to me was about to be stolen away. A strange grinding arose inside my head, like gears on a new machine moving for the first time. I reached for a slim hope.

"Can you tell me about the inscription?"

"Yes, certainly. It says 'To L.M.—A Killer is Born'."

L.M.

Not M.S. An exhilarating surge of energy pulsed through me.

"That's not it!" My voice betrayed the excitement I was feeling.

"It is!" he said. "I've read it a dozen times."

"Well, I'm looking at it right now, and the initials are not L.M."

"It belongs to me!" he yelled weakly. "If you try to keep it ..." I could hear the old man struggling for breath on the other end of the line, "...your life will never be the same." It sounded as though he were trying to summon a menace that had once bent others to his will. "I'll find you."

There was a time I may have been intimidated by his threat; I think that time must have passed less than two days earlier—when I picked that clip out of the ice. The words that answered the old man certainly wouldn't have come from the man I had been before I picked up the money clip.

"Fine," I screamed into the phone, "come find me. You'll get a double tap for your trouble!" I'm not even sure what "double tap" means, but I don't think "two mugs of beer" is it.

I should have gotten rid of the disposable phone number right after the call; still don't know why I didn't. The days that followed were a bit of a blur. My wife noticed that something was different about me, but I refused to talk about it; told her everything was fine.

Even though I was sore from that twelve-mile run, I managed to get out every day. Funny thing is, I *couldn't* get out the door unless I had that money clip slipped into the waistband of my running shorts.

There were more calls from people hoping to claim money that wasn't theirs. I dealt with them easily.

But there were also calls that were eerily similar to the one from the old man. The area codes were from all over the country; L.A., Dallas, New York, Boston, Miami. Not all of the callers were old, but they all clearly knew the money clip. Each of them described the hidden chamber, and the inscription. They all sounded like tough guys.

And the boneheads all got the initials wrong.

You may be thinking that there had to be other money clips like this one, clips that had other initials inscribed in them.

Really? And they all got lost? At the same time? Something strange is going on; I just can't figure out what it is. Now that I've had some time to mull it over, I wonder why none of them mentioned the money. Even more curious; at the time, I never even thought about the money myself. The clip was the only thing on any of our minds.

Yesterday, circumstances took a turn for the worse. That was when I realized that I wasn't going to let anyone take that clip away from me. It all started with another call. Breakfast was finished; Katie had just left for work and I was about to clear the table and follow her out the door when my cell rang.

When I answered, the guy started right in before I could even say hello.

"So, you're the one found my money clip." His voice sounded young and cocky.

"Yeah," I replied, "yours and about thirty more, from all the calls I've been getting."

"Oh, there's no mistaking this clip," he said. "It's big for a money clip … has two big jewels on the front, along with a freaky two-faced guy."

"Don't think that's going to impress me," I said. "I've heard it all before."

"No doubt." He sounded as if he knew something I didn't. "But I'm sure no one else could tell you about the money."

I held my breath. This sounded like it might really be the owner of the clip.

"Bet those had you worked up." The guy laughed. "Thirteen hundred in Franklins and two Hamiltons, not the ten spots either. Ya never saw any of those before, am I right? I can even give you the serial numbers."

"That won't be necessary; you've obviously seen this clip before."

"Of course!" he quickly answered, "it belongs to me. I'll even let you keep one of the hundreds as a reward. So where can I come to pick it up?"

"Well, I do need one bit of information first," I said.

"What's that?" he asked hesitantly.

"Can you tell me about the inscription?" There was a long pause. "Hello?" I heard him cough, then say ...

"So you found the compartment."

"Yeah. I'm afraid your coke didn't handle the moisture very well."

"Too bad," he said, "that was some good shit. But there's plenty more where that came from. At least you're admitting the clip's mine."

"Not so fast. What about the inscription?" At that point, I knew it didn't matter what he said, but I went through the motions anyway.

There was some static on the line, and then another moment of silence before he answered,

"A Killer is Born."

A haunted tone colored his words and the hair on my neck straightened. When my voice came back I whispered, "What about the initials?"

"I'm Manny Shelstein," he said. "My initials are M.S."

For some reason, hearing those initials spoken made the chill on my neck disappear and my spine straighten. "So are mine," I said.

"Don't even think about keeping my clip, punk." He growled. "I've got the resources to hunt you down ..."

"I've heard that one before, too." I held the clip up and twisted it in the light of the sun through the kitchen window. The red-eyed leer stared at me. I smiled back. "Manny, my boy... I think this belongs to me now."

"No fucking way! I want that clip and that money now, you little prick! It won't be hard to find you, asshole. I'll ..."

I hung up on him. The old me would have, too. He never put up with being cussed at, not by anybody. Especially some jerk on the phone. Now, though, I'm not sure why—that language doesn't bother me anymore.

Strangely enough, I wasn't too worried about this guy. I was sure I'd have to deal with him, more likely sooner than later; but I was sure I could handle it. Where this confidence came from, I have no idea; in the past, I would have been trembling in my shoes.

My cell rang again. I ignored it and, as it rang and rang, I had a brief period of lucidity. I could see that violence would be at the end of this game I was playing. Violence that would forever alter the life I led, no matter who got hurt. When the ringing stopped, I dialed the State Police.

I told the officer who answered that I had found a money clip and started to give him a brief description. The words began to stick in my throat as I regretted making the call; at the same time I heard a click on the line.

The officer said, "Sir, can you start again, please? We need to record this for accuracy."

I thought the police recorded all incoming calls, and immediately suspected that he might have turned the recorder off. There was no grinding in my head this time; the gears were whirring smoothly. Like a movie preview, I could see exactly where this would end. After describing the money clip, I told him about the classified ad and the response I had gotten.

"We have lots of resources," he said. "I'm sure we'll be able to find the true owner. Go ahead and give me the inscription."

When I gave him the inscription, I told him the initial were R.T. instead of M.S. He took my name and said that when the real owner was found, they would be in touch.

৯৫

Before going to bed last night, I laid down on the living room floor, carefully massaging, stretching, and foam-rolling my sore muscles. My running has never been logical. I break a lot of the accepted "rules" of training. Obviously, no running authority would recommend putting in fifty miles in the first week of any training program. But I use what resources I have, and being obsessive and stubborn are resources. Once I start running, running long every other day is a compulsion. I knew I'd be headed out for a long run the next day, regardless of any threat. The more stiffness I could work out that evening, the better I'd feel during those long miles.

While rolling and stretching, I considered Manny Shelstein. The guy was surely searching for me right now. If he really did have resources, it wouldn't take him long to find out where I lived. I had no illusions that this problem would just go away. I thought about how to be best prepared at home and at work, wondering where I'd be the most vulnerable if this guy came after me. Of course I'd be least able to defend myself when I was out on my long run. I imagined lots of scenarios and I was surprised at how easily I thought of a few tricks that might pull me out of trouble.

❧

Despite the painful foam rolling last night, I was pretty stiff when I woke up this morning. Moving around at work was hard, but I got through without straining anything. I even came up with another idea that would help me if I was accosted during my run.

Once home, I changed into my running clothes quickly, but then took a little longer getting loose. As I ran easily down the driveway, I took stock. All my muscle groups were hurting, as were my knees, my hips, my shoulders. Working from the top down, I determined that all the pain I was feeling was just soreness, not injury, and figured that most of it would go away as I got into my run, with a little help from the two Nuprin I'd taken earlier. With my anatomical inventory complete, I shook out my arms and settled into a steady, relaxed pace. Soon I was in cruise control and my mind turned to the events of the last week and what effect they would have on my life. My overactive imagination led me through a series of entertaining and highly improbable plays in which I was the star, handling all sorts of evil schemes and schemers. The fantasies were so involved and varied that I blew by the eight-mile mark still on auto-pilot. Dehydration finally brought me back to the real and now. As I ran along, I took some water from one of the flasks in my fuel belt, being careful to avoid the gray Teflon bottle. Then I sucked down a packet of power gel and washed that down with some more water.

Properly refueled, I reached the nine-mile mark and turned for home. Idling on the left shoulder on the other side of an intersection about a quarter-mile down was a faded black Caprice. As I approached, the car moved up to the intersection and turned right, the engine rattling roughly as it accelerated away.

Unless I have a really wide shoulder to run on, I always run on the left side of a road, facing traffic. That way I have a little warning when some ignorant kid and his drunk friends come barreling down the road in their oversize pickup, blaring their horn and yelling obscenities. And unless I'm off on some flight of fancy, I usually am hyper-aware of vehicles approaching from either direction. So I heard the Caprice and its engine rattle long before the driver went past me and pulled over on the right shoulder. He rolled down his window and called out.

"Hey, I think I'm lost. Could you tell me where this address is?" He waved a piece of paper in my direction.

This guy certainly looked stupid enough to be lost, but he also seemed like the type with too much ego to admit it. And he sounded just like the guy who I'd hung up on the day before. We were on a deserted section of road with no houses visible from that particular spot. I crossed the road toward the car, reaching for the gray flask at my hip as I did. I even pretended to take a drink.

"Hey, thanks for stopping!" he said.

I popped the top off the flask as I approached the window.

A sly and self-satisfied grin spread across his face and the driver held out the paper, "I'm looking for this address. The fuck-up who lives there has my money clip."

Without pausing, I took the paper from his left hand and sprayed the flask of hydrofluoric acid all over his face.

He screamed, dropped the gun he was hiding in his right hand, and put both hands to his face, thereby getting the corrosive liquid on them, too. Opening the car door while staying as far back as I could, I put my foot on his shoulder and shoved him flat across the front seat. Holding my breath, I reached in and turned the car off and took the keys, then picked up the gun that had fallen on the floor. I stepped back, rolled up the window and closed the door, with the man inside writhing on the seat. Then I quickly went back across the road and continued on my way.

I knew the fumes from the acid would already be making it hard to breath and destroying his lungs, that his eyes were permanently blinded and that the pain he was experiencing everywhere the liquid had touched was driving him quickly toward unconsciousness. Before I was around the next turn he would be dead.

After I tossed the car keys far into the woods, I tucked his gun under the back of my fuel belt, pulled my shirt over it, and picked up the pace. The whole incident had happened in a flash and should have left me shaking in my Saucony Trigons. But I felt strangely calm, maybe just a little euphoric. A bit like I had just won a race I was sure I'd win anyway. I had never intentionally killed anything before. I even swerve to miss little animals in the road and feel genuinely depressed when I fail to avoid hitting them. Now I had killed a human being and felt good about it.

Each stride ate up the ground toward home and what now seemed to be a very troubled future. I had my second energy gel with about five miles to go and that got me through to the finish, barely. Eighteen miles and killing a man had left me drained and numb—physically, mentally, and emotionally. The gun digging into the small of my back didn't help either.

◡◠

As soon as I got inside, I went upstairs to run the water for my ice bath. I dropped the gun on the bed then went back down to the kitchen to get a bottle of water from the refrigerator. I was drinking deeply when there was a knock on the door.

I could see through the glass in the door that the man knocking was large and had an authoritarian posture. When I opened the door he said …

"Good afternoon, sir. The State Police gave me your name and address. They said that you had found my money clip."

"That might be true." The movie that had played in my mind the day before began to run. "Can you describe it?"

With a firm, polite voice, he went on to describe the clip and the money and even volunteered the inscription.

"To R.T.—A Killer is Born."

"Are you sure that's right?" I asked. "R.T.?"

"Yes, sir!" he answered. "That's me, Robert Tobin."

"Well, I guess it must be your clip," I told him. "I have it out in my shop behind the house. I just started running a bath; let me turn the water off and we'll go get it."

I went up and turned the water off ... and put the gun back under my fuel belt.

As we walked around to the shop, he went on with a story about how he had lost the clip. I nodded politely but was, in truth, hardly listening. I was too busy visualizing what would happen when I shot this pretender in the head.

About one hundred meters behind the house is my woodshop, in what used to be a detached two-car garage, although I don't know why anyone would put a garage so far from the house. During inclement weather, I don't enjoy going out there to work. But it is remote enough that my noisy woodworking equipment doesn't bother my wife or our neighbors. I was pretty sure a gunshot would go unremarked, if not completely unnoticed.

Inside, the shop is a disaster area. Equipment, scrap wood, boxes of supplies, half-finished projects and sawdust clog almost all the floor space. Only the area around the main work table is relatively clear. I led him along a serpentine path to the table.

"Sorry about the mess," I said, "I never seem to be able to make time to clean up."

I had stashed the money clip in a drawer built into the underside of the table. I took it out and laid it on the table in front of him. As he picked it up to examine it, I slipped the gun out of my waistband, quickly put it to the back of his head, and pulled the trigger.

The next hour was crazy. I felt like Super Mario on crack. As soon as the guy hit the floor, I took his keys from the clip on his belt, locked the door of the shop and ran back to the house. I grabbed my bike and put it in the trunk of his car, jumped in and tore off down the road. Driving as fast as I could without attracting too much attention, I headed for the state park in the next county over. There I got my bike out of the trunk, left the car and called my wife on my cell.

"Hey, sweetie! Are you on the way home yet?" I asked.

"No, but I'll be leaving soon," Katie answered, "I just have a couple of things to clear off my desk."

"Would you mind picking up something for dinner on the way home? I did another long run today and I'm exhausted."

"You crazy man! You're gonna wear yourself out! Sure, I'll pick something up and be home as soon as I can."

"Take your time," I said. "I may pop over to the health club and get in the whirlpool for a bit."

"Well then, I hope I'll see you at home sometime tonight!"

"Don't worry, I won't be long. Love you!"

"Love you, too!" she said.

With my wife sufficiently delayed, I began the long ride home.

⁖

So, that brings us up to now. Here I am writing this at my computer in our den, full from the delicious Fazoli's spaghetti dinner my wife brought home, while she's at her own computer just a few feet away. I'm considering what to do with the dead guy in the shop. I'm wondering how I'll be able to sell those Hamiltons. And I'm imagining what I'm going to do to the next guy who comes looking for that clip.

A moment ago, right after I typed that last bit, I picked the money clip up off the desk and pushed open the medallion.

"To M.S.—A Killer is Born."

I know what it says is true; it's what I feel like now, a killer. And it doesn't bother me.

"What's that you have?" my wife asked a moment ago.

In the instant the thought popped into my head I knew it was a foolish way to think. Still, I had to hide a suspicious and hostile reaction that was directed toward the woman I've loved for twenty years. As I write these words I'm worried about how this little piece of metal might change our marriage.

"Oh, just something I found on my run." I palmed the clip and slipped it into my desk drawer.

And that's my story for now. I can't pretend that this is the end. Something big is coming, I can feel it.

∽

As obsessive as my husband was, I'm sure he would have liked to see this little story finished. I've reached that age where hot flashes usually wake me at least once during the night. Often, Melvin wakes up when I get out of bed for a glass of water. Last night he must have been so tired from all his running that he didn't even stir.

I was drinking the water and flapping my nightshirt to cool off when I thought of the money clip. I'd only gotten a glance at it and I was curious. Making my way quietly to the den, I turned on the desk lamp and took the strange object from the drawer. As I moved it under the light, I saw the smiling face ... and the red-eyed devil. I was about to set it down when the chamber slipped open and I read the inscription ...

"To K.S.—A Killer is Born."

THE END

RUNNER'S HIGH

CHAPTER ONE

The Redeeming Ponytail

The deadly yellow beast seemed to assemble itself, piece by piece, from the blizzard. It towered above the terrified runner as desperation teased a bit more speed from his tired legs.

To his left and to his right, cliffs of white over-topped his own height of six-two by several feet. Heavily falling snow had made him invisible to the driver of the huge plow. His only chance was to get to the intersection just a few meters ahead.

Thoughts of his wife and the unborn child he might never know helped him surge forward, driving his arms and lifting his knees.

❦

"Look at those legs move!"

Jason's large, coarse hands rubbed the last of the moisturizing lotion into her drum-tight skin as he followed the bumps on his wife's swollen belly. The tiny feet raising those bumps ran down her left side before they vanished, only to reappear further up and repeat the journey.

"What foot speed!" He leaned forward and carefully placed his left ear against the mottled, sensitive skin of her stomach. A look of mock-horror played across his face as he looked into the soft brown eyes of the woman who had changed his life.

"My God! What if he's a sprinter?"

He ducked, but wasn't quick enough to keep Jill from grabbing a handful of his dark brown hair. She pulled his head up and growled into his face.

"This *girl* is going to be a distance runner and you better not forget it!" After kissing his crooked nose, she pushed him away and pulled the yellow maternity sweater down over the Energizer bunny that had taken up residence in her tummy.

"That kicking has been going on for two hours," she moaned. "I think she's going to be a marathoner."

"In that case, I better get my run in." He smiled, kissed her on the forehead and signaled his surrender on the gender/running issue. "One of us needs to be in shape enough to keep up with her. By the looks of it, she may skip the crawling and walking stages and go straight to running."

"Be careful," she said as she tried to push herself out of the rocker, "another storm system is moving in. I don't want you getting lost in a blizzard."

Slipping two strong hands under her arms, he helped her up. With a pat on a still-athletic posterior, he sent his wife down the hall toward the bedroom.

"Don't worry," he said. "I won't go far."

"Yeah, right! I've heard that before."

"No, really. I'll be back before the storm comes ... and before you're up from your nap."

From the back, except for the slight waddle, she looked like a top-ranked road runner, which she had been more than eight months earlier. From the front or the side, she still looked like a top-ranked road runner ... one who'd swallowed a basketball.

It was amazing to him, how she looked more beautiful with each passing month.

Her long ponytail swayed as she made her way down the hall. The movement was just as hypnotic as it had been when he'd first seen her three years before. She had passed him in the early stages of a 5k race that raised funds for the residential treatment program where he was a patient. His counselor had talked him into running the race because Jason was one of the few recovering addicts with a chance of making it to the starting line.

He had chased that swaying ponytail all the way to an improbable finish.

Bringing out the best in him turned out to be only one of her talents; within a year, they were married. Although the treatment program deserved some credit, he believed Jill's swaying ponytail was the reason his life was now drug-free.

She turned the corner into the bedroom and the spell was broken.

CHAPTER TWO

The Past has Teeth

Stepping to the edge of the porch, he looked out over a frosted landscape. Even his young, skeletal red maple trees carried ridges of snow balanced precariously on their thin branches. Like white-plumed palace guards, they stood sentry on each side of the front walk.

On the left sentry a single, red leaf was still clinging stubbornly to a branch near the crown of the tree. Finding inspiration in small things, Jason used it as motivation to resist the temptation of going back inside and skipping his run.

If that tiny leaf can handle all this cold and snow, so can I.

For the past two weeks, the white stuff had fallen every day. His two beautiful Douglas firs by the driveway were half-buried. Broken by the weight, a branch near the top dangled from a string of Christmas lights the snow had kept him from taking down.

More than six feet since New Year's Day! From where he stood his driveway, and those of his neighbors, looked like dead-ends in some cruel, frozen maze.

They'd planned on having a home birth. Even though Jason had memorized the Emergency Childbirth manual front to back, he'd made sure the county road crew knew about his wife's impending delivery. That road crew had done a good job keeping the narrow road to their little development plowed so the midwife could make it in.

But, so far today, they hadn't made it the half-mile off the main road. From the porch, he could tell that last night's eight *more* inches still paved the lane in white. Shaking his arms and legs to loosen up, he walked down the short driveway he'd shoveled first thing this morning.

Jason reached the point by the road where he had stopped shoveling and did a few easy trunk twists, a couple relaxed toe-touches. He'd always thought his neighbor's monster truck was a bit loud and extravagant, but today he was thankful for its big, dual rear wheels as he stepped into their tracks and began jogging slowly up the road.

Walls of white had been built high by huge snowplows, making the road feel like a tunnel. Low clouds gave the tunnel a ceiling, one heavy with a burden about to be delivered. The world was painted in shades of white and gray; an ambiguous palette that rendered depth and distance into a mystery.

A flash of color drew his eye. High atop the snow bank on the opposite side of the road was a sight that made him shake his head and blink. When he looked again, it was gone. But for a moment, perched on a chunk of ice, he was certain he'd seen a huge green tropical bird.

At the main road he stepped aside and waved as a snowplow made the turn toward his house. The tall, precisely-curved blade slammed into the snow and fired clouds of white into the air, building the wall along the road even higher.

When the plow passed, his eyes locked on the phone booth at the gas station across the street. Tattered remnants of concert posters and lost dog notices cluttered the glass and, backlit by the weak interior light, looked like teeth—long, jagged, grinning teeth. He kept hoping some drunk would jump the curve some night and wipe that anachronism away, removing the temptation it presented.

A number leapt into his mind, along with a desire to dial it. That jittery itch still lurked; a reminder of the snow that had almost buried him. As Jill's due-date drew closer, Jason had worried more and more about what kind of father an addict would make. Because that's what he was, an addict. Resisting that siren's call had become a little easier as months turned to years, but he couldn't forget the phone number that could bring all that horror crashing back into his life. Gritting his teeth and shaking his head, he turned away.

The plow was already nearing his driveway. With his lane cleared, Jason had one less thing to worry about and stepped back into the road to begin his run. After a deep breath in and a quick, powerful exhale, he crouched over his left foot. His upper body began to drift forward; he pushed off strongly and hit the start button on his Garmin.

He accelerated steadily, waiting for the moment when his intuition said, "This is the pace you can handle today."

Whether it was the soft cushion of snow on the asphalt, or the crisp clean air, intuition failed. Before long, he'd reached a pace that was faster than normal for his training.

Jason was about to back off when he realized that this was one of those rare days when, not only didn't anything hurt, everything actually felt fantastic. His stride was smooth and efficient. Lungs and heart were working like a well-tuned engine. Ignoring the cautionary thoughts, he powered down the road.

He was headed for Route 444, a state road that rolled along in a mostly straight shot into the hinterlands, passing towns that were increasingly smaller and more widely spaced. When he reached it, Jason had planned to make a series of rights that would take him around a five-mile loop and back to his lane.

Though a light snow was beginning to fall and he'd told his wife he wouldn't go far, Jason was like a thoroughbred itching to run.

He turned left instead of right and ran into the storm.

ᘒ

Since he was working hard and sweating; Jason enjoyed the cold touch of the fat, soft flakes on his face. They were coming down steadily now, painting the exhaust-tinted drifts on the shoulder of the road with a fresh coat of white .

Every landing of his foot made a squeaky crunch in the snow followed by a light swish as he lifted a powdery swirl in his wake. The sound of his stride and his fast, rhythmic breathing seemed amplified compared to the serene silence of the alabaster landscape.

Many miles had swept by under his exuberant feet. The endorphins his pituitary gland injected into his bloodstream acted as an analgesic and covered the stress his muscles were experiencing. The effect of the endorphins produced by his hypothalamus was different. They caused a euphoria that made him feel as though he were floating through a white cloud.

It was better than any drug-induced high the razor-cut line of a different snow had ever given him.

Millions of unique crystals dropped one after another to the road. Cruising along, the ribbon of asphalt ahead of him had become a thick blanket of pure white in the rapidly failing light of late afternoon. Behind, his footsteps were quickly filled, leaving only a series of dimples on the smooth surface.

Through the heavily falling snow, he could barely make out the flashing red of the stoplight at the junction of SR 444 and SR 5. A glance at his watch showed him that he was about to reach the ten-mile mark in a time far faster than he had ever achieved in a race.

With enthusiasm, he looked ahead once again. The flashing red was clearer and it had been joined by a larger, rotating yellow light. Recognition of what was approaching unleashed a torrent of adrenalin.

There was no time for him to cross the road; reaching the finish line represented by the break in the wall of snow to his left was his only hope for survival.

The plow in the intersection was bearing down on him with a merciless haste.

Driving his arms and lifting his knees, he dove toward the shrinking space between the deadly yellow blade and the icy wall. Even with an imminent death staring him in the face, he still remembered to hit the timer on his watch as he flew through the air.

CHAPTER THREE

The Outline of a Man

A raucous cawing made his eyelids flutter. Dazed by the hard landing on the freshly plowed asphalt, Jason had, for a long time, lain spread-eagle over the double yellow line in the middle of the road. "Mmaacck aack aaaacck!"

The sound was insistent and irritating. It refused to let him fade away.

Stiffening muscles resisted, but Jason rolled over and pushed himself to his knees. Like an outline at a murder scene, his body had left its mark behind. At once, falling snow began to erase the evidence.

"Aacckk!"

Sitting back on his heels, Jason opened his eyes and looked up. On a high, white wall above his head was a bird at least three feet tall. A Great Green Macaw with a bright red, ridged forehead and blue-tipped wings opened its curved black beak and squawked.

"Get up!" his ringing ears heard.

With his head swimming and his body beginning to chill, he crawled to the edge of the road and began to climb the snow bank. Dizzy and aching, he gritted his teeth and fought the temptation to yield to the spinning gray fog that beckoned.

As he reached the top, a low rumble made him turn toward the road where another plow was driving over the spot where he had just been lying. It threw cold, wet slurry into his face that hit like an Ernie Shavers punch. His surroundings, like some snowy image on Outer Limits, went black. He tumbled backward into the deep, fresh snow.

∽

Glaring sunlight gave the inside of his eyelids a rose glow. A nearby rumbling built into a thunderous roar, then faded, only to build again. Sunshine hit his bare chest while a deep chill kept hold of his bones. A smell of salt water scented the warm breeze that ruffled his hair. A lyrical sound struck his ears.

"Hey! Get up! This is no time for a nap!"

Sand shifted beneath his head as he turned toward the sweet, teasing voice. Shielding his eyes from the dazzling sun, he opened them and saw a young girl standing on sand so white it could have been snow. With an emerald green swimsuit and bright red hair, the child would have stood out on the most crowded beach. This one was wide, straight and smooth ... and empty all the way to the horizon.

"C'mon, lazy bones!" With her hands on her hips she continued in a mock-severe tone. "You've still got ten miles to go before you're done."

Rolling onto his knees, he blinked and shook his head, trying to remember who he was ... where he had come from ... and why he was here.

To his right, a kaleidoscope of colors bordered the beach. Palm trees, their ringed, ivory trunks as straight as telephone poles, lined the beach into the distance. Delicate vines graced the palms with a garland of lavender blossoms. A screaming palette of blooms decorated the undergrowth that filled the spaces between the trees. Beyond the wall of color was a dense, dark jungle.

On his left, one after another, raging blue waves soared high and then raced toward the beach before collapsing into a foamy sheet of white that left glistening bubbles on the little girl's toes. The bubbles reflected the bright riot of the rain forest.

Every color was radiant ... sharp, hitting his eyes like sparkling knives that sliced into his brain. An earthy scent rolled heavily out of the jungle and fought with the salty tang of the ocean. The undulating roar continued incessantly. His senses were overwhelmed.

"Wow, am I ever confused!" He closed his eyes, covered his ears with his hands and tried to block out the sensory overload ... and gain time to think.

"So, what's new?" Laughing, the girl ran up and took his large left hand with both of hers and tugged him to his feet.

"That's never kept you from running before." She reached up and poked his belly-button before running happily down the beach.

He staggered, then started after her.

Although there was something familiar about her face and she acted like she knew him, his brain could retrieve nothing of value from its muddled files. Some instinct told him that he'd never seen this girl before.

One thing he learned about her right off ... she was fast.

"Wait up!" His legs responded with a sluggish reluctance as he gave chase.

∾

As he made his way down the beach, his muscles loosened and his stride became strong and smooth. Amid the confusion, running felt real. It calmed the upheaval in his mind and allowed him to think.

He hoped he was dreaming; none of the other possibilities was particularly appealing. Amnesia, a drug-induced hallucination, or a psychotic break with reality were ideas that ran through his mind. The only source of information available to him was the girl who seemed to be skimming above the sand just ahead.

Warm sun on his skin and the effort he put into his running chased the cold from his bones while he caught up with the speedy sprite. Though he was working hard, he was surprised to find that he could talk without his normal huffing and puffing.

"Who are you?" he said as he pulled alongside. "Do you know me?"

The peal of her laughter echoed off the thick vegetation and momentarily drowned out the crashing waves.

"Of course I know you, silly Daddy. I'm your little girl ... I'm Emily."

On the edge of memory was a taunting voice that rose up through his subconscious. It was the voice of doubt and self-loathing that had plagued him since he was a teenager.

That can't be true! You're a loser, always have been. You don't deserve the privilege of being a father; and you know you'll never live up to the responsibility.

Back-alley memories bubbled to the surface like sewage backed up in the drug-plagued tenement that was once his home.

His stride faltered as those thoughts hit hard. He began dropping behind once again.

Emily turned and gave him the serious look of an adult.

"Don't slow down, Daddy," she said. "The monster will get you."

"There are no monsters," he responded automatically, as if just being called Daddy forced the comforting, fraudulent words from his mouth.

Then his ears picked up a higher pitch that was different from the roar of surf. Without words, this sound called to him, understood by some dark part of his soul. Cold and cruel. Depraved. Seductive.

The sound drew his eyes to the right. At first he could see nothing. Then there were flashes—narrow bands of white. Like some child's flip-card movie, it appeared in fits and starts through the heavy foliage.

Beyond the colorful border at the edge of the beach, something big was tracking his progress. Through a gap in the foliage he caught a glimpse of what pursued him. Yellow eyes in an icy misshapen head topped a wraith-like form that regarded him with a conspiring, gleeful evil. Teeth—evil, white fangs that sparkled in the shadows—snapped hungrily and he saw black numbers written upon them. A new chill crept down his spine.

He felt insubstantial; an outline of a man with nothing solid inside. An ugly urge, deep within, pulled him toward the jungle, promising to fill him. Cold fingers wrapped around his will and deafened his ears to every-thing except the siren's call; blinded him to all but that thin line of white drawing him to the darkness.

Resisting with every fiber of his being, he stumbled and his soul cried for relief.

Emily called ... she shouted ... and her voice broke through his deafness. "Daddy! Look at me!"

He turned, and the sight of her washed away his blindness.

"It's time," she said, "We have to hurry!"

Turning from him, she raced up the beach and shouted, "I'm on the way, Daddy! You need to hurry!"

Following with all the speed he could muster, he watched in wonder as the green from Emily's swimsuit spread up her neck, across her arms, down her legs. Her skin became ruffled and plumed; a rich, textured green. She no longer left footprints in the sand as her arms lengthened and spread, lifting her from the ground.

As she glided above the beach, she turned to look back at him. A bright, horizontal ridge of red topped a large, ebony beak on a sleek green head.

But the eyes were human and shining with a love that urged him on.

"Faster! I'm almost here!" The confusing words were delivered in the same, musical, childlike tones that had come from the girl who'd said she was his daughter.

Like a tiny green angel, she flapped her wings and pulled away, getting smaller as she vanished into the distance.

He strained for more speed, but his legs were growing heavier, exhaustion setting in.

Light-headed, he struggled up the beach as everything around him turned fuzzy and white. The sun disappeared and he was suddenly chilled.

Emily's voice echoed from the void.

"Keep running, just as fast as you can."

Putting one foot in front of the other, time after time, he forged on.

"Don't stop 'til you reach the end."

Flecks of something soft and cold hit his sweating face. He struggled forward through hot sun and blinding snow, though his direction was unknowable, meaningless.

The end came when his muscles refused to lift his feet for one more step and he fell down into a soft, cold blanket of white.

Rolling onto his back, he stared into a brightness from which poured a multitude of perfect crystal snowflakes. His eyes followed a beautifully patterned sample as it glittered in the sunlight and floated toward him. Its exquisite form was the last thing he saw.

CHAPTER FOUR

Numbers That Matter

When the first thump hit his chest, he knew he was on the edge of consciousness, lucidly dreaming. When the painful thumping continued, he opened his eyes and the dream was confirmed.

A Great Green Macaw was sitting on his stomach. The bright red ridge between its eyes was unmistakable. With a distressing regularity, it pecked his chest with its large black beak.

Jason was sure it was a dream because here, in this dream, he was on a beach with a warm sun shining down, instead of sprawled on a snowbank freezing to death. Reality, which he could clearly remember, was diving out of the way of the monstrous plow. Less clearly, he recalled climbing the wall of snow. His last memory was one of falling backward into darkness.

"Wake up!" said the Macaw, then it thumped him again.

He closed his eyes and shook his head. The result was immediate. A deadly cold replaced the warmth. Just as deadly were the thoughts that began racing through his mind.

I'm ten miles from home, probably suffering from a concussion.

My arms and legs are stiff, almost frozen.

I'm alone, exhausted, in the dark ... in the middle of a blizzard.

I'm as good as dead.

The sound of tires crunching slowly over crusty snow caused him to open his eyes. Light reflected off the snowflakes falling toward his face. He rolled over and pushed himself to his knees.

Jason knelt on a high bank of snow. Below him was the driveway of his home. The light on the front porch was shining brightly. Getting out of the car that had just arrived was Martha, the midwife they'd chosen for their baby's home birth.

"Why are you playing in the snow at a time like this?" she said, when she spotted him above her. "You better get your butt down here! We've got a baby to deliver!"

The adrenalin this news engendered drove most of the pain and exhaustion from his body. Though still confused, he scrambled down and limped through the blizzard with Martha.

"Jill is going to strangle me." The dangerous moods of a woman in labor had been stressed over and over by the teacher of their natural childbirth class.

"I'd say you darn well deserve it," the stocky Mennonite said, "You're a fool for bein' out in weather like this." She thumped him on the arm and then pushed him through the door.

"Likely she'll let you off easy … under the circumstances."

As they shed layers of outerwear, she peered up at him.

"Say, you been to the tanning parlor?"

"Huh?" he replied, "What do you mean?

"Just that you're lookin' pretty dark for this late in January."

Jason was about to turn to the mirror by the front door when the sound of a desperate woman echoed down the hall.

"Will you two quit chit-chatting and come help bring this baby into the world!"

He hurried down the hall and into their bedroom. When he looked at his wife on the bed, he was crushed by the realization that he hadn't fulfilled any of his duties. While he'd been out in the snow, Jill had been forced to get ready without him. The towels, bowls, hot water, ice chips … everything was set to go.

Already he had failed as a husband and a father. Tears welled in his eyes as he sat on the edge of the bed.

"Honey I'm so sor—"

Jill reached toward her husband.

"Stop. It's all right sweetie. Everything's fine. There's still so much for you to do. Help me. Hold me. Love me." She squeezed his knee and smiled. "I knew you'd be back in time. I had a dream about it."

"A dream?" He took her hand as the back of his neck tingled and memories tickled at the edge of his mind.

"Yes." Jill's face was glowing as she told him. "Our daughter told me that you beat the monsters and that I shouldn't worry, you'd make it home before her."

Jason sat on the edge of the bed as images took shape in his mind. A frightening visage with black numbers written across sharp teeth tried to form, but was wiped away by a bright, redheaded angel.

"Our daughter?"

"Emily. She told me in the dream that her name was Emily."

Stunned, Jason put a hand to his chest and stood as a flood of memories washed over him. He lifted his shirt.

Jill's breath caught as she stared at the deep red bruises on his chest. "My God! What happened to you?"

Jason closed his eyes. The weakness, the ugly stain on his soul that had so long been a burden to bear, a temptation to resist ... was gone; replaced by a contentment he'd never before experienced. As he fingered the marks on his skin, he caught a glance at the time on his watch and smiled. On it were numbers that brought a smile to his face. They told the story of the race he had won.

"I'm not sure, but it was worth it."

THE END

DRIVEN

CHAPTER ONE

To Adam Cannaday, the scene brought to mind a Christmas from his childhood and the powdered sugar left behind on his mother's kitchen counter when she'd made chocolate mint snow cookies. He hadn't called her yet this week and made a mental note to correct that oversight.

The victim's body had been carefully removed by the medical examiner's crew; despite the green, white, and red colors on the ground, what was left did not resemble a holiday sweet. The impressions of arms and legs were a clear indication that the dead woman's last moments had not been pleasant.

A late spring flurry outlined the patch of crushed green grass. A tall border of dense holly, dusted in white, separated Adam from the backyards of an exclusive country-club community. Tall oak trees were widely spaced in the park through which the popular biking and running route passed. Flashing red and white lights cast shadows from the spectral trees that stretched into the distance and danced on the stately brick homes.

There was a charming beauty to the setting that the lanky detective appreciated despite the grim circumstances. It wasn't enough to improve his mood. He pulled a notepad and pen from his sweat jacket; he'd just gotten back from an evening run when he'd gotten this call. The captain knew he was a runner and wanted him on this case, no matter whose shift it was. Adam turned toward the asphalt community trail where there was a yellow crime-scene barrier and a cluster of people gathered around the pulsing lights of an ambulance.

Cannaday's demeanor appeared calm and his long stride was unhurried, but his wife would have recognized the slight tightness in his jaw as anger and the fingers run through his sandy brown hair as frustration.

"Getting a little ahead of ourselves, aren't we?" he said to the gathering. Two uniformed cops, an ambulance driver and the EMT looked briefly at the approaching detective and then turned to the fifth member of their group.

"Don't blame me, Rock." Gary Trouter was the youngest detective on the force; the harder look of a veteran hadn't yet lined his face or grayed his sandy hair. Cannaday had been his partner when he was a rookie three years before and Trouter was still searching for some sign of approval from the older man. He pointed to a brightly-lit extravagance beyond the holly hedge; the throbbing bass beat that emanated from the home could be felt as well as heard.

"That's the mayor's house and he's got a party goin' on. I guess he thought this murder was puttin' a damper on the festivities."

Rock was a nickname that had always irked Cannaday, but it wasn't revealed on his granite-like face. He'd been given that handle as a rookie, seventeen years earlier. A veteran's prank fell flat when Adam had calmly lifted one foot and then the other to douse his flaming size thirteens in the water fountain, then continued about his business without showing the slightest emotion.

"He's got as much emotion as my pet rock," the disappointed perpetrator had said.

So Cannaday became known as Rock and his near-rage at finding this crime scene disturbed was initially undetected.

"The Mayor, the Pope, and the President *together* don't have the authority to have that body moved from the crime scene," he said calmly. "Until I arrived, only you had that authority."

Trouter knew to ignore the moderate tone of Rock's voice and focus on the words. And those words showed that the senior detective was pissed. His shoulders slumped.

"C'mon, Rock," he said, "the Mayor can get me fired. He told me to have that ambulance out of here before eleven o'clock. Don't worry; I took a ton of pictures, we were real careful."

Cannaday looked at the rest of the group; all of them were nodding their heads in agreement. He gave them a disgusted shake of his own in return, pushed between the EMT and the driver, then jerked open the back door of the ambulance.

"You're not leaving until I say so," he said to the EMT. He delivered the words without force or inflection.

Trouter rushed to Cannaday's side and put his hand on the detective's shoulder.

"It's eleven right now," he said nervously. "The Mayor said ..."

"The Mayor can shove it." Adam calmly removed the hand from his shoulder and ducked into the back. "I'm in charge now. Let him try firing me." He pulled the door closed in the young detective's face.

Sitting back on his heels next to the stretcher, he studied the sheet-draped body. The petite form looked almost childlike. If the door had been open Trouter would have seen a crack in Cannaday's stony visage as he hesitated before uncovering the victim's face.

Although the pretty features weren't as young as he had feared, they were familiar to him; a picture of an awards ceremony popped into his head. It was the Pear Blossom Run down in Medford three weeks earlier. He could remember the scenic ten-mile course, the guy he out-kicked to claim second in the 45–49 age group, and he could remember this woman at the award ceremony accepting the prize for first female finisher.

But he couldn't recall her name. He wasn't one of those godlike movie cops whose instinct, intellect, and photographic memory made the successful resolution of even the most byzantine cases a foregone conclusion. Cannaday had to work hard for every break; whether it was physical or mental, his approach to each challenge he faced was one of mule-headed determination.

He studied the face carefully and his workmanlike mind hammered out some clues. She was a serious runner; the thin, strong face, ponytail and lack of makeup screamed "athlete." Adam rubbed his finger across a white, chalky spot on her cheek and touched it to his tongue.

"Distance runner," he murmured as he tasted the salt residue from her sweat. He thought she must have run hard and long—at least ten or fifteen miles—to have built up that much in such cool weather.

The angry red line around her neck was the likely cause of death. Cannaday remembered two cases; one involving the rape and strangling of a jogger up in Portland three months earlier and an identical one last month in Corvallis. He jotted a reminder to have the coroner look for connections.

After checking her wrists, he found what he was looking for tied under her shoelaces. It was another sign that she was serious about her running. The Road I.D. gave Adam the name his memory could not; as well as an address, phone number, emergency contact, and blood type.

Heather Templeton. She was new to the area, he was sure; otherwise, he'd have remembered her name. He didn't know every runner; after all, McCarthy was a populous university town and had a big community of runners. But he knew all of the good ones.

He stepped out of the ambulance and bumped into a large, round ... and angry Mayor Haggard.

"Listen, Cannaday." The bluster in the man's voice grated on Adam like no one else ever had. "I told your man that ..."

Handcuffs waving in his face shut the mayor up.

The senior detective filled the resulting silence. He made sure he was loud enough for everyone to hear.

"If you're still in my way ten seconds from now, I'm cuffing you, charging you with obstruction of justice, and taking you downtown. The voters have already given you your walking papers. You can party away your last month as mayor or spend it in a jail cell. Do you want to choose ... or should I?"

Adam took a deep breath to calm down. Not that the mayor could see a trace of anger on the man in front of him. Then he started counting at seven.

"Eight, nine ..." Haggard jumped back and Adam headed for his car.

Cannaday looked at his watch and sighed. It was late and he wanted to go home. If it had been a stranger, he could have sent Trouter to Templeton's address with the terrible news. She wasn't a stranger ... she was a runner; in Adam's mind that made her family.

෧෨

CHAPTER TWO

Each step groaned loudly as Cannaday walked up onto the darkened porch. Being a Clydesdale had never bothered him, since his two-hundred ten pounds were well distributed on his six-foot-seven-inch frame. He was about to knock when he heard a voice. It was muffled, but he could understand the words clearly through the door.

"That's probably her right now."

He took his badge from his pocket and took a deep breath. The porch light came on and Adam watched the expression of the man who opened it change from relief to confusion when he saw the detective's shield. The cell phone in the man's hand snapped shut.

"Kurt Templeton?"

"But ... bu ... How did you get here so fast? I was just on the phone with the County Sheriff's office. My wife is missing."

"I'm not with the Sheriff's office. My name's Adam Cannaday, I'm a detective with the McCarthy Police Department."

The confusion on Templeton's face grew. "But we live outside the city limits," he said. "Why did they send you?"

"We share jurisdiction with the county for neighborhoods that are adjacent to the city."

At times like these, Adam wished his face was easier to read. The sorrow and discomfort he was feeling was tearing him up, but no one would know from looking at him. While he put his shield away with his left hand, he held up and opened his right. In it was the Road I.D.

"Oh my God! What happened? Is she hurt?"

Templeton stepped toward him. Adam handed him the small metal tag and put his hand on a broad shoulder that was just starting to tremble.

"Can we talk inside, Mr. Templeton?"

It had been a half-hour and Cannaday still could not get a coherent word from Templeton. He'd tried to comfort the broken man, but Adam felt that any and every word that came from his mouth sounded weak and trivial.

He looked at his watch. It was after one a.m. In an obvious case of wrongful death like this, Cannaday had called the coroner in for an immediate autopsy. It would be starting soon and Adam wanted to be there. But he needed answers to a few simple questions before he left here.

"Mr. Templeton, please!" He gave the man a gentle shake. "The first twenty-four hours are critical if we're going to catch the person who did this. Can you tell me when she left the house? Was she with anyone?"

With a deep, shuddering breath, Templeton pushed off the couch and walked unsteadily into the foyer and picked up the cell phone that had fallen from his hand after Adam had delivered the awful news. He returned to his seat, punched a few buttons and handed it to the detective.

On the screen was a text message: "Left at 6. Running with a new friend."

"Do you know the name of this new friend?"

Templeton's body was bent forward, his head once again buried in his hands. They moved in concert with his face as he shook his head no.

"Is there anyone who would want to hurt your wife?"

"Had she mentioned any suspicious persons watching her?"

"Have you noticed anyone watching her or the house?"

While every question Adam asked was answered with a morose shake of Templeton's head, it appeared the man was slowly getting control of his emotions.

"When did you realize that your wife was overdue getting back from her run?"

Templeton's whispered response was slow in coming.

"I worked late tonight."

Cannaday interrupted. "Where do you work?"

"Jensen and Haverford; it's a land survey company in McCarthy."

"And you arrived home from work when?"

"Got home around ten and saw she wasn't home. Went back out right away and started driving routes I thought she might use. I was worried …" His voice cracked and he clenched his fists between his legs. After a moment, he continued, tears dripping onto his hands. "I was worried she might have slipped on the snow and gotten hurt or something."

"Thank you Mr. Templeton. I know this is hard to deal with. That's all the questions I have for now, but you need to come down to the Coroner's office, to identify your wife's body."

Sobs wracked the distraught husband and Adam took pity on the man.

"But that can wait until morning. Can you be there at nine o'clock?"

With an effort, Templeton put his hands on his knees and pushed himself up. His face was wet and his eyes closed when he nodded his head.

"Do you have someone you can call? Someone to stay with tonight?"

His reply was strained. "Yes, thank you detective."

"We'll find whoever did this." Adam squeezed Templeton's forearm. "I promise you."

Rafe Brillson distrusted most thin people, especially thin white people who spent their weekends sweating buckets and running around in skimpy shorts that barely covered their bony butts; they were everywhere in McCarthy. Rafe played tennis under the lights twice a week and basketball on Saturday afternoons. The shorts he used for both sports reached below his knees, his butt was a far cry from bony, and he ran as little as he possibly could.

But, for some unknown reason, he liked and trusted Adam Cannaday; even though Cannaday was one of those bony-butt people.

And he knew Cannaday was a guy who preferred to get his information straight from the horse's mouth. That's why Brillson was sitting in the lobby of the municipal building at two a.m. when his friend came sprinting through the doors.

"Whoa, there!" Brillson called. Adam skidded to a stop and walked over to the bench where Rafe was waiting. "Didn't your teachers ever tell you there's no running in the halls?"

"I did indoor track in high school," Adam said. "We were *encouraged*, no … we were *forced* to run in the halls."

Brillson cackled. He had learned a long time ago to look for the humor in Adam's words, since it never seemed to show in his face.

"Are you done already?" Adam asked. He was tired and not as disappointed as he thought he would be about missing the autopsy.

"I knew you'd be eager to get home to that pretty wife of yours, so I did a very thorough and *efficient* examination."

"Do you think it's the same as the Portland and Corvallis cases?"

"Well, I'll put it this way." He stretched his legs out and balanced the file on his ample paunch. "The victim profile is the same, it looks like a latex condom was used like in Portland, and she was strangled with some type of plastic-coated wire, same as the others."

Adam liked Rafe. The McCarthy City Coroner was good at his job, always followed his words with action and threw a mean elbow under the basket. But it creeped him out a little that the man could talk so coolly about such a heinous crime. Of course, Adam was also considered to be exactly that cold and unemotional. It was one reason he hated his nickname … inside, he was anything but a rock.

"So we have a serial killer on our hands."

"Every coroner in the state would probably agree with that statement." Brillson stood up and slapped Cannaday on the head with the file. "Good thing for you I'm better than all of them."

Adam knew what his reply was expected to be.

"Huh?"

"Huh, indeed." Brillson grinned as he began to pace back and forth in front of Cannaday. "There was vaginal tearing as would be expected in cases such as these. But there was only a small amount blood. I found a welt on the back of the victim's head, one that might have been administered by a sap of some kind. There were two small wool fibers embedded in the scalp. Was a wool cap recovered from the scene?"

"Not that I'm aware of. I'll check with Trouter." Adam tried and failed to suppress a yawn. "So, what are driving at?"

"I believe she was stunned, strangled and then … *not* raped."

"*Not* raped?" Adam had been going for twenty hours and was way short of his daily allowance of caffeine. "But what about the latex … the tearing?"

"In addition to the tearing, I found some very tiny punctures. After a microscopic exam, I discovered several small wooden splinters. Oregon white oak splinters." The look on Brillson's face was just short of celebratory. "The victim was penetrated shortly after her death by a stick over which a latex condom had been applied."

On top of being exhausted, Cannaday was in a foul mood as he made his way back to Kurt Templeton's house. Someone had attempted to make Heather Templeton look like the random victim of a serial killer. In a great majority of similar cases, the perpetrator was the husband or a scorned lover. If it turned out that Templeton had killed his wife, Adam would be embarrassed that he had been taken in so completely by the man's sorrowful act.

The house was dark when he pulled up in front. It stayed dark while he pounded on the front door. Cannaday thought that Templeton might have taken his advice and spent the night with a friend or relative. Or he might be guilty and on the run. If it was the latter, Adam would be more than embarrassed; he would be furious at himself for letting it happen.

With his hands on his hips, Adam stood on the porch steps and considered his options. The ensuing silence showed that his pounding hadn't yielded the result he was looking for, but it had roused the neighbor next door.

Her frail, reedy voice was amplified by the crisp night air. "You better quit all that noise or I'm calling the police."

Adam left the steps and crossed the dark, dew-covered lawn to the neighbor's porch. He looked up at an elderly woman; one knobby hand was on the railing while the other held the neck of her quilted pink housecoat closed against the chill, damp air. Her wispy white hair was rolled in curlers and her expression was stern.

"I'm sorry ma'am ..."

"You should be!" The voice was frail, but there was an iron will behind it. "I've got a busy day tomorrow and I need my sleep."

You and me both, Grandma, thought the tired, but amused detective. He could imagine her puttering in a garden or gossiping with friends over tea while they played canasta.

"Kurt, this is the second night in a row you woke me up; you should know better."

Adam took another step, into the glow of the porchlight.

"Ma'am, I'm not Kurt, I'm Detective Cannaday, with the McCarthy Police Department. And you are ...?"

"Mrs. Hazel Kinton." She straightened her spine and glared as she made the introduction.

"As a matter of fact, Mrs. Kinton," he said, "I'm looking for Mr. Templeton."

"Oh!" She took her hand from the railing and laid it on the side of her wrinkled face. "He left earlier. I thought you were him, coming back to make up with that lovely wife of his."

"You said there was a disturbance on another night?"

"My goodness, yes there was!" Despite the late hour and cold air, Adam could tell the old woman was going into gossip mode. "Kurt and Heather had quite a row, night before last. Front yard, back yard, slamming doors ... the whole she-bang. I couldn't make out everything they said, but it sure sounded like one of those 'other woman' type of fights."

"Kurt isn't in any kind of trouble, is he?" Hazel made a cast for a new gossip tidbit, but Adam wasn't biting.

"I'm sorry, Mrs. Kinton. I'm not at liberty to say."

"I hope he isn't," she said and dropped from gossip to good-neighbor mode. "The Templetons really are good neighbors and a lovely couple, just a little fiery, that's all. They look so happy when they're out running together."

Cannaday felt a shiver of anticipation.

"They run together often?" he asked.

"Almost every night."

After putting out an APB on Kurt Templeton and his blue Outback Sport, Adam went home for a few hours sleep. In his gut, he was sure the case would be broken during the coming day.

∽

CHAPTER THREE

Liz Cannaday stood at the foot of the bed and dressed for her pre-dawn run by the light from the bathroom. She watched her husband's eyes flutter as he struggled to drag himself out of bed to join her. Two quick steps brought her to his side.

"Don't even think about it," She pushed his head down to the pillow and tucked the covers back around his shoulders. His resistance was halfhearted.

"I know it was three-thirty in the morning when you finally got home. If you try to run now, you'll probably fall asleep on your feet and get hurt."

"Can't run alone," he mumbled.

"Lucy and Tom are meeting me here," she looked at her watch and gasped, "in two minutes!"

She kissed his forehead and chuckled. He was already drifting back to sleep. "I'll wake you after the run and fix both of us a fruit smoothie."

Streaming through the tall windows of the breakfast nook, the first rays of dawn brightened the mountain-cabin décor of the cozy space. It was his favorite room in their little home and kept alive the dream that one day he and Liz would have that cabin, high in the Cascades where long trails, blanketed in pine needles, ran for endless miles from their front door.

Adam stood in front of the glass, closed his eyes, and enjoyed the warm caress of the morning sun. These might be the only relaxing moments of his day and he was determined to make the most of them. He set the empty smoothie glass on the rough pine table he'd made with his own hands and his long arm pulled Liz closer.

"Oh, Adam," she said, pushing against him, "don't! I'm gross and sweaty. I was about to jump in the shower."

Ignoring her protests, he held her tighter and inhaled a long, exaggerated breath, held it a moment, and then sighed.

"You know I love how you smell after a run." It was true. Adam thought it was an honest, healthy smell; evidence of hard work and dedication; a musky, sexy scent that spoke of reaching for one's dreams.

"Yeah, and I know you're cracked, too!" Still, she gave in and wrapped her arms around him.

He tilted his head down, rubbed his cheek against hers and then kissed her neck.

The taste of salt was one that usually accelerated his desire. But this time, it derailed his train of thought, jumping his mind from one track onto one completely different. In his mind, he saw the cold, lifeless body of Heather Templeton.

Liz Cannaday was an exceptionally perceptive woman. Back when she was Oregon sophomore Elizabeth Alcorn, this ability had allowed her to see into the soul of a stiff and lonely criminology major. What she found was a caring, passionate man unreasonably crippled by a rare, congenital neurological disorder that left his face unable to show the emotions he was feeling. Although he had learned to live with his disorder, Liz taught him to triumph over it and helped him become the man standing beside her now.

"What happened last night?"

Adam squeezed her tight and then stepped away. How easily, and quickly, she could read the changes in his mood never ceased to surprise him. He picked up his glass and headed for the kitchen.

"Do you know Heather Templeton?"

"Yes," Liz said, following him. "She's the new top gun on the local road-racing circuit. I think she moved here from the East Coast a few months ago. I'm glad she's not in my age group; she might be the fastest woman in the state."

"Not anymore," Adam replied. He put the glass in the dishwasher and turned toward Liz. "She was murdered last night."

The look on his wife's face was shocked, but Adam thought something else was there as well. Not for the first time he wished he was as perceptive as she.

"Someone tried to make it look like those murders in Portland and Corvallis. I'm thinking it might be the husband."

"Oh no, Adam. Really?"

The doubt on her face was clear. Again, one or more emotions were added to the mix.

"Why?" he asked, "Do you know him?"

She shook her head firmly. "No. It's just that ..." Liz hesitated, then turned to the counter and started fiddling with the blender.

"What?" Adam looked at his watch. Jensen and Haverford would be opening soon. Templeton's place of work would be his first stop on the way into headquarters.

Liz shook her head again. "Nothing ... it's just so awful."

Adam put his hands on her arms and kissed the back of her head.

"Don't worry," he said. "I'm going to catch whoever did it." He glanced at his watch again and didn't notice the slight stiffening across her shoulders. "And I better get moving."

"Be careful out there," Liz said quietly as he left the kitchen.

CHAPTER FOUR

It wasn't quite nine a.m., but clouds were already gathering to choke the promise of the sunny morning as Adam drove into the business development he thought of as "upscale commercial." The landscaping, modern sculpture, and striking architectural features of the buildings called out "we are solid and prosperous businesses" while the low occupancy rate and the two going-out-of-business signs screamed "the overhead is killing us!"

The firm of Jensen and Haverford was located in one of the buildings where the tenants did indeed appear to be solid and prosperous. Polished marble glistened throughout the lobby and healthy paper birch trees stood as impressive sentries in each quadrant of the glass-ceilinged circular atrium.

From the center of the atrium, Adam could see through glass walls into four separate businesses. The two that were on each side of the center of the building, opposite the entrance didn't open until ten o'clock and were dark. On the far right, a receptionist was busily preparing for a nine o'clock opening; brewing the morning coffee, setting out the daily newspapers.

The scene on the far left was much more interesting.

Beyond the glass walls of Jensen and Haverford, Kurt Templeton was having an animated conversation. His hands were firmly grasping the arms of a lovely, and obviously distraught, young woman in a lacy lavender tea dress. Cannaday thought that finding his newly installed prime suspect like this, at his workplace, the morning after his wife was murdered ... it was almost too good to be true.

Adam scurried over to the wall, disabled the flash on his camera phone, snapped a picture and texted it to Gary Trouter. "Get over here and question this girl," was the simple message that accompanied the photo. Since Trouter had spent the early morning at his desk doing research on one Kurt Templeton, Adam was pretty sure the young detective could figure out what questions to ask.

Eager to see how the "distraught" husband would react, Adam pounded on the glass.

Liz Cannaday's acute perception wasn't necessary in order for Adam to recognize the emotions that raced across Templeton's face. The blood draining from his face left him pale and shocked. Then the blood rushed back and showed his embarrassment. Fear flickered in his eyes, which darted immediately back to the girl.

Thirty feet and a half-inch of plate glass separated him from his suspect, but Adam knew what was being said because the girl's reaction mirrored those of the man holding her arms. She spun away from him and rushed into a back office while Templeton made his way to the front door.

"What are you doing here?" he said.

"Funny," Cannaday replied, "I was going to ask you the same thing. Having one's wife murdered is a pretty good reason for missing a day or two of work, don't you think?"

Templeton began stuttering an excuse, but Adam ignored him.

"Besides, aren't you supposed to be at the Coroner's office?"

The man dropped his head and began fidgeting with his wedding ring. "Last night was just one awful blur. I don't remember ... am I?"

"Yes it was awful ..." Adam said gently. Then he delivered his next words with a hefty dose of hard steel in them. "... and yes, you are. Don't worry, though. I'll take you there myself ... *right now.*"

The man's head came up quickly and it was easy for Adam to see the wheels turning. Templeton looked cornered and he was trying to get a read on a man whose face was incapable of showing anything. It was one of the few times Adam was glad of his condition.

"That's fine," Kurt said, and began to turn away from the door, "just let me get ..."

Cannaday's firm hand halted the turn.

"No, Mr. Templeton. We are leaving here this very moment. We'll go together to the Coroner's office. And on the way, maybe you can tell me who would try to make the murder of your wife look like the random act of a serial killer."

Although no one would know it, as he led a stunned Kurt Templeton out of the building, Adam was smiling. *Maybe I'm getting better at this perception stuff after all,* he thought. To Cannaday, it seemed that guilt and regret were flowing from every pore of Templeton's body.

It was a silent drive to the municipal building, just like he planned. Adam wanted the guilt-ridden husband to stew and he wanted every word from that murdering bastard's mouth to be recorded. They were pulling into the parking lot when Trouter passed them on his way to fulfilling his assignment.

Templeton broke down again when he had to identify his wife's body. But Cannaday was becoming inured to the man's emotional displays.

His confused and angry protests when Adam read him his rights fell on deaf ears. The stone-like expression on the detective's face wasn't just because of his mild Moebius syndrome. It was as much a result of his rock-hard determination to force Templeton to admit his crime.

"You are one cold-hearted son-of-a-bitch," his suspect had said as Adam handcuffed his right arm to the chair in the interrogation room.

That Templeton could be so wrong was a paradoxical result of Cannaday's condition. While they are young, children learn to exert some control on their emotions to avoid being called "cry-baby." That learning experience was something Adam never had. He didn't have to hide emotions that couldn't show anyway. Being upset or angry with a playmate, parent, or teacher never showed to start with. He could be furious at his parents for their refusal to let him get a tattoo and never a hint of that rage was revealed on his face.

But that lack of practice at controlling his emotions was sometimes a burden. Right now, impatience was driving him to start the interrogation, even though he knew he should wait for Trouter's report on his interview with the girl. How he would frame his questions might change depending on her side of the story.

Trouter hadn't shown up by ten-thirty and Cannaday's impatience finally got the better of him. He had the technician start the recording, grabbed his file and a hot cup of coffee, and stepped quietly into the interview room. Templeton was at the table in the middle of the room, his head on his folded left arm ... sound asleep.

Adam picked up the chair opposite the slumbering suspect. When he slammed it back down, Templeton jerked his head up, confused and groggy.

"You must have a clear conscience," the detective said, "sleeping there like a baby while your wife is lying dead on a slab just a floor below us."

"Wha ... I ..." he bent his head toward the handcuffed right arm so he could massage the sleep from his eyes with the palms of his hands. "No, I don't have a clear conscience, I just ..."

"Hold on, don't say another word." Cannaday didn't want to hear a confession that might get thrown out later by a judge. "For the purpose of accuracy and fairness, this interview is being recorded. I mirandized you earlier. Do you need me to repeat those rights?"

"No, I under ..."

"So you are giving up your right to remain silent and your right to an attorney of your choice, is that right?"

"Yes," he said. Fatigue accompanied every syllable. "I don't need an attorney."

"Mr. Templeton, from where I'm sitting, I think you definitely need an attorney."

Templeton's anger flared and he slapped the table. But then it flickered out as quickly as it had arisen.

"I did *not* kill my wife!" His words were tired and defeated.

"What did you and your wife fight about the night before last?"

"Huh? That ... I uh ..."

"Why did you go to work this morning?"

"I had to ..."

"Who was the woman I saw you holding?"

"What? No, it wasn't like that ... Sherri is just ..." Templeton ran his hand through his mussed brown hair.

"I have pictures." Adam took a photo from the green file folder and slid it across the table. It had the effect he wanted.

Templeton's head sagged and he rubbed his temple, as if fighting back a headache.

"Listen, I haven't slept in two days. I'll tell you everything. Just let me tell it my way."

CHAPTER FIVE

"We moved here for work, Heather's work really. Her degree in environmental studies and her work with the Forest Service landed her a position with the Institute for a Sustainable Environment.

"I have an engineering degree, but all I've been able to get out here so far is a job as the head of a surveying crew. Jensen and Haverford lay out land for big box stores, malls, new housing developments. They cut up big swaths of forest for parking lots, warehouses, and McMansions.

"The company I used to work for designed and built wind turbines. It was like Heather and I were on the same team. When we got here, it suddenly felt as if we were on opposite sides of a raging river gorge. We could see each other, but not hear or understand what was going on in our lives.

"She loved her job; admired and respected the people she was working with. I was just collecting a paycheck, one that was just a pittance compared to hers. For a time, it made me jealous. She was doing something rewarding, what she wanted to do; but the move had forced me onto a path that made me feel trapped, unhappy."

Cannaday looked at his watch. He was about to tell Templeton to stop with the sad story of drifting apart and get to the facts. That's when Trouter knocked at the door.

"Let's take a short break," Adam said.

"Can I get something to drink?"

Adam shoved his untouched cup of coffee across the table.

"This'll have to do until were finished," he said and then stepped into the hall.

"Don't even say it," Gary said, before Cannaday could complain about his tardiness. "After talking to Sherri, I had to interview everyone else in the office to confirm her story. Here's my report."

"What about the crime scene? Did you send a team over to search the area around where the body was found?

"Yes, Rock. I do know how to follow orders. The snow was melted by eight o'clock. They found dozens of likely candidates. Rafe is sure that none of them are the one we're looking for."

"Sorry, Rock." Gary turned to leave and then paused. "How's it going in there?"

"I think he's close to confessing." Adam held up the file. "I was hoping we might find something to push him over the edge."

"Oh," Trouter said as he walked away, "I don't think that would have happened anyway."

For the second time that morning, Cannaday was glad his face was no better than a frozen mask. When he walked slowly back into the room, scanning the statements of Sheila and her co-workers caused a war of emotions that Templeton could have easily read.

As it was, Kurt was clueless.

"Let's continue," Adam said as he plopped down in the chair. "You were saying you felt trapped and unhappy."

The coffee must have provided some lift to Adam's beleaguered suspect, because he seemed eager to continue.

"Yes, there was tension. There were fights about my job, about the move, about meaningless little things that were a proxy for the bigger hurt inside of me.

"But when we ran, all that was forgotten. Heading out on a run with Heather at my side was a joy that took the hurt away, like a warm spring rain washing the ice from a mountain brook. Among the tall Douglas firs, along the soft, needle-covered trails, we talked, we found common ground, and we found solutions to our problems.

"I was only weeks away from leaving Jensen and Haverford and starting my own company in partnership with a local green architect. We were going to build earth-friendly homes. Heather and I had almost worked through all the issues that were dividing us.

"Sherri was my problem. She'd been throwing herself at me from almost the first day. For a while, my ego liked the attention, maybe I even encouraged it a little. But I was never unfaithful; it was just a stupid flirtation. Heather knew I loved her … and only her.

"Weeks ago, I started giving Sherri signals that the flirtation had to end; that I wasn't about to fool around with her. It only seemed to make her more determined. But I was resolved to end this once and for all. I decided to take Sherri out to a public place, a restaurant, and make the situation crystal clear. It was over and I would be leaving the company."

The regret he felt was clear as Kurt shook his head.

"That's what the fight was about two nights ago. Heather didn't like my plan. She thought that the dinner might encourage Sherri or make her more desperate. After the dinner, I saw that Heather might have been right, that Sherri might never give up.

"That's why I went to work this morning, to confront her; to see if she was the one who'd …" Kurt's voice began to break, "taken away the person I loved most in the world. If I'd been able to tell for sure …"

Anger surged so strongly through Templeton's body that Adam could feel the temperature in the room rising.

"…I'd have strangled her with my own hands right there in the office."

Cannaday looked again at the file that Trouter had prepared. In each particular, Templeton's story was supported by the interviews inside. He had given his four weeks' notice almost two weeks earlier. Sherri Krause had thrown herself at every man in the office. In Trouter's opinion, all of the men at Jensen and Haverford had succumbed to Sherri's advances, all but Kurt Templeton.

If it wasn't the husband, who did that leave? Did Templeton's suspicion of Krause have some validity? Adam held out some hope that something could be salvaged from this investigation.

"What time were you at dinner with Miss Krause last night?" he asked.

"We met at Olive Garden at eight o'clock. It was about nine forty-five when we left."

That cinched it. Now he had no suspects at all. The coroner had put the time of death at nine o'clock.

৶৹

CHAPTER SIX

"Out with it," said Liz. "Why are you so worked up?"

After two hours of beating his head against a wall, Adam Cannaday had failed to come up with any potential suspect or even another avenue of investigation. Trouter had canvassed the neighborhood around the Templeton's home. Two teams of uniformed officers had covered all the homes along possible running routes that Heather Templeton may have used. Her co-workers at ISE had been interviewed by two of his department's veteran detectives.

It was times like these that he was glad his wife was close enough to meet for lunch.

The storm front had deposited enough rain to clean the streets and then promptly blown out over the Cascades. Sunshine, a brisk warm breeze, and some cotton towels had rendered the outdoor patio of their favorite vegetarian restaurant suitable for a quiet meal.

He'd thought that he just wanted to get his mind off this morning's collapse of his investigation. But his wife knew him too well; he was incapable of diverting his thoughts from the murder. It was simply uncanny how she could read him like an open book when, to everyone else in the world, it was a book written in unbreakable code.

The waitress took their order and left before Liz renewed her effort to open him up.

"Come on, don't just sit there and stew ... tell me what's wrong."

"You were right," he said. "I saw the doubt on your face this morning, and you were right."

"About what?" she said.

"Kurt Templeton. He didn't murder his wife and now I don't have a clue who did."

Adam detected a strange, cautious look on his wife's face. It left him befuddled. He stared at her as he tried to figure out what was tickling the back of his mind.

"What is it?" For once, Liz wasn't sure what was going on in her husband's head, and she didn't like it; she'd always been able to see past that rigid mask.

"If I didn't know better," he said. "I'd think you know who the murderer is."

In the instant before he realized what it meant, Liz's wide-eyed, deer-caught-in-the-headlights reaction gave Adam a brief moment of pleasure; it wasn't often he surprised her.

Twenty years ago this short, freckle-faced girl with frizzy hair the color and appearance of a corn broom had stepped in front of him as he was heading for Law and Sociology 301 class.

He'd been so hot with anger that he thought his shoes might melt the asphalt of University Street as crossed the road. Criminal Justice class had been torture, with the professor baiting him, trying to punish him for challenging some revered, and now long-forgotten, tenet of criminology. Dr. Henderson sought to elicit an emotional reaction from Adam that was there from the start, but couldn't be seen by the people around him. Or so he thought.

Textbooks held demurely across the front of her track team jacket, her pale gray eyes had met his brown ones in a way that said "I know just what you're thinking."

"Since your face won't show him what you're feeling," she'd said, "you should just punch him in the nose."

Adam hardly ever laughed. He'd learned at a very young age that the unnatural stiffness of his face made him look like a zombie trying to imitate human laughter. It frightened his kindergarten classmates, who often responded cruelly, in the direct, innocent manner of five year olds.

So he tried not to show his amusement to the pretty young girl. But the thought of punching Henderson in the nose broke his anger and his rock-hard reserve. He turned away so she couldn't see his face as he laughed.

"You don't have to hide," she said. "My brother had Moebius much worse than you do."

Finding someone who understood what his existence was like changed everything. It wasn't long before the young Adam Cannaday was gripped by the certainty that his life would not be complete without Elizabeth Alcorn by his side.

Now it was fear and confusion that gripped him. Like any loving spouse, he was absolutely sure his wife was incapable of violence such as he had seen. But there was something in her eyes, some shadow that made him afraid to find out what was behind curtain number three. As an officer of the law, tearing back that curtain was his duty.

Their favorite grilled Portobello, roasted red pepper, and mozzarella sandwiches were delivered as they stared at one another. Adam waited until the waitress was beyond earshot before he leaned over and whispered urgently,

"What do you know about any of this?"

"I know who did it!" she said defiantly.

"How could you?" Adam glanced around to make sure no one could overhear their conversation. "Who do you think murdered Heather?"

Liz dropped her eyes and twisted the napkin in her lap. "Never mind ... you wouldn't believe me anyway."

"That's not fair," he said. "Besides, it's too late for 'never mind'."

The silence stretched out as Adam watched his wife worry the paper napkin to shreds. His concern built as he imagined his wife unwittingly involved in some monstrous, byzantine plot.

"You have to tell me who you think did it, Liz."

The name burst forth like a quail flushed from a bush by a prize bird-dog.

"Judy Crawford."

Adam was astonished, rendered momentarily speechless by the audacity of his wife's allegation. Then, like the first time he had met her, he was unable to hold back his laughter.

Her head shot up. "Don't laugh!" she said. The defiant look was back.

"But Liz," Adam protested, smothering his amusement, "You can't be serious!"

"I am! She was the one, I'm sure."

"C'mon honey, I know she's a hard-nosed runner who keeps beating you … but that doesn't make her a murderer."

"Crawford's always been the queen bee in Oregon running, a jealous queen bee. Until Templeton came along, no one had beaten Judy in five years. I saw how she looked at Heather when they were leaving the awards ceremony at the Pear Blossom Race; there was murder in her eyes, I'm sure of it."

Adam reviewed the mental picture he had of Heather Templeton at the awards ceremony. An unhappy Judy Crawford was in the background. He didn't see a murderer, he saw a winner who didn't like getting beat.

"Really, Liz?" He was sure that Liz would soon see how absurd the idea was. "You think she's capable of strangling someone just to win a road race? Do you think any woman wants to win that bad?"

Liz's anger flared. "What kind of sexist statement is that? You think that because we don't have a pair between the legs, that means we don't want to win just as desperately? I work hard so I can kick your butt and any woman who comes along. Don't think I'm not pissed as hell when Judy beats me, even if she is younger. I'm as driven as any woman … or any man."

"Whoa!" Adam held his hands up in surrender. "I know you're always striving to be better, to win. But would you kill to do it?"

"No." Liz let her anger cool a little. "But that's because I was raised a certain way. I know there is a right way to strive for the top … and a wrong way. But a woman who wasn't raised to recognize those limits? Who knows how far she might go?"

"Look, Liz. I understand what you're saying; I'm just not sure I buy it."

"What about that Olympic skater; the one that tried to have her rival's leg broken?"

"Tonya Harding?"

"Right. That shows that a woman can drive herself too hard, go too far … doesn't it?"

"But they were Olympians," he said. "The stakes were so much higher."

"Just because the Olympics aren't in the cards for us, doesn't mean that competitive fire isn't burning just as bright in our hearts."

"Ok, Ok! I get it." Adam ran a hand through his hair. He still had trouble believing a woman was capable of this crime. "Maybe Crawford is the type who could do something like this. But I'll need more to go on if I'm going to make her a suspect."

Liz took a bite of her sandwich and glanced at the time on her Garmin 405. Then she lit up like a light bulb as an idea popped into her head.

"What are you thinking?" Adam said.

She made a dramatic show of chewing her food, while her husband waited for his polite wife to finish her bite of sandwich. After a swallow of water, the way to prove Crawford's guilt came pouring breathlessly out of her.

"Crawford loves her Garmin. She's way worse than me, which is saying something. If she was the 'new friend' that Heather ran with last night, I bet she logged the run on her 405."

"But that's crazy," Cannaday's police instincts initially were telling him that no criminal would be stupid enough to record evidence of her location during such a heinous crime, and then leave it on a GPS device. Then he remembered how obsessive his wife was about logging her miles. How much of a habit it had become, even for him. If Crawford was confident of not being associated with the crime, maybe it *was* possible.

"Even if I could get a judge to give me a search warrant and obtain the watch, there's no way she didn't erase it."

"My Garmin ANT Agent uploads all my workouts automatically anytime my watch is within range of my computer." Adam smiled. Liz was eager and hot on the trail, like a rookie detective. "I know Judy has the same setup."

"So? I still have to get a search warrant for the computer."

"No!" Liz jumped up and waved at the waitress. "The workouts get uploaded to the Garmin Connect site. You can choose to make them private if you want, but Crawford has an ego the size of Mount Hood. I know her workouts are public. She wants everyone to know how hard she works. The evidence might be as close as the nearest Internet browser."

As the waitress arrived, Liz pointed at the Internet Cafe across the street.

"Can we get some to-go boxes please," said Adam, "and the check?"

CHAPTER SEVEN

"I don't believe it!" said Liz, after she scrolled down the screen to the heart-rate graph. "See here, her heart rate was between 155 and 160 beats per minute for most of the run." Her finger pointed at the chart. "Right here it dropped to 117 bpm in the blink of an eye before it gradually rose back to 160. Crawford even stopped the timer while she was killing her ... didn't want the time it took to commit murder to mess up her pace per mile."

Cannaday could sense the attention of the crowd in the chic coffee shop had been drawn to them. He put his hand on her shoulder and leaned over.

"Explain that to me," he whispered. "But do it *quietly*."

Liz moved back up to the top of the screen and clicked on the 'player' button.

"Once it loads," she said, "I'll put the map on hybrid mode. You'll be able to see her progress throughout the run."

Adam stared in awe at the wonder of technology that resulted in a little marker following a red line across the map on the computer screen. Liz dragged the icon in order to skip the long miles from Crawford's home in the foothills near Lookout Lake. She had run 17 miles just to get into McCarthy where she met Heather Templeton near the doomed runner's home.

When Liz paused the player, the red marker was in the park behind the Mayor's house.

"See right here?" She moved the mouse so the pointer hovered over the blue pace line on the linear chart above the map. "Except for a tiny dip, her pace doesn't change when she reaches this spot." The arrow on the screen moved straight up to the red heart-rate line. "But look at this. Her heart rate drops like a rock at that exact moment. The Garmin continues to monitor heart rate, even when the timer is stopped, but it doesn't record it. After she killed Heather, she restarted her watch and went on her way, while it recorded her heart rate, now much lower because of the time she'd been stopped."

With a strong sense of revulsion, Adam tried to imagine how a woman could become so twisted, so obsessed with her training, that she would take that into consideration while she murdered another human being. He'd always held the opposite sex in awe; consider women to be purer, kinder, even stronger in many ways than men. This was hard to accept.

"She probably did it more out of habit, than thought," said Liz.

"Yeah, like the time you got struck by that car and had paused your Garmin before you even landed on the ground ..." He had been half a block behind when he'd seen the car roll through the stop sign and hit his wife. It still gave him chills even though she'd only been a little bruised.

He gave her an affectionate kiss on the neck. "...I think you are all crazy." Even though he logged 25–30 miles a week, he knew he wasn't the same kind of runner as his wife and most of the other fanatics in McCarthy. But he was a good detective; much better than he gave himself credit for. And that was about to be proven once again.

"What's that?" He pointed to a small jig in the red line on the map. "Can you zoom in there?"

As Liz enlarged the location on the map, Adam saw the jig become a line that led briefly away from the path and then circled back to it. He could imagine Heather Templeton lying on the ground. In his mind, he could see Judy Crawford kneeling over the brutalized body. Her taut muscular form stands up with a piece of an oak branch in one hand. She strips the condom from the stick and puts it in the pouch at her waist. With the touch of a button, she starts her Garmin; subconsciously she doesn't want to miss getting credit for each step as she runs toward the holly hedge behind the Mayor's house. The oak stick flies through the air into the mayor's back yard.

Judy Crawford turns and starts her long run home. But, in Adam Cannaday's mind, her destination became Salem, Oregon. There he imagined her, old and grey, running laps around the Coffee Creek prison yard. He was coming to accept that a woman was capable of the cold, callous violence done upon Heather Templeton.

The jittery excitement that had taken hold of her husband was evident to Liz in the ratta-tap drumming of his hands on her shoulders.

"Get going, detective," she said. "You've got a bad guy to bring in ... or girl, I should say." She grabbed his hand as it landed on her shoulder and kissed it. "I'll get all this on a memory stick and drop it by the station on my way back to work. Now go!"

Adam's phone was against his ear before he left the coffee shop.

"Gary," he said, as he ran across the street, "Take a squad car and a couple of uniforms over to the Mayor's house. Search the southwest corner of his back yard for that stick."

He dodged a cyclist and listened to a protest from the young detective on the phone while he opened his car door, jumped in and gunned the motor to life.

"I'll call for a search warrant as soon as I get off the phone with you. If the Mayor is there and gives you any trouble at all, I'm *ordering* you to bring him back to the station, handcuffed." Adam's tires laid a patch of rubber as he pulled away from the curb. "You can even gag that lame-duck s.o.b. if you need to."

The smoke from his spinning tires drifted across the busy street and, even though it didn't show on his face, Cannaday was grinning inside.

"I always wanted to do that," he said to the empty car, "just like in the movies."

The drive was hurried and full of anticipation, but pleasant nonetheless. Along narrow back roads, he sped into the foothills; tall, evergreen forests pressed in from all sides as he neared the Crawford residence. When he rounded a bend in the road, the cabin in the woods he'd always dreamed about appeared on the ridge ahead. As he got out of the car he saw that there was even a view of snow-capped Mount Hood far to the northwest. The pine scent on the soft breeze made him feel like lacing up his running shoes and hitting the trail. He wondered how someone could live in a place so clean and pure while maintaining such a corrupted soul. In his opinion, the almost holy essence of the place should wash away any evil.

According to his Mobile Data Computer, the muddy Range Rover he'd parked behind belonged to Samuel and Judy Crawford. His MDC had also shown him Judy Crawford's license photo. So her narrow face and short auburn hair were familiar to him as she opened the front door. The thin legs, barren of fat, with wiry muscles that dropped out of hot pink running shorts were known to him also. They looked just like his wife's ... and Heather Templeton's.

The alarmed look when she saw his detective's shield gave Adam a sense of satisfaction.

"Good afternoon, Mrs. Crawford. I'm Adam Cannaday from the McCarthy Police Department. I need to ask you a few questions."

"But I ..." Flustered, she glanced back into the house, pausing as she tried to think of some way to stall the detective. "... I don't have time now." She grabbed her car keys from a hook by the door. "I have an appointment in town."

"It wasn't a request." The stern tone of his voice froze his suspect in her tracks. "If you'd prefer, I can take you into McCarthy myself ... to police headquarters. I can ask my questions there if you don't want to do it here."

The threat didn't unnerve Crawford as Cannaday expected. Instead it seemed to awaken the competitor within her. Her eyes acquired a steely glint.

"I'd be careful if I were you, Detective Cannaday." She stepped back and opened the door to let him in. "Threats like that against an innocent citizen could backfire on you."

Adam was getting what he wanted, so he didn't feel the need to banter.

"I'll beat a hasty exit and you'll get a sincere apology," he said as he looked around the entrance foyer, "if you can give satisfactory answers to my questions."

She showed him to an Adirondack chair next to the flagstone fireplace in the living room while she sat to his right on a country-style upholstered sofa. It was a friendly, open space. He even liked the Remington landscapes that decorated the walls.

"Well then, what can I do for you?" The ice in her voice chilled the room, despite the warm sun shining through the picture window opposite the fireplace.

"You can start by telling me where you were last night between the hours of eight and eleven."

Crawford didn't hesitate. "I was here all evening, with my husband."

"Where is your husband?"

"Working in the backyard."

"I'll need to speak to him before I leave."

"Of course."

Adam could see the confidence growing in her face. She actually thought she was going to get away with this. Little did she know that Trouter was, at that very moment, picking up the stake that Cannaday would drive through the heart of that hopeless expectation.

"Do you know Heather Templeton?"

"Certainly." she smiled. "Templeton is a runner like me."

"Not like you," Adam replied. "Not at all."

Crawford took the words as a challenge.

"What do you mean?"

"She's dead," he replied. "Heather Templeton was murdered last night."

The attempt she made at looking shocked was laughable.

"That's terrible." she said.

"Yes, it is. And I have reason to believe that you are involved."

"How ridiculous!" Crawford tossed her head, the cocky lack of concern evident in her tone and on her face. "I have no idea what would lead you to that conclusion."

Cannaday looked over his shoulder toward the wrought-iron and glass entrance table in the foyer. On it was a Garmin 405, clipped into its charger.

When he looked back, his confidence wavered slightly. Judy Crawford had followed his eyes, yet her cock-sure attitude hadn't changed. Then his cell phone rang. He walked into the foyer as he answered.

"Give me some good news, Gary," he said.

"I've got it ... and the Mayor." The tone of the young detective's voice was exultant and the sound of an affronted politician was clear in the background.

"Good man! Take it to Brillson so he can ..."

"I had Rafe with me. He's already confirmed that this is the one we're looking for. Do you want me to bring it to you?"

"No, you keep it. Rush it to the F.B.I. fingerprint lab in Portland. The murder happened before that flurry started to fall. That stick was dry when it was used. There's a good chance they'll find a print. And oh ... Gary?" Adam paused to make sure his former student was listening.

"Yes sir?"

"That was stellar work. Really. Bringing Rafe with you was brilliant."

Cannaday enjoyed the happiness that wove through Trouter's simple "thank you."

CHAPTER EIGHT

Adam shut his phone and reached for his cuffs. He didn't need to wait for the prints to come back. He was sure. Turning back to the living room, he found a pale and shaken Judy Crawford. Next to her was a stocky, balding man in work boots, jeans, and a flannel shirt. His arm was wrapped protectively around his wife's shoulders.

"Judy Crawford, I'm arres—"

"Detective Cannaday?" The man stepped forward and held out his hand. "I'm Sam Crawford. I think an awful mistake is about to be made." He looked pointedly at the cuffs in Adam's hand. "Can I speak to you alone?"

Adam ignored the extended hand. "If I'm about to make a mistake," he said. "it's one that can be easily corrected ... downtown." As he moved toward Judy Crawford, her husband put his hand on Cannaday's forearm.

"Please, Detective. You must hear what I have to say."

"Fine," he said. He knelt in front of his suspect and cuffed her ankles together. "You wait right here." Then he followed Sam Crawford out the front door.

"Talk fast," he said as they stood on the deep front porch.

"My wife is innocent," Crawford was wringing his hands, "She couldn't have ..."

"Mr. Crawford, this is a waste of my time. You'll get a chance to defend your wife on the witness stand. We have evidence that ..."

"I know you do. But it isn't proof of my wife's guilt."

Adam stared at the nervous man pacing in front of him. "What are you saying?"

"I'm saying that I killed Heather Templeton."

The stone features of the detective couldn't change, but Crawford's statement had taken him by surprise.

"How do I know you aren't just saying that to protect your wife? You're trying to muddy the waters of this investigation."

"No, it's true. Judy doesn't know anything about us. Last night wasn't the first time I'd run with Heather. We met at a race shortly after they moved here. I don't know how or why it happened, but there was this attraction from the first moment. We both resisted at first, but then she started having marriage problems. She thought her husband was fooling around and turned to me for comfort … for affirmation that she was still desirable. It was easy for me to give her what she wanted."

Cannaday interrupted. "I'm not buying this; we *know* your wife was there at the scene."

"Why? Because of this?" Crawford held up his right hand. On it was a Garmin 405. "My wife and I have matching Garmins. I grabbed hers by mistake last night."

Adam was bewildered, floored by what this man was telling him.

"But why? Why did you kill her? And if you did, why are you admitting it now?"

"The answer to both questions is the same," Crawford said. "I love my wife. I always have and always will. What happened with Heather was just a sex thing. A short-term attraction I couldn't resist. When she started talking about leaving her husband … and me leaving my wife, I knew how it would end up. If my wife had found out, she would have left me."

"Now I'm going to lose her no matter what I do. But I can't let my wife go to prison for the mistakes I've made."

He'd never wanted to believe a woman capable of the crime, so the confession was beginning to feel right to Adam. For a long moment, he looked through the gap in the pines at distant Mount Hood. Then up at the trees, their long green needles rippling gently in the breeze. His mind was made up.

"Don't move from that spot," he told Crawford. He went back inside and uncuffed the newly cleared suspect. "My apologies, Mrs. Crawford."

He walked out of the house and off the porch.

"Samuel Crawford, you have the right to remain silent ..."

From the living room window Judy Crawford watched the scene; relief was the strongest emotion she felt.

༄

Crawford took full advantage of his rights; they rode back to McCarthy in silence.

They reached University and 13th Street; Adam glanced down the road to the spot where he had first met Liz. He drove through here several times a week and it always brought the same feeling; one that told him his life was everything he had hoped it would be.

When his phone rang and he saw it was his wife, he took it as a sign of the connection they had, of the synchronicity that had brought this day to such a successful conclusion.

He answered the phone with a question. "How did you know I was looking at the very place where you first spoke to me?"

The sound of Liz's laughter brightened an already glorious afternoon.

"It must be that invisible, infinite fiber-optic line connecting my brain to yours," she said.

"So that's your secret! No wonder you read me so well." They amused each other by having this same conversation at least twice a month.

"You sound happy. Does that mean mission accomplished?"

"Yes," he replied, "but not like you expected. Her husband confessed to the crime."

"Oh, Adam!" Her voice sounded more concerned than congratulatory.

"What?" he said.

"I was calling to tell you that I found two more instances where it looks like Judy ran with Heather. I think she set this up over several weeks' time."

"But I know all about that. Sam Crawford admitted to accidently using his wife's Garmin." As soon as the words were out of his mouth, he realized they didn't sound right.

"Three times? And only on days that the runs went near the Templeton's house?"

Adam glanced at Sam Crawford in the rearview window. He was sitting rigidly still, his head bowed.

"Think, Adam!" his wife continued. "How hard is it for you to keep up with me when we run together?"

"I can do it," he said defensively, then he chuckled, "for a half-mile anyway."

"Well, I have a hard time keeping up with either Judy or Heather."

"So?" He knew this was taking him somewhere and he wouldn't like it when he arrived.

"Did you take a look at Sam? Does he look familiar?"

Another look in the rearview confirmed that Adam could not remember seeing the man before this afternoon.

"Of course you don't recognize him. He doesn't run much; I don't think he's ever run more than a 5k and he's never come within minutes of you in any race the two of you have ever done. He was always way *behind* you.

"You're the detective, sweetheart, don't you see? That page on the Garmin Connect site shows that there is no way Sam Crawford could have run that far or that fast. He's lying to protect his wife."

There was a strong dose of sympathy in his wife's voice that was clear in her next words.

"She's a runner, honey. Judy Crawford is going to run."

CHAPTER NINE

Cannaday worked the police radio and his cell phone hard. City and county as well as United States Forest Service and National Park rangers were alerted. He even had an assignment for his wife. After turning Sam Crawford over to Trouter, he started back toward the mountains.

He didn't get far before his hopes for a quick apprehension of his suspect were dashed in a variety of ways.

A noisy metal canvas of modern art was rolling relentlessly along in front of his car. Cannaday silenced his siren and shut down his dashboard police beacon since it was having no impact on the Union Pacific freight train. While he waited at the railroad crossing, Adam scrambled to change into the running clothes he kept in his car for the occasional times he squeezed in a lunchtime run.

Dispatch connected him with the Lois County sheriff, who delivered more bad news.

"Sorry Cannaday, Crawford must have heard us coming, we could see her running for the woods as soon as we came around the turn." County Sheriff Tim Harden sounded sufficiently contrite. "But we kept her from getting out of here in the Range Rover. It was packed up and ready to go. Fifteen minutes later and she would have been headed for the interstate. At least she's on foot; she won't get far."

The Crawford house backed up to the Willamette National Forest; almost 1.7 million acres covered with trees. North of that was Mount Hood National Forest; south was the Umpqua. In all, the national forests in

Oregon comprised over 16 million acres; 25,000 square miles. The sheriff could hardly have been more wrong.

Not for the first time, or the last, Adam cursed the train. "Did anyone go after her?" It wouldn't matter if they did. With their soft body armor, firearm, police radio, cuffs, and assorted other encumbrances, no one in uniform had a chance to catch her. He finished stripping out of his trousers and yanked on his running shorts.

"Sure, four guys are on her trail and I have more coming."

"Was she wearing anything?"

Harden snorted. "She wasn't naked, if that's what you're asking."

"On her back." The frustrated detective pounded on the steering wheel. Any runner would have known what he meant. The continuing clatter of the endless train only added to his impatience. "Was she wearing anything on her back?"

"A skinny little pack. Don't know what she could fit in the thing. Why?"

"That's a hydration pack." That skinny little pack could hold three liters of water, assorted energy bars and gels, electrolyte tablets, emergency gear; everything Crawford needed to keep her going for hour after hour.

"It doesn't matter how many guys you send after her, she'll be long gone." Adam got his shoes tied and looked at the network of National Forest fire roads on his MDC screen. He only had one shot at this. Guessing the trail she would use was key to his slim hope of catching her before nightfall. His odds would improve if Liz came through for him.

"Psshaw!" The sheriff scoffed. "How far can she go?"

"She has run one hundred miles before, Sheriff ... for fun. If she has a headlamp, she'll be on the other side of the Cascades by morning. With her freedom at stake, I imagine Judy Crawford could keep going for a lot longer than that."

"What a crock! This is a woman we're talking about, right? My men will catch her, you can count on that."

It was obvious Harden wasn't married to someone like Judy Crawford, or Heather Templeton, or Liz. He wouldn't have survived long with thoughts like that running around in his head. Adam wasn't sure how the man had held on to such chauvinistic ideas in this day and age, but he didn't have time to argue the point. He could finally see the end of the train.

"I hope you do, Sheriff. Good luck."

The last, colorfully gang-tagged railcar cleared the crossing, the red-and-white barrier rose, and Cannaday jammed his foot to the floor. He raced out of the valley, topped a ridge and let his car drift to a stop. Ahead of him was an ocean of green.

It was a daunting haystack. Judy Crawford was a very tiny needle. This was literally her backyard and she knew the hundreds of miles of trails that wound through it as well as, or better, than anyone. He would need help and a lot of luck to find her.

Cannaday hadn't hesitated before getting his wife involved. If anyone had a chance of predicting where his suspect would run, it was Liz. Both took their running very seriously, both loved the Willamette trails and both women were driven to succeed. The two competitors had gone head-to-head in some epic races over the years.

At the Mackenzie River Trail Run, the two women had battled for thirty-one miles over rocky, rolling and winding trails through some of the most breathtaking scenery in Oregon. In the end, after four hours of knee-pounding, quad-mashing, lung-bursting effort, two seconds was the margin of Crawford's victory. Liz had taken that loss particularly hard. Although his wife had never beaten Judy Crawford, maybe even because of that fact, there was no one he trusted more to help him in this situation.

When his cell phone buzzed, he wasn't surprised to see her name on the screen.

"I hope you have some good news for me," he said.

"Why don't you ever say something like 'hello, sweetheart'?" she asked.

"Next time, I promise. I am kind of anxious to find out where in this infinite green wilderness you think I should go to find a murderer."

"Well, I wish you had given me an easier assignment, like telling you where to find D.B. Cooper." Liz had spent a frantic half-hour studying topo maps and using her knowledge of her competitor and the terrain to come up with the winding escape route she thought Judy would follow.

"I tried to estimate what her pace would be and where you had the best chance of intercepting her. If you drive fast, I think you'll reach the western edge of the Rebel Rock Loop about the same time she does. She may have already gone by; if so, you may be able to tell. It's still wet from snowmelt up there ..."

The thought she'd put into this scouting report made him appreciate even more what an amazing woman he had married.

"... She'll probably be wearing Adidas Kanadias; she uses those for longer trail runs. The studs on the shoe will leave a bunch of little round indentations, about the size of the tip of your pinky. I don't think it will be as easy as just following her shoeprints, but you should be able to see if she's used the trail. This is the route ..."

Adam took careful notes while his wife gave him the list of trails and junctions that would lead him into one of the most remote areas in the state.

"If I didn't know better," he joked, "I'd think you were trying to get me lost in the wilderness." He already had the car moving toward National Forest Road 19; his destination was the Red Diamond Campground where he would head out on the Rebel Rock Trail.

"This isn't a joke, Adam." White noise degraded the connection as he made his way into the mountains. "You'll be ...sss... alone, a long way ... sss... back-up ...sss... water at Beeler ...sss... I ...sssss... head for Pacific Crest ...ssss... Elk Lake, other ...sss... meet ...sss..."

A "no signal" message showed that he wouldn't be talking to Liz again anytime soon.

Whether his chances at catching Judy Crawford were good or not, at least now he had a plan, a way to move forward. By the time he reached the trailhead, Crawford would have already run almost thirty mostly uphill miles over some pretty rugged country. Adam hoped she'd be dragging if he had to chase her down.

An hour later, he slid to a stop in front of a sign that directed hikers to the Rebel Rock Loop. Eager to get the hunt started, Adam jumped out of the car, at the last moment grabbing a half-empty plastic bottle of water.

After only four running strides, his well-developed common sense regained control. He'd spent much of the last three hours in his car. Slowing down to a walk, he made his way to the trailhead, shaking out his legs and swinging his arms as he went. He would not catch her if he cramped up a quarter-mile into the chase.

Cannaday leaned against the sign-in station, stretching his calves. Bear warnings, leave no trace postings, and cautionary notes about being prepared when entering the wilderness were spread liberally across the four-foot-by-four-foot bulletin board.

The loop trail crossed only a dozen feet away. A thrill climbed up Adam's spine.

In the soft, moist dirt of the junction, exactly like Liz had described, was the imprint of a Kanadia shoe.

CHAPTER TEN

The majestic, old-growth forest with its towering green canopy filled Adam with awe. He wanted to stop and soak his soul in the natural spirituality of the quiet glade. Instead, he took what energy he could from the place and pressed on. Likewise, he ignored the riotous color of wildflowers in the meadows. Without pause, he crossed deep, emerald canyons and clear, rushing mountain streams as he pushed toward Rebel Rock. As he neared the ridgeline, scuffed pine needles on the trail ahead showed that another had done the same.

When the mitten-shaped rock outcropping finally came into view, climbing three thousand feet in just over five miles had taken much of the freshness out of Cannaday's legs. That Crawford had followed the same torturous route did not keep some negative thoughts from creeping in.

He'd run hard and yet never felt that he was anything but alone in the wild. No other person had come along the rough, lightly used trail. Any other time, he would have considered it a blessing; a rare chance to commune with Mother Earth. But the sometimes faint prints on the forest floor gave him no clue as to whether he was gaining on his quarry or not.

An old lookout cabin, just southwest of Rebel Rock, gave him a chance to take the lay of the land. At least that is what he told himself, denying that it was just an excuse to allow him to catch his breath. From that small frame building, teetering on the edge of a rocky slope, he would have a view of the deep wilderness awaiting him, even an occasional glimpse of the trail ahead.

Three Sisters greeted him as Adam stepped up to the northeast window. The trio of peaks was due north of Elk Lake, which lay more than twenty trail miles east of his position. The area was a spider's web of intersecting pathways, with the Pacific Crest Trail serving as the wilderness "interstate" for hikers. If Judy Crawford was able to reach there, it would be hard to guess in which direction she might go next.

A flash of movement pulled his eyes to the switchback slightly north and downhill from the cabin. For a moment, there was nothing ... and then Judy Crawford emerged from a bend in the Beeler Springs Trail. Though she was headed diagonally downhill, the zigzag of the trail made it look like she was approaching. She looked so close; Adam was tempted to jump from the window in pursuit.

Her face was focused and relaxed; she cruised smoothly down the rocky trail without a single errant step. As she was about to disappear around the next turn, she turned her head toward the lookout and looked directly in Cannaday's eyes.

The smirk on her face spoke her thoughts as clearly as if she were broadcasting with a megaphone from the top of Rebel Rock.

"You are a fool and you have no chance," that look said, "I'll run you into the ground and spit on your shriveled, exhausted body."

If his own face had possessed the capacity to respond, it would have shown Adam driven into a fierce and unflinching temper; a near-fey mood gripped him as he rushed from the cabin. As it was, in her brief glimpse, Crawford was not intimidated by his stony, unemotional mask that could have hidden defeat as easily as determination.

Cannaday reached the junction in moments, leaping over the sharp angle of the switchback and plummeting down the steep trail. He wished for the courage and balance that his wife had when she ran the downhill portions of her races; gliding effortlessly as though on a rail.

"There is a rhythm to trail running," she told him once, "it comes from letting your body feel the course, not fight it. Relax and let instinct direct your feet. That loose rock in the middle of the path isn't there to turn your ankle. It's there to tell you to stop over-striding; let your reflexes shorten your step and guide you smoothly down the trail."

Now, in the moment of utmost need, he finally got it. The thrill almost unbalanced him, but his feet found their way and kept him flying in pursuit. Almost before he realized it, the switchbacks ended and Beeler Springs became a downhill roller coaster. It was easy to let each drop push him into a faster pace and the whooshing sound as he tore through the dense forest only added to his feeling of speed. He topped a prominent rise and spotted Crawford on the trail ahead as she caught airtime on the next camelback and disappeared beyond the crest.

She looked strong and fast; she looked confident. She also looked closer. Adam convinced himself he was gaining and pressed even harder. Minutes later he reached the spot where she had dropped from sight. In the long swale that descended between two hills, he caught brief hints of activity among the thick trees and undergrowth.

There was no doubt in his mind; he had gained an enormous chunk of ground in just a few minutes. Cannaday knew how much his body had to give and parceled out a little more.

As he raced along the shady hollow, a signpost in a small clearing ahead pointed right, directing hikers to Beeler Spring, a place to replenish one's water supply. It was only a short distance off the trail.

Adam's pace faltered. From the multitude of knobby footprints on the ground, he could tell that Crawford had taken the time to refill her pack. That was how he had gotten so much closer. He looked at the plastic bottle in his hand which held, at best, two or three more swallows.

If he stopped, there was no doubt that the durable ultrarunner he was chasing would pull ahead, probably beyond any hope of catching her. If he didn't, he wouldn't last more than five or six more miles on the water he had left. Once dehydration set in, he would slip farther and farther behind and Judy Crawford would escape from his grasp all the same.

A bear cub wandered out of the huckleberry and into the clearing behind him. The frisky black ball of fur was as surprised as Cannaday and his squeal brought a chuffing response and a louder crashing from the undergrowth to the south.

That made Adam's decision simple. He ran.

CHAPTER ELEVEN

By the time he came upon the junction with the Olallie trail, the woods were silent except for the soft, rapid patter of shoes along the trail. Adam grabbed a sapling and whipped himself into a sharp turn to the north. Although he never saw the bear, the sounds from the angry mama had been enough to send a surge of adrenaline coursing through his veins that was still giving him an extra boost.

He was getting closer; he could feel it. The half mile to French Pete Creek flew by and then he turned east again, onto the Wildcat Swamp Trail. Long stretches of smooth footing led gradually downhill and allowed him to use his long legs to settle into a quick pace that Adam felt would bring Crawford within reach before his water ran out.

But an increasingly noisy dialogue had begun inside his head. One in which his jealous, underused, impetuous side was arguing strenuously for a dramatic surge, a sprint if need be, to catch Crawford quickly. The risk-reward factor for that course of action was great. She wasn't yet within view; he had no way to judge the length of her lead. It was all or nothing.

The stronger, plodding, determined part of his character won out and remained true to the course he was following; a fast but sustainable pace that would draw him within a certain range before he attempted that final sprint.

Four more miles had flown by beneath his feet before he began to seriously doubt his decision. Cannaday had covered almost fifteen miles at a speed far above any race he had ever run. His approach to the open, grassy expanse of Wildcat Swamp was painful. His legs ached and his lungs had grown tired of the reduced amount of oxygen in the air he was breathing at 5,000 feet. Through sheer willpower alone had he been able to drive himself for so long at such a pace.

Quit was a word that had never entered his vocabulary. In elementary school, when school-yard toughs thought he was easy prey, he kept getting up and hitting back; the pain and fear never showed in his face and the bullies were unable to fill their need to terrorize and belittle.

As a freshman, Adam collapsed during the first mile of his first high school cross-country practice. He spent three days in the hospital while doctors labored to find the cause of the breathing difficulty that had led to his fainting. When it turned out to be another effect of his Moebius syndrome, they told him he might never be able to engage in strenuous physical activities.

The challenge was formidable but the determined teenager researched every possible way to make his lungs stronger and develop the muscles on the right side of his chest. With the bull-headed determination that became his trademark, Cannaday applied what he learned and was running on the varsity team by the time he was a senior.

Continuing that regimen throughout his adult life had allowed him to become a competitive runner in his age group, even if it left him a little short of being able to keep up with his wife.

But a lifetime of developing that willpower and determination could not save Adam from the crash that was approaching. He'd finished the last of his water miles earlier. His body had been consuming energy at a prodigious rate for over two hours without any carbs to replace what he was burning.

An introduction to that hideous "Q" word was facing Cannaday as he burst out of the trees on the south end of Wildcat Swamp. In a month or two, it would be a huge patch of golden grain in the middle of bright green wilderness; visible from airliners passing at 40,000 feet. Right now, it was a catch basin for snowmelt; a wet, boggy mess.

Much like his experience coming down from Rebel Rock, Adam's feet now dodged puddles of water instead of rocks as he followed the trail along the tree line.

It would have been too much … except for one thing. The open expanse gave him a clear view of Judy Crawford. After miles of chasing a ghost, she was a physical reality that was struggling through the marshy fringe of the swamp less than one hundred yards in front of him.

For once, his plodding, methodical side and his impetuous, risky side were in agreement ... the time for letting go was here.

Cannaday charged ahead, dancing past the roots and puddles, drawing closer to the tip-toeing woman who was still unaware of his presence. He was only yards behind when she reached the end of the swamp and the drier trail leading away from it.

When she glanced back, the shock and fear that sprang upon her face was satisfying to see, but Adam would rather she had not looked at all. Alerted to his closeness, she turned and streaked out of sight down the path.

Seconds later he, too, was out of the swamp. Driving his arms to force his heavy legs faster, he continued to pull closer. He could picture Russ Sellers, his old cross-country coach, standing by the trail, urging him on while hauling on an imaginary fishing pole. "Reel her in," he yelled, "she's on the line, just reel her in."

Twenty yards ... ten yards. As they wound through the woods he was sure he would catch her. The fish was almost in the boat.

Then Adam felt the line about to snap. Even though she was so close, he couldn't hear her footsteps or her labored breathing. The only sounds he could here were the hammering of his own heart and ragged gasping of his lungs.

Five yards. No amount of effort could get him closer. He could feel even that margin about to slip away when he spotted the shallow gully ahead and a stream running through the center of it. They'd covered the mile from the swamp to Bill Gott Spring in a handful of minutes.

The small ravine was only three feet deep, but it was at least fifteen feet wide; she'd have to run down into it and then out again. But he would jump it.

Judy Crawford leapt into the gully and splashed across the stream. She was climbing the other side when Adam reached the edge. Sixteen miles of rugged trails had stolen the spring from his legs; the fastest mile he had ever run had robbed his lungs of their last breath; as soon as he was in the air, he knew ... he wasn't going to make it.

Crawford was back on the trail when Adam's knees caught the edge of the ravine; he reached out desperately and grabbed at her ankles as he hit the ground hard. Stunned, he struggled to push himself to his hands and knees. Even that tiny effort left him on the verge of blacking out. He looked up in time to see a blurry, muddy foot coming straight for his face.

Shockingly cold water washed the blackness from his mind and kept him barely conscious. He was lying on his back in the middle of the ravine. The icy flow was only four inches deep and gurgled around him as he watched Judy Crawford step up beside him.

She bent over and picked a stone precisely the size of his head out of the rushing water and began to lift it over her head.

If this was the movies, he thought, she'd taunt me; give me a few more moments to live while some miracle comes along to save me.

"Is at all ya gah?" His mumbles didn't provoke her or slow the upward progress of the rock. The blur of movement meant the coming of more pain, so Adam Cannaday closed his eyes, surrendered to the dark ... and learned the meaning of the word "quit."

CHAPTER TWELVE

A splash of water pulled him from the darkness. Adam lifted a stiff, cold hand out of the stream and rubbed it uselessly across his face. "About time," he heard his wife's teasing voice say, "I was going to hit you with the next rock, instead of just splashing you."

He turned his head toward the sound and was rewarded with a nose full of water. After pushing up on one elbow, he shook his head and looked again.

Liz was sitting in the water downstream. Beneath her was a struggling form. His wife was smiling like an adrenalin-pumped bull rider. She had a handful of hair in her right hand and pulled a spluttering head out of the water.

"This is the only way I can get her to shut up," Liz said. "Do you think we could just let her drown?"

"Oh, I'm afraid I couldn't let you do that," said a pleasant, laid-back voice, "at least not in my neck of the woods."

Liz's right arm around his waist felt heavenly. Not just because of the support it provided as he walked along on gimpy knees, but also for the warmth it was helping to put back in his chilled carcass.

Ahead on the trail Forest Ranger Brett Smith was leading a cuffed and hobbled Judy Crawford across the Pacific Crest junction and on toward Elk Lake.

The wet, spent, and bedraggled detective hugged his wife closer.

"You are amazing, you know that?" He kissed the side of her head.

"Why?" She looked at him with amusement glittering in her eyes. Liz knew what he was about to say, but wouldn't spoil it for him. "Because I drove like a NASCAR maniac for two hours, ran from Elk Lake back along a murderer's escape route that I had predicted, saved my husband and captured the bad guy?"

"No," he replied. "You are only amazing because you love me. So you better not ever stop."

"What can I say?" Liz stopped and put her arms around his neck. "There's just something about your face."

Adam Cannaday tilted that face forward and kissed the woman he loved; secure in the knowledge that she, and only she, could see every emotion written there.

The End

PROGRÁMMED

Prologue

The power of the human mind has been the subject of study and an object of wonder for centuries. After decades of effort by brilliant scholars and researchers, much is understood about which processes take place and *where*. But we are not very much closer to knowing *how* or *why* our brains operate the way they do. One fact is certain; no one has realized the full potential of the human mind.

A few people, perhaps as the result of good genes, excellent nurturing or just lots of hard work, come closer to maximizing the potential of their brains than do the rest of us. One couple learned how dangerous exploring that potential can be.

CHAPTER ONE

She Laughed at Herself

T he late spring cold snap was taking a toll on flowers throughout the Denver area and making runners once again bundle up. For Colleen, picking just the right outfit for a training run had nothing to do with color coordination or current fashion trends. When the weather was really cold and windy like today, she had a furry cap with ear flaps, a hat that would have looked good on a Russian tank commander. On this small woman, the style was eccentric—at best. She had a hole cut in the top to let excess heat out and the hat was a color no self-respecting Russian would be caught dead in—lime green. Wearing that hat, stuffed over her bright red hair, she looked to be about three miles passed eccentric. She laughed at herself when she passed the mirror in the front hall.

Colleen stepped out the door into a bitter west wind, slicing relentlessly down from the distant, snow-shrouded Rocky Mountains. With it came fine, powdery flakes that collected around curbs, behind trees and sign posts, and in the smallest depressions in the land. Her hat was well-secured, flaps down. Along with down mittens on her hands, the parts that could not suffer the cold were well-covered. The rest of her body parts could take care of themselves. Long, black tights, a sports bra and a blue, long sleeve Bolder Boulder t-shirt were the only protection they got.

As she turned her compact, muscular body onto the wind, a fierce, happy grin transformed her pretty face into one that showed her true strength and beauty. The effort of going against the wind would warm her up quickly and the wind would be at her back for the return. Colleen loved challenges because they helped expose the weaknesses she had, even though her husband Gary would swear that her only shortcoming was that she was perfect.

Runners in general tend to be a cerebral bunch and Colleen was certainly that. A part of her mind constantly monitored the time, noted the distance and computed the pace of her runs. She eschewed the fancy watches that would do this for her because her most versatile running aid was setting on her shoulders.

Colleen knew her body well. So well, that she stopped doing prediction runs because she always won and didn't like the "she must be cheating" looks she'd often get.

Her job at the Space Science Institute in Boulder entailed monitoring and maintaining the many computer programs that are the lifeblood of modern astronomy. The complexities and pitfalls of long-running programs were her specialty. But her hobby was the working of the human mind, in particular, her own. What power the mind had over the body and how that related to her running was of special interest.

She was still a teenager when she discovered that she had the ability to work out complex problems while she ran. It was an advantage that she used to full effect in earning a full scholarship to M.I.T. and then on into her career. After one exceptional run in which she had worked out a new algorithm for controlling the cameras on the Cassini Saturn mission, she found herself striding up her driveway with no idea where she had run or for how long.

In her running log she kept short notes about her efforts to "program" herself while running. Considering it a form of self-hypnosis, she never thought about where her efforts might take her.

With her stride carrying her smoothly down the windswept shoulder of the road, Colleen began to "program" herself for the day's run.

She pictured herself standing in a large, dark room. In front of her was a huge, floor-to-ceiling, computer monitor. At eye level was a bright blue "START" button. After she put her hand flat against it, a real-time picture of her running along the road appeared. She noted the head bobbing up and down a little too much and touched her back on the screen, mentally straightening it. Then she touched the shoulders to relax them and the hands to drop them slightly. Next, she touched her hips and shifted them slightly forward so that her body's center of gravity was directly over the place her foot hit the ground on each stride.

Noting that the head bob was gone, Colleen took a step back and examined herself again. With an approving nod, she stepped up to the screen again and put her hand against a "special commands" button that had just popped up on the screen. A console window appeared, cursor flashing in anticipation of a command. She quickly entered,

> KEEP RUNNING

As the console spat out a warning message and a chance to abort, she impatiently mashed the enter key, not even pausing to read the output.

> COMMAND ACCEPTED

flashed briefly on the screen then vanished as Colleen continued striding down the road.

Standing in the dark room, she saw her husband's car on the screen, coming down the road toward her as he returned home from work. She heard the short beep of his horn. In the control room, she smiled and raised her hand to wave, but the runner on the screen just kept on running.

෭

Gary recognized her lime green hat floating just above the crest of the hill. He smiled affectionately as the rest of her came into view. The strong pumping of her arms and the quick, efficient lift of her heels at the back of her stride made her easy to identify, even without the hat.

Though he was a cyclist and not a runner, he understood the dedication it took to get out in conditions like this and loved his wife all the more for her toughness and determination. No way was he going for a ride today. His bike was set up in the basement and that suited him just fine.

He tapped his horn as he approached, and then made a rueful shake of his head as she ignored him. They'd had a rare spat the night before—it had ended almost as quickly as it had started—and he'd already forgotten the cause. Now it appeared to Gary that the cooling off period had not yet run its course.

〰

Colleen sat cross-legged on the floor, leaned her head back, and closed her eyes. Control of all the processes necessary for running had been relinquished to a carefully compartmentalized part of her brain; she was free to turn her thoughts to other matters. She knew Gary probably thought she was still mad about that silly argument. Well, *that* would be easy to remedy when she got home; she'd just ask him to join her in her post-run shower.

With one problem solved Her mind turned to a particularly vexing issue concerning the effect of electro-static emissions on the DC power production of the Radioisotope Thermoelectric Generator aboard the Cassini. Out on the road, her legs and arms worked in perfect harmony to carry her farther and farther from home.

CHAPTER TWO

Without Conscious Thought

With Led Zeppelin blasting from the speakers, Gary worked up a good sweat spinning. He always got the Led out when he was ticked off. He knew it was silly, but it bothered him that Colleen sometimes held onto little hurts longer than he felt necessary.

After a quick shower, he got dinner started, the cats fed and his e-mail checked. An hour and a half after he arrived home, he glanced at the clock in the kitchen as he carried the scraps for composting out to the bin in the backyard. *She must be putting in a few extra miles.* His jaw clenched briefly as he wished she'd left him a note letting him know.

Back inside, he put the bowl of pasta in the oven and set it to warm. The sauce on the cook top he put on simmer. In the living room, he picked Danyers' "The Watch" off the coffee table and sat down to read.

~∞~

Though she ran on under low, fast-moving clouds, the approaching mountains reached proudly into sunshine. The spring melt was well under way and the winter snow shed drops of water that sparkled in the late spring sun. This brief cold snap couldn't halt the changing of the seasons. Drops joined to form quiet trickles, which became bubbling rivulets, then rushing streams and finally a crashing river. Like the water beneath her,

Colleen moved as though she were part of an unstoppable flow. Without conscious thought, she crossed the bridge over the roaring river below. And the miles rolled by, bringing the majestic barrier of stone closer.

ᐁᔕ

Along with Peter, a character in the book, Gary was finding out about "accidentals" when he realized the afternoon had gone and evening had crept in to steal his light. It hadn't stopped him yet, but the words on the page were getting harder to make out.

Dark thoughts rushed up from his subconscious as he looked at his watch. Colleen had not returned, even though several hours had passed. When a picture of her injured by some inattentive driver flashed through his mind, he grabbed his car keys and rushed for the door. Although the clouds remained dark over head, in the west the sun pulled free of them before slipping behind the mountains.

ᐁᔕ

Sunshine and a small, hand-written sign that said "People's Republic of Boulder" welcomed Colleen as she crossed the Foothills Parkway. She cleared the road looking strong as a State Trooper sped past. Her body was still cruising along at peak efficiency, but with almost thirty miles gone under her fleet feet, her lips were drying out. The stores of fat that were now her primary fuel were getting low. Like a jet on auto-pilot, with no one watching the gauges, Colleen moved into the shadow of the mountains.

ᐁᔕ

Gary expected to see her returning almost as soon as he started looking. As he drove longer and farther without finding his wife, he became seriously worried. Once he had covered the maximum distance he thought she would run, he turned around, checking side roads and alternate routes as he headed back toward home. What helped him avoid panic was the hope that he would find her there.

When that hope proved false, he left a note on the door and went to the police.

摸

She opened her eyes to a wondrous landscape of ghostly shadows and starlight. The full moon was rising behind her and its soft glow lit the winding road as it climbed before her. Only a guardrail separated her from the torrent cascading through massive boulders in the cavernous ravine on her left. The pounding water threw up a damp mist that coated the canyon wall. Thousands of glistening crystal droplets decorated the hardy evergreens clinging to the rock face. Through the mist, the mountains towered over her, their white tops glowing magically. An immense cliff rose straight up along the right side of the road. Long, sparkling icicles hung from every protruding rock that her steadily pumping arms and driving legs carried her past.

Awe was mixed with confusion as Colleen struggled to give the astonishing scene some context. She had begun to assemble the memory of leaving her house for a run, when, like an alarm clock slowly penetrating the fog of sleep, her body's needs began to clamor for attention.

She felt the stinging cold of the air she was breathing into her lungs. Blisters on her feet sent waves of pain radiating up her legs. Every breath she exhaled stung her cracked lips. Her chest ached with the rapid pounding of her heart. Though the moisture of the waterfalls was chilling, it did give some small relief to her terribly dehydrated system.

A break in the cliff revealed a pull-out for slow vehicles. There, off the shoulder under a stark, sodium-vapor lamp was an emergency call box. Relief helped dull some of the pain that was over-loading her senses.

Colleen turned to cross the road toward the light, or, at least in her mind, that is what she attempted. Her arms and legs kept her running steadily up the left side of the road.

The scream she made was given voice only in her mind. She tried again and again to force her tortured body toward this chance for deliverance. As the light drifted towards the limit of her peripheral vision, she couldn't even turn her head to keep it in view.

CHAPTER THREE

Deep Into the Program

If Colleen had been twenty years younger, her description and last known whereabouts would have been instantly broadcast throughout the region as part of an "Amber Alert". As it was, Gary was being treated as though he should feel lucky the officer was doing him the grand favor of taking a report. He tried to remain calm as awful possibilities battered his morale. But images of those ugly possibilities zapped what little patience he had.

What happened next was some minor destruction of public property, verbally abusing everyone within earshot and almost assaulting a police officer, but it finally got him the attention he needed.

It had been full dark for hours before the advisory went out asking that all law enforcement personnel keep an eye out for the missing runner. Gary had stayed busy by calling all the local hospitals and urgent care centers. Since she wore a Road ID bracelet, he was certain that his efforts would be fruitless; if she was at a hospital he would have been called, since his contact info was on the bracelet. In his heart, he knew that something was seriously wrong and his anxiety had developed into an almost physical heaviness that he could not shake. The guilt he felt as a result of their meaningless argument made it worse.

After she had been missing for eight hours, a case number was assigned and Officer Al Naylor was put in charge. He suggested to Gary that he go home and look for anything that might help him get a handle on what might have happened. Although it seemed like an obvious effort to get him out of their hair, Gary had begun to feel useless at the stationhouse, so that's what he did.

Meanwhile, Naylor began compiling notes for the new file.

After two in the morning, a state trooper, upon his return to the District Six headquarters, remembered seeing a runner with a green hat earlier in the evening, crossing west over the Foothills Parkway. Far from looking in trouble, the runner had seemed in control. Besides, the city of Boulder had the highest percentage of runners of any city in the US. And, he had seen this runner approximately thirty miles from where the subject had been reported missing. He logged the sighting all the same, but marked it low-priority.

❧

Rarely, a headlight flashed in and out of view as it came down the curving mountain road toward her. Colleen knew she wasn't dressed for running at night and wanted to move further onto the shoulder. She also knew that she desperately needed help and wanted to go out into the road, waving her arms for the car to stop.

Neither was an option.

No matter how furiously she tried, none of her efforts had the slightest affect on her steady, rhythmic stride as it took her deeper into the mountains.

❧

He wandered from room to room, feeling lost. The empty feeling in the house was matched by an even emptier, hopeless feeling in his heart. Eventually, he found himself at her desk, staring down at her running log. The tears he had dammed up all evening broke free and flowed down his face. He fell sobbing into her chair.

When he had finished crying, he opened the log and started to read. It wasn't long before he began to realize that the margin notes about programming might be important.

"I'm constantly awed by the capacity of the human mind," his wife wrote. "Mozart, Einstein, even modern savants like Nash, Peek and Tallent seemed to have the ability to devote large portions of the natural processing power of their brain to one problem while allowing the rest of the mind's function to carry on."

"My progress in compartmentalizing certain operations of the brain have me amazed at how much we as a species could accomplish if only we could unlock all the power of our minds."

Gary was amazed, too, and frightened, by the detailed description of the mental exercises she had performed. They sounded much like mind control or hypnosis. He skipped ahead to the last entry.

"After success at self-programming pace, distance and time, I'm interested in seeing what effect a more open-ended command might have on endurance.

"Could I program myself to just keep running?"

Gary called the station to tell Officer Naylor what he suspected. Naylor told him of the report that had come in from Boulder. In moments, Gary was headed west for the mountains.

↬

Dehydration, fatigue and altitude sickness had kept Colleen on the edge of delirium for hours. During her few lucid moments, she could feel herself dying. Her heart, lungs and kidney struggled to function under the strain of non-stop running. Her muscles had begun cannibalizing their own mass for energy. She'd lost fully twenty percent of her body weight. Because she had no fat remaining for insulation and no energy to produce heat, she was developing hypothermia.

Despite being on the edge of death, the programming held.

On she ran.

↬

Gary had been driving all night and he was one hundred and ten miles from home. Hope had once again started to fade. As he guided his Subaru through the mountains, he kept checking the outside temperature. Again and again it registered in the single digits. Even in mid-summer, it often dropped below freezing at this altitude. Every spring, hikers died from exposure when they were lost and unprepared for the Rockies. It seemed impossible that Colleen had come this far, but if she had, she might already be dead.

As he neared the top of a high pass, the sight of the full moon dropping behind the mountains brought an aching tightness to his chest. When a lime green hat came briefly within reach of his high beams, that tightness exploded into elation.

⁊

The moon was falling slowly between two magnificent peaks on the western edge of the Rockies as Colleen crossed the summit of another mountain pass. The vast, intense beauty of the rugged wilderness below her brought a few moments of clarity. She was staggering now and felt the unrelenting hand of death pulling her down. Magnified by the earth's atmosphere, the moon looked like a huge white balloon hanging in front of her face. If only she could reach out, she was sure she could touch it. But even now, when every part of her body was failing, the programming held.

The man in the moon looked like an excellent charcoal sketch on the balloon. Colleen was sure the delirium was returning when the balloon moon began calling loudly to her. Her foot slipped on the edge of the roadway. Muscles that had been ravaged by the body's desperate search for a source of energy could not react to counter-balance the slip. The pain that ripped through her body was unbearable. Her eyes watched black asphalt replace the white moon as she fell prostrate in the dirt beside the road.

Arms and legs writhed on the ground as her body refused to stop running.

The programming held.

❦

Gary's relief at finding his wife was quickly overwhelmed by horror. His strong, muscular, determined wife had been transformed into a thin caricature of the woman he loved. Face, arms, legs; every part of her body was wasted. She was little more than a skeleton.

And still she was trying to run.

"Colleen, please! I'm so sorry. Honey, come back to me." Her face showed no reaction and her arms and legs continued to flail. "Stop the program," he screamed, "Find a way to stop the program."

❦

She opened her eyes in a dark room. In front of her was the computer screen, with ethereal white error messages floating across it. At the center, her husband held her fragile body as it struggled feebly to continue running. In the control room, Colleen pushed herself to her feet. Stumbling to the screen, she pounded on the shiny surface that showed the man she loved begging her to come back to him.

The picture went black. A moment later, letters began rolling down the screen.

Colleen stepped back and then cried out, before crumpling to the floor as the same two words flashed over and over ...

"Keep Running"

"Keep Running"

"Keep Running"

Gary wrapped Colleen in blankets and carried her back to the car at the top of the pass. He poured a sip of Gatorade between her dry, cracked lips and then rubbed her back through the blanket. He had been unable to find a pulse, because he couldn't find a big enough vein in her wasted body. If her heart beat, it was so weak he couldn't hear it. But he knew she was still alive by the feeble motion of her arms and legs.

The sun was rising in the east, over mountains his wife had conquered in a single night. He sat at the top and held her as the dawn light reached their faces. He stroked her sunken cheeks, softly murmuring of love and loss. Tears slid down his cheeks when he closed his eyes and turned toward the increasing warmth of the sun.

CHAPTER FOUR

Two years later

Gary smiled as his hand brushed across her cheek. He sat beside her and held his wife's hand; the face he beheld was the one he had loved from the moment they first met, her eyes just as green. He swept a wisp of red hair from her face. No tears fell from his eyes—he had run out of tears many months before. "I'm sorry. I can't take it anymore. I miss you so much." Standing, he crossed the basement floor to his bike.

Colleen couldn't turn her head as her husband left her field of vision.

The programming still held.

He looked back to the bed and watched for only a moment as his wife moved constantly beneath the sheet. He recalled the last consult with her doctor before their coverage for long term care had run out.

"This case is the most intractable I've come across. I've tried everything." The man had looked harried and frustrated as he looked down at his clipboard. "Any treatment that's been attempted has failed. Drugs are only effective when they put her out completely. Once she's conscious, she immediately attempts to begin running again." He shook his head. "In her mind, I'm sure that's what she thinks she's doing. Taking her home might be for the best."

So Gary had brought his wife home, hoping for a miracle. After a year of desperate prayer, he was ready for desperate action.

"I'll be with you soon, dear." He climbed onto his bike and his legs began spinning around and around. He thought he knew what he was doing; he had practiced for months—and the descriptions in his wife's logbook were clear. When the screen came up in a darkened room he had built within his mind, he nervously touched the "special commands" button. A console window appeared, cursor flashing in anticipation of his command. Gary entered,

> KEEP RIDING

As the console spat out a warning message and a chance to abort, Gary hesitated. He touched the head of the picture of him riding on the screen, turning it to look at his wife one last time. He had long ago abandoned hope and what he saw was affirmation that he was making the right choice. His fist slammed against the enter button.

> COMMAND ACCEPTED

flashed briefly on the screen.

In her own control room, which had long ago become a cell that she believed she would never escape, Colleen stood and screamed, "NO! Gary you can't!" The prison kept the words from escaping her lips. She knew where this would end for her husband and couldn't bear to see him trapped the same way. Stepping as far back as the imagined room allowed, she ran and leapt headfirst into the screen.

The atrophied muscles in her neck screamed in protest when Colleen turned her head toward Gary. He was peddling madly on his bike. Her arm and leg muscles were more forgiving; they had been in constant motion for two years, though they had grown unaccustomed to supporting her weight. She stumbled to the corner of the room and threw her arms around her husband.

"Gary, I'm here … I'm back!" Tears soaked into his shirt as she held him. "Please don't leave me!"

With his eyes fixed on the wall, Gary kept spinning; his legs pumping at a furious pace.

The programming held.

THE END

THE GHOST
RUNNERS

The Ghost Runners

Every time you win, you're reborn; when you lose, you die a little.—George Allen

❧

I have to hand it to you; you're a brave one to go through so much to get my story. Most people wouldn't have come this far. But you've earned a story, so here it is ...

It's a cautionary tale for people like me—people who believe in winning. I mean, it isn't likely that you are—or could ever be—a runner like me. I'm a serious athlete; but you might be able to learn something from this story anyway. My name is Gabe Hastings. If circumstances had been different, I'm sure I would have been an Olympic champion.

Like I said, I'm serious about my running; I had a drawer just for my running socks, organized by their suitability for various temperatures and distances. The same for my shirts and shorts; if the temperature was thirty-seven degrees and there was a fifteen-mile-an-hour wind blowing, I could go to a shelf in my closet and the perfect gear would be sitting there waiting for me.

My logbook was custom designed. Heart rate, time, and distance were just the beginning. Every environmental factor for all of my runs for the last seven years is in that book; temp, humidity, wind speed and direction, dewpoint, percentage of cloud cover, altitude, ozone level, and more.

I had a special blood meter and I monitored my glucose level, red blood cell count, and oxygen content before and after every run. The recorded mileage for each of my twenty-three pairs of shoes was accurate to within a quarter-mile.

Every meal I put into the temple of my body was carefully planned. The vitamins and supplements that I used covered the alphabet from A to Z. I even had a nutritionist design a personalized protein shake specifically for after my weight-lifting workouts.

And I am *fast*. Before I moved to McCarthy, Oregon, I was *the* badass of Maryland road running. All the slow people say that running is about self-improvement, that the clock is the only competition.

Horseshit.

The Lombardi-Allen school of running is the one for me. Sure, they were football coaches, but they understood what mattered. "Winning isn't everything, it's the ONLY thing." Old Vince knew his stuff. And George was talking about me when he said, "The winner is the only individual who is truly alive."

I run to beat people. If you're in the race, count on me being the guy who runs you into the ground. And don't expect any empty platitudes from me as I buzz by your sorry, gasping, defeated carcass.

Right about now, you're thinking, "I really don't like this guy, he's a conceited prick." Yeah well, do you think I give a rat's ass what you think? Besides, the only reason you're not like me is that you don't have anything to be conceited about. Every other fast runner is just as egotistical as me, but they all cover it up with a phony veneer. Did you think they really *meant* it when they said "nice race" after kicking your butt? They say all that friendly crap, smile, and try to avoid doing anything that might motivate you to get better and beat them the next time.

But me, I'm honest about this whole racing scene. I don't believe you have a cat's chance at a dog show to beat me. If you think you do, come and get me. A challenge is better than caffeine for making me feel awake and alive ...

... and that's how I ended up in McCarthy.

Some loser, some guy I *demolished* in a race, was crowing about his big PR. I laughed in his face. Then he tried to make himself feel better by calling me a medium-sized fish in a little pond. "If you think you're such hot stuff, why don't you move to McCarthy?" he said. "The runners out in Oregon would spank your skinny ass."

So ... here I am. And my skinny ass hasn't been spanked yet.

❧

My first few races were just scouting expeditions. I used them to measure my competition, find their weaknesses. There are a bunch of good runners in McCarthy, I'll have to admit, but I wasn't worried. I was confident that I would beat them all when I chose my "coming out" race.

There was something interesting that I noticed in all of the races; many of the top finishers were wearing matching singlets that intrigued me.

On the front of the white singlet, in the center, was a gray-scale figure of a runner on a trail that was passing through a stand of trees. Among the trees was the barest hint of a phantom, more than one actually. Slim, Casper-the-ghost forms that eyed the runner eagerly. Above this scene, like a monogram, were the interlocked letters *G* and *R*.

The back of the shirt had a short list of names.

Steve Post

Dave Bowden

Gerry Moore

George Mazzoni

Allen Graham

I recognized the first name, of course. Post was known everywhere. The former Olympian is venerated in McCarthy; he's almost a patron saint to the running community. The names Bowden and Moore also rang a bell; highly regarded runners from the last couple of decades. But Mazzoni and Graham were completely unfamiliar.

There was a tree in the middle of a broad, grassy lawn alongside the course near the finish line. Leaning against it was an ancient-looking guy with a shiny aluminum cane. His thin, lined face was topped by a shaggy white fringe that made his tanned, balding head look like a brown egg in a bed of cotton. Dressed in tan slacks and a white, button-up shirt and tie, the old guy still had the spare form of a runner, although the cane that was helping to keep him erect indicated otherwise.

I walked over and asked if he knew what club was represented by the shirts. He looked me up and down before freezing me with a penetrating stare.

"You must be new in town," he said. "Those guys call themselves the 'Ghost Runners'. It's more of a semi-secret society than it is a running club. They won't even talk to you about the group until you prove you're a winner. There's even a special initiation race."

"An initiation race?" I said. "You've got to be kidding. They look a little old for kid's games. Do they have a private tree fort? A special handshake? Secret password?"

"It's no joke," he said, his white eyebrows raised at my dismissive tone. "Someone I know went through the initiation. He would never talk about it, but I know he had the living daylights scared out of him."

"Did he win?"

"Win? Win the initiation?" The old guy shook his head and looked at me like I was stupid. "Not every race you run is about winning."

"It is for me," I said.

"Really?" A toothy grin flashed across his face and his eyes kind of glazed over, as if he was remembering an entertaining scene. "Well, I suppose ... every once in a while, someone comes along who's fast enough to make it exciting."

"That would be me." I pointed to a group of guys wearing the singlets. "How many people are in the club?"

"That might be all of 'em over there." The five lean, muscular guys were standing near the awards podium. One of them had his back toward us.

"What's with those names on the back?" I asked.

"It's a list of the presidents of ..."

"Steve Post was a Ghost Runner?" Post had been dead for more than thirty-five years.

"Nah," the old guy said irritably, "I was about to say, except for Post. I think they kinda look at him as their ghost-emeritus ... the first, honorary, president of the Ghost Runners."

"And the rest?"

"Oh ... the rest had to *earn* their way onto that list."

A woman with a bullhorn called our attention to the awards ceremony that was just beginning and I turned toward the podium to watch.

"You seem to know a lot about the Ghost Runners," I said. "How about introducing me to them?" When he didn't respond, I turned back to repeat my question.

The old guy wasn't there. I walked around the tree, and then surveyed the wide expanse of grass. He had just disappeared.

⁊

My next race was the Monster Mash, a 5K event in celebration of Halloween. I wanted to find out what this "semi-secret" runner's group was all about, so I decided this was to be the race that would show the McCarthy running community how good Gabe Hastings was.

The rolling course followed a dirt road through a shady forest reserve. I pushed hard on the downhill slopes and even harder on the climbs. Some of the Ghost Runner dudes made a contest of it and hung with me until the final quarter-mile; then my stellar kick buried them.

After the awards ceremony, I saw the same group of five gathered under a shade tree near the refreshment table, chowing down on bananas and bagels. They all looked strong and wiry. Dressed in their distinctive singlets with matching gray racing shorts, they looked like a runner's version of the Stepford Wives.

Leaning against the tree was one of the people who'd hung with me until the end, "in third-place, Derek Fuller" the announcer had said. He was the tallest of the group at almost six feet, six inches tall, with a narrow face and short, black hair. Like lightning strikes in a night sky, broad streaks of white hair flowed back from his temples and stood out against the black.

Standing to Fuller's right were a couple of six-footers; strawberry-blonde mop-tops that had to be twins. Their wide foreheads and dimpled chins ... even the freckles on their pale faces seemed perfectly matched. But it was easy to tell them apart; the one closest to the tree had a lock of white hair that hung just above his left eye. His twin didn't seem to have a similar white marking, until a closer look revealed a chalky sprinkle in the light red on the right side of his head.

The dude to the left of the tall guy had a dark complexion, black eyes, and a short, white rat-tail dangling from his close-cropped, curly brown hair. Silas Kiptao had been the fourth-place finisher. The last member of the group was the shortest, a couple inches shorter than my own six feet, one inch, and he had his back to me. But I recognized the runner-up anyway. I couldn't tell if Jason Marley had a white marking; every hair on his head was the color of bleached bones. His shoulder-length locks were pulled into a ponytail.

I elbowed my way into their tight, small circle. I didn't bother introducing myself, since the emcee of the festivities had recently broadcast the name of the winner—me, of course—to the large crowd; I just held up my first place medallion.

"I understand this qualifies me for admittance into your little clique," I said. "When do I get my secret decoder ring?" I thought it was funny, but I could tell from the frozen smiles on their faces that maybe they didn't.

I had expected Fuller, the tall one against the tree, to speak for the group, but it was Marley who responded.

"It isn't nearly that easy," he said. I turned toward him and saw a pair of bright blue eyes that looked both haunted and hostile. "And winning a race isn't really a requirement."

I guess the old guy had been pulling my leg. "Yeah, well, I heard there was an initiation ... sounds kinda juvenile to me."

If Marley was offended, he hid it well; a manic smile split his face. He looked like a Mayan priest about to perform a human sacrifice.

"It's more like a team tryout than an initiation." Marley looked around the circle and the others gave a negative shake of their heads. I don't know whether it was in disagreement or a vote on some unspoken proposal.

"The funny thing is ... you don't really need our approval to try out, or to become a member. You just have to know when and where the tryout takes place."

"Don't do it, Marley," Kiptao said.

"I agree with Silas," said Fuller. "What if he wins?"

The twins piped up in unison. "You really think he could win?" They both had an eager look on their faces.

"Look at the time he ran today," Kiptao said, "Graham didn't run that fast, but he won."

I got tired of them talking about me like I wasn't there, so I interrupted. "Winning is what I do; you can bet I'll win."

Fuller looked at me with what looked like a trace of compassion. "You don't have to win the test to join our club ..."

"Derek, that's enough!" Marley's anger was evident as he stared at Fuller.

"But you should tell him," Fuller said defiantly.

"Tell me what?" It sounded like Marley was trying to freeze me out. "What happens if I win?"

"Go ahead, tell him!" The twins were nodding enthusiastically, but Kiptao and Fuller were still shaking their heads.

"You chickenshits are trying to keep me out," I said. "You know I'll be the fastest in this sorry excuse for a club."

Kiptao glared at me for a long moment and then turned to Marley and gave a brisk nod of his head. Meanwhile Fuller was watching me as if I were a child in kindergarten who had just insulted the class bully.

I returned his stare defiantly until he dropped his head.

"Fine, tell him." The reluctance in his voice was clear.

"Yeah, tell me." I turned to the man I had beaten once again.

Marley was looking at me with an evil gleam in his eye. He didn't look beaten.

"If you win, you become the next president of the Ghost Runners."

Fuller's head snapped up. "Jason, you can't ..."

"Aha! Well, I guess you losers better get ready for some new leadership." I could tell from the frown on Fuller's face that he didn't like being called a loser. I looked around and saw the twins, Kiptao, and Marley smiling. "I take it you guys don't think I can win?"

Marley looked down and shrugged, but I could still see the smile on his face.

I wasn't sure that I cared about being the president, but I was ready to wipe the smiles off their faces and show them what it means to be a winner. Besides, I figured I could always quit their little club whenever I wanted. I asked him where the tryout was held, and when.

"It only happens once a year ..." Marley held up his hand because he could see an objection forming on my lips. I figured they were going to tell me it was yesterday and I'd have to wait a whole year.

"…but you're in luck, that day is tomorrow, October 31… Halloween. Be at the Post Trail before midnight. Stand at the white pillar that marks the beginning of the 2,000-meter loop. The bell of St. Mark's Episcopal Church always rings the end of All Hallow's Eve; when it tolls midnight, start running. All you have to do is finish five laps … 10,000 meters."

"Which one of you do I have to beat?" I asked.

"None of us will be there," Marley said.

"Oh. Now I see. Fresh legs, huh? You figure I can't race on back-to-back days and still win against your exalted leader. What if he's late?"

"When the bell strikes midnight, start running; like I said, you just have to finish. Don't worry, you'll have plenty of competition."

I decided to head home and get an ice bath and start resting up for tomorrow night's race. I walked out of the circle and started jogging away.

"Gabe, wait!" Fuller wanted to make one last attempt to halt the inevitable.

"Save your breath," I called back. "Just go tell your current president that his term is about to end."

❧

So, on Halloween, just before midnight, I was standing right here, at this tall, white pillar. Pretty much exactly where I'm standing right now. The lights above my head revealed the writing on the massive pillar, just like they do now:

> The Post Trail
> In honor of the
> most courageous runner
> who ever lived.
> Do you have
> the courage
> to run with him?

Night or day, the Post Trail is the best place in the world for a person to run. The fine, wood-chip surface is easy on the legs; there are a variety of loops that can be combined into different lengths. They are all fast, but they aren't so flat as to become boring.

During daylight hours, there are patches of cooling shade; at night, there are lights along the path. Although they aren't bright enough to banish the darkness, the lights push against the shadows and provide a circle of comfort. The stream and its bridges; the trees and ponds, the green lawns and gentle curves, all work to allow one's mind to relax while pushing one's body to the limit.

Halloween night was turning brisk. There had been a light, warm shower earlier in the evening, but a cold front had moved in and pushed the clouds away, revealing a dark, moonless sky. A ground-hugging mist was rising from the stream that bordered the park on the north side, and from every damp, grassy expanse that dotted the park through which the Post Trail meandered.

The path was speckled with moisture, creating a pattern of light and dark, but recently fallen leaves were dry enough to crunch beneath my feet while I completed my warm-up. As midnight approached, there was no one in sight. I stepped up to the line, ready to start, with or without any competition. To me, being sportsmanlike meant starting on time; it didn't require waiting for your opposition if they were late. I was sure I could beat him straight up, but I wasn't about to pass up the chance for a head start.

When the bell began to ring, it sounded as though it were tolling inside my head. I felt a chill down my back as I started my watch, pushed off, and ran down the path. The first one hundred meters were straight and covered by a low fog that was well-lit by the metal halide lights in the parking lot. Besides the ringing in my ears, my shadow was the only company I had as I raced away from the starting line; that shadow was a ghostly patch of darkness shaped like a runner that stretched out on the fairy vapors in front of me.

The ringing had faded by the time I left the light of the parking lot and sped along a series of gentle curves that carried me through a gloomy stand of trees. Except for my own breathing and the whispered sound of my footsteps over the leaves, all was silent. Halfway through the trees, a bench and a pathway light lined the trail, illuminating a sign that marked 500 meters; the brightness faded as quickly as it came, my shadow again gaining on me before leaping ahead and then disappearing as I entered the dark woods once more.

After a while, the trees thinned and the trail came along a broad stream on the left before turning across a wide wooden bridge, which had lanterns on both ends. The center of the bridge was the halfway point of the course. Each of my steps, though quick and light, returned a thumping echo off the water below. On the other side, the path crossed a grassy open space before it entered a natural tunnel through a grove of bog birch, its leaves glowing orange in the light from the bridge.

As I emerged from the dense grove into another open space layered in mist, I could hear the faint thumping of another runner crossing the bridge. I wasn't sure how large my lead was, but I did know that this wasn't just a solo run anymore … and that I hadn't been punked by those guys when they sent me out here at midnight on Halloween. The race was on!

The low fog swirled as I sped through it. Ahead was a stand of maple and Oregon oak trees where the fog ended. Just inside the trees, another pathway light was shining on a bench and a sign that let me know I had 500 meters left in my first lap.

I was a little startled to see—sitting on the bench—the same old guy I had talked to at the race the previous weekend. The cane, white fringe, and gleaming bald head were unmistakable. He was even wearing the same pants and shirt.

"Let's go, boy." He used the aluminum cane to stand and then slapped his hand against his thigh. "This is one footrace you do not want to lose."

Now that I knew I had some competition, I picked up the pace and raced past the old man and into the trees. In a short time, the maples and oaks thinned on the right, but became thicker on the left. After a hundred meters, the trail came out of the woods and ran straight along the edge of the forest; dew on a wide, grassy lawn to the right reflected the faint light from buildings beyond the border of the park. As I neared the end of my first lap, the path curved sharply to the left at a fork in the trail. Going right led to the south end of the parking lot. It was a heavily used area where the wood chips had been worn away, leaving a stretch of dirt that would have been dusty except for the earlier rain. Drops of water from branches overhanging the trail had given the dirt a textured finish.

Although I was tempted to glance over my shoulder at my competition to see how far behind he was before I rounded the turn, I resisted that temptation easily.

"Never look back," my high school coach always said, "that's like telling the runners behind you that you're worried. It gives them hope." Whenever I was in a race and saw someone ahead of me look back, I knew I had them. So, I cruised around the bend, past the pillar, and started my second lap without a backward glance, enjoying the cool night air, moving fast but relaxed … feeling confident.

Again I chased my shadow away from the parking lot, admiring the smooth, ethereal form as it flowed across the waist-high vapors. I hadn't noticed the electric hum of the lights when I started, but after the silence on the back portion of the course, I did now. It sounded like a distant, cheering crowd and I imagined it so, with thousands of adoring fans … all rooting for me.

As I pounded across the bridge at the halfway point for the second time, I began to count the seconds. I was in the tunnel of bog birch when my challenger reached the bridge. The echoing thumps sounded through the night. Twenty-four seconds! That's how far ahead I was. At the speed we were moving that was almost one hundred and fifty meters, more than a full straightaway on the track. I couldn't hold back a broad smile.

"What are you smiling about?" yelled the old man as I approached, "He's closer than he was on the last lap. Come on! If you want to win this thing, you got to pick it up a notch."

"It's in the bag," I called back as I passed him.

"Hah!" His short bark of laughter and the words that followed were designed to rile me—and they did. "Talkin' isn't gonna win this race."

Running harder, I sailed toward the end of my second lap and followed my tracks from the first loop over the textured patch of dirt near the end of my second loop. It wasn't until I was into my third time around that I realized that I had seen no prints except my own in the damp earth.

The buzz of the parking lot lights seemed louder still and my imaginary cheering section urged me to up the pace some more. Winding through the first stand of trees, it sounded as though the electric hum hadn't faded; instead, my phantom fans had filled the woods on each side of the trail and continued to exhort me to go faster.

At the bridge for the third time, I again began my count, not expecting to hear my adversary for a long time, certain that my surges had widened the gap between us.

I had barely reached the bog birch tunnel before footsteps rumbled over the water, more than one set by the sound of it. My lead had been narrowed to fourteen seconds, maybe eighty meters. Not only that, but it appeared other people had joined the pursuit; my challenger had help. With pacers to push him, chasing a solitary leader was much easier.

Still I wasn't worried. The pace was fast, yes; but I had a couple more gears to use … and lots of gas in the tank. Half the race had gone by; I had a substantial lead and my legs were feeling strong.

A raucous, gleeful cry reached me even before I left the tunnel. "They're getting closer!"

The fog swirled around my legs as I sped into the open. Across a smooth, velvety expanse of gray, set aglow by the lamplight, I could see the old man waiting at the edge of the trees. His left arm was moving in windmill fashion, as if that could make me move faster. On each downward swing, his hand would disappear into the mist, and then raise a plume of moisture as it swept above his head.

"You're gonna lose this race, if you don't get the lead out!" As I ran toward the light, I thought his face looked more hollow and sunken, his toothy grin wider than on the prior lap. When I blew by him, the wake of my passing seemed to raise a puff of loose white hair from the fringe around his bald head. The skin on his shiny dome was cracked and hints of the white skull beneath showed through. A cold finger of fear traced a line down my back.

Once in the woods, I tried to dismiss my fear, laughing at myself for mistaking the sharp shadows and whirls of mist as something more sinister and haunted. That's when I heard the old man cackling again.

"He's just ahead of you, boys," he said. "Fresh meat!"

The response was an eerie mix of demented laughter and ferocious, eager longing. If there were words among the howling sounds, the trees and the mist had rendered them unintelligible. By the time the end of my third lap was near, I had increased my pace again, determined to leave that raucous pack far behind.

At the final turn of the loop, I saw that the clear impressions of my Hatoris from the previous two laps were still the only marks in the dirt. I had begun to consider the possibility that my pursuers were cutting the corner—cheating—when I noticed a rising clamor as I rounded the bend.

The hum of the lights had increased to a warbling buzz that sounded more than ever like the excited undertone of a crowd in anticipation of a thrilling show.

The layer of fog on each side of the trail beyond the starting line was no longer smooth and still. It roiled and stirred. Silvery mounds of vapor writhed and twisted into vaguely human shapes. As I raced between the swelling mists, a ripple of eerie cheers rolled along beside me. On the heels of that, a raucous wave of sound crested and followed me into the woods.

The chase pack was getting closer.

I surged ahead and found that, when the clamor had faded in the distance, it had been replaced by the faint echo of footsteps and rhythmic, heavy breathing on the trail behind me. With my legs churning, I raced along the stream and powered across the bridge. I pushed hard toward the tunnel of bog birch, listening all the while for the inevitable reverberations of my relentless antagonists.

Seconds ticked by...

...not enough seconds.

An unbounded confidence in one's ability to handle any challenge is one thing that allows a runner like me to reach for the stars ... to dream impossible dreams ... to push beyond physical and mental barriers that stop lesser athletes. My faith in my potential for greatness had always been like an eternal flame, bright and unwavering.

A thunderous noise followed at my back only a handful of seconds after I had crossed the stream. It sounded as if the pack chasing me had swelled to a horde.

The first dark flicker of doubt wormed its way into the brightness of my confident flame ... I began to consider the possibility that I might lose this race.

"Don't be thinking like that, boy!"

From nowhere, the words filled my ears. I was still in the tunnel, the old man wasn't even in sight; but he seemed to be inside my head, hearing my doubts ... and answering them.

"You can't quit on me yet."

Though I was nearing my top speed, I responded by inching a little faster still. When I burst out of the tunnel into the open space, I saw that, here too, those human-shaped tendrils of mist were rising from the layer of vapor. Wraithlike arms waved while a warbling hum of ghostly cheers drifted on the night breeze.

Atop the bench at the entrance to the woods, I saw something that was even more bizarre.

The old man was capering back and forth, shaking his cane at me and screeching. The skin of his bald head was coming loose in strips and bounced around his face like the dreadlocks of some pale Rastafarian.

I watched his feet, bare and skeletal, as they clicked like dancing taps while he leaped and twisted from the bench up to the seat back and then down again, over and over.

"Fahsta man! Fahsta man! Fahsta!" He sang as he danced ... a strange blend of Bob Marley and Fred Astaire.

I sprinted by this Tim Burton nightmare and into the woods, sure that the blood rushing to my legs had deprived my brain of the oxygen necessary to accurately process the images it was receiving. It was either that, or accept the likelihood that I had run straight into my own version of the Twilight Zone. At the time I wanted to believe that I was only experiencing the weirdest runner's high ever.

The sweat dripping down my face, my labored efforts to draw ever more oxygen into my lungs, and the lactose-driven burn that was building in my legs served to remind me that I was in a race. It had become a race in which I was driven by my fearful imagining of what might happen were I to lose.

The rapid cadence of my pursuers' speedy feet on the trail behind me made losing a real possibility. Their measured, forceful breathing sounded like the relentless chugging of a steam engine drawing closer with every passing second.

But I refused to look back.

When I turned the corner toward the pillar, with my last lap about to start, I was greeted by a scene that convinced me that this wasn't just some hallucination brought on by oxygen deprivation or the endorphins coursing through my bloodstream.

The fog along the trail had transformed itself into a spectral mass of people that crowded up to the path, like savages lining a gauntlet. Hollow, empty eyes stared out from gaunt, gray faces; gaping, toothless mouths emitted an unearthly howl. I couldn't tell if they were cheering for me or for the pack that was now only spitting distance behind me.

"You got yourself a race now, boy." It was impossible, but the old man was leaning against the stone pillar. The strips of skin from his head had peeled down his face; a tattered, flesh-colored beard for his gleaming skull. The lipless teeth moved and his gleeful taunting continued.

"Don't matter what your coach told ya," His high cackling was clearly audible above the incoherent roar of the crowd. "I say you *should* look back ... so you can see why you don't want to lose this race."

I cast a quick glance over my shoulder. The glaring light of the parking lot was shining on the group of runners behind me like a theatre spotlight. That snapshot look gave me all the motivation I needed to release the governor that had held my speed to a sustainable pace.

As I plunged into the horde of phantoms, their arms reached out and attempted to clap me on the back, push me on my way. I felt their hands as an icy chill up my spine, but it was nothing compared to the arctic glacier that had wrapped itself around the very fiber of my being.

What chased me was human only in that two legs propelled the creatures across the ground; two arms swung in smooth counter-balance with each stride; a head sat upon the shoulders between those arms.

My own arms and legs, earned through years of high mileage and tons of lifted weights, were like cooked spaghetti next to the chiseled ropes of steel on the running machines that were closing on me. Teeth, chiseled to fine points, grinned from drooling mouths. The desire, energy, and pride that burned so brightly in my chest paled when compared to what I saw in those hungry, fiery red eyes; eyes belonging to creatures that had once been men.

Doom was in those eyes ... my doom.

◌

"Limits are for sissies," Post said. "There are no boundaries for someone like me, someone with the courage to push beyond the limits that keeps the rest of the world from achieving something magical."

That final lap taught me that Post was both right ... and wrong.

The echoes of my pounding heart rang in my ears and my lungs were burning; I ran faster still. Hot, feral breath blew across my neck and the air became close and fetid; I ran faster still. The night produced horrors which were strewn along my path, and I ran faster still.

I had become part of the pack ... ahead, but only by the barest of margins. I didn't have to turn my head to see the eager, red glow of their eyes. An earthquake rumble split the night as we thundered across the bridge for the final time. For me, the rumble didn't recede, but grew stronger as the hammering of my struggling heart replaced the pounding of feet across the wooden planks of the bridge.

I ran faster still.

We blew through the bog birch tunnel; the hurricane wind from our passing shook the last leaves from their tangled branches. Another unearthly throng of spectators buried us with deafening cheers when we emerged into the open. Despite their vaporous form, the ground shook with the stomping of their feet and the air vibrated at the clapping of their hands.

I'd never run so fast, but I couldn't pull away from that growling, grunting, drooling pack. How could I hope to win? My body was giving all that it could possibly give; it had reached its limit.

"There are no limits."

I wasn't sure if it was the old man's voice I heard, or only my own thoughts. Nothing should have been able to penetrate the wall of sound that was assaulting my ears. The loudest sound was the throbbing pulse from the Herculean pumping of my heart.

"You said you were a winner!" The skull of the old man appeared over my shoulder; his words were infused with impelling, angry passion and his bony finger pointed toward the finish line.

"NOW PROVE IT!"

Somehow, though my vision was fading and my body failing, I ran faster still. Fear, and my boundless ego, pushed me on. Using a will-to-win that overcame all my instincts for self-preservation, I drove toward the finish line.

As darkness slowly closed in, the steady tha-whump that shook my body was the sound of my heart finding its voice ...

"No limits ... no limits ... no limits ... no limits ..."

My awareness returned and I found myself leaning against the side of the granite pillar where I had started this paranormal competition. I wasn't even breathing hard and I felt surprisingly fresh. The adrenaline-rush of winning often does that.

The waist-high fog was once again quiescent and still. No spectral crowds cheered; none of my unearthly challengers were gathered around the finish line. The skeletal coach who had pushed me through the race wasn't there to tell me if I had won or lost.

Do you think I fell asleep against this pillar? Was it all just a Halloween dream?

I was close to accepting that it had all been a nightmare, when I heard voices. I glanced around the granite corner and saw Jason Marley, Derek Fuller, and the rest of the club walking up from the parking lot. I ducked back behind the pillar, preparing to put a fright into them for being so late. As they got closer, I was able to understand their conversation.

Fuller was talking to Marley. "Don't you even feel a little guilty?"

"Guilty?" Jason replied. "Why the hell should I feel guilty? No one told me before I ran with the ghosts."

"Still, you should have explained things to him, let him know the consequences."

"Ease up, Derek," Silas Kiptao said. "You know that conceited prick wouldn't have believed Jason."

"Yeah, you heard him ..." Jason changed his voice into a sarcastic falsetto, " 'winning is what I do'... what an asshole. Do you think he would have listened to me if I had told him that this isn't the kind of race you want to win?"

The group was almost even with the pillar and I got ready to scare the shit out of them.

"But he did win ..."

I screamed and leapt in front of them. "Yes, you butt-heads, I won. Now, bow to your new presi—"

They ignored me and continued walking. Derek kept talking like he hadn't seen or heard anything.

"... and, since his name will be added to the list, we'll have to get new shirts."

The five runners gathered around a form lying in the low fog beyond the finish line.

Derek leaned over. "C'mon, give me a hand. He may have been a jerk, but he did run himself to death for the privilege of being our new president."

The others bent down and helped Derek lift a body out of the mist. My body. I stared into my own lifeless eyes as they carried their new president toward the parking lot.

"Ya know, Jason, this could have been you," Silas said. "You were only a stride away from winning your race and becoming a 'past president'."

One of the twins snickered. "Yeah, instead you ended up looking like an albino."

Marley flicked his ponytail. "I like my white hair," he said. "It proves I got closer to winning than you guys. That little spot of white in your hair just shows how far back you were when you tried out."

Derek shook his head. "Yeah, well ... we knew that was one team we didn't want to make."

"What was his name again?" the other twin asked.

"Gabe Hastings." Silas said.

Derek bowed his head; there was a trace of regret in his voice. "Well, Gabe Hastings ... I hope you enjoy being the new president of the Ghost Runners."

"Yeah, Hell to the Chief" Jason said. "Get it? Hell to ..."

The rest of the crew moaned, their good-natured protests fading as they disappeared down the hill and into the fog.

A metal tapping drew my eyes to the far side of the pillar. The old man was leaning against it, rapping his aluminum cane against the granite. He looked dapper in his tan pants, white shirt and yellow tie. The bald head and white fringe were back, and two little red bumps above his forehead. He looked at the watch on his wrist.

"Congratulations on an excellent tryout. Welcome to the team." he said. "And now it's time for the next interval."

"Huh?" I said. I admit I was a bit befuddled.

"Practice isn't over." He pointed behind me. I turned and saw the group of ghost runners waiting behind me. Their red eyes were gleaming and they were licking their lips.

"In fact, it's never over. You've joined a team that loves to run ... twenty-four hours a day, seven days a week."

When I looked back at the old man, his aluminum cane had become a pitchfork and two bright red horns grew out of his forehead. My new coach grinned and yelled.

"Now RUN!"

I took off down the trail, the pack at my heels.

As the mist swirled, I heard him call after us.

"Remember ..." he screamed.

"No Limits!"

So, there it is—the tale of how I became a Ghost Runner.

Do you want to take a shot? Are you ready to prove that you're a winner? Come on! Let's race!

THE END

Dear Editor,

Attached you will find the manuscript that Dylan left with me. Although Dylan had chosen not to submit this in order to protect me, I believe it is a well-told story and give my blessing for its publication. I'm sure no one will believe it anyway.

Sincerely,

Cowboy Joe

COWBOY JOE

CHAPTER ONE

The Man in the Mud

When I first arrived at his ramshackle prairie hut, the man I came to interview was waist-deep in a muddy ditch, digging up a busted water line from his well. The tawny mud of Wyoming was baked on the upper half of his body and wet red goop covered the rest of him. Only the muck clothed him. Otherwise, he was naked except for a ragged pair of running shoes.

The sun was at my back and he squinted into the shine and grinned, breaking flakes of mud from his face. Intense blue eyes danced in deep sockets and held no trace of guilt or sorrow.

Below me stood a man who'd gone from reclusive unknown to world-renowned ultrarunner in less than a year. Then he went from budding entrepreneur to an accusation of fraud in a matter of days. It was said that he had returned to obscurity in disgrace.

He didn't look broken or disgraced. What he appeared to be was elemental; a part of nature, strong but guileless; so in tune with Mother Earth that she cradled him against her rough bosom as one of her own.

At least that's the way I'll see him in my memory, now that I've come to know the man called Cowboy Joe. At that moment, though, I thought he just looked filthy.

Standing in that hole, he looked up and said,

"Young man, to get what ya want, you gotta be 'ware what ya want."

It was a curious greeting and the words were barely audible over the sing-song whir of the wind turbine spinning on a nearby ridge.

I wanted a story; it was why I'd come all the way from New York. But I came to realize that he always saw a deeper truth, even if he occasionally missed some obvious details. Young was one thing I certainly was not, although I could understand why he might think so. It wasn't the only detail he missed.

I grabbed the hand he held up and gave him a boost out the hole.

"Trip tallable?"

After a moment's thought, I decided that he was asking if my drive had been tolerable.

A glance at the battered rental car I'd picked up in Denver six harrowing hours earlier made me shudder. I'd followed Interstate 25 to 80 and then onto a state route. Once across the Snowy Range, the directions had taken me off that main road onto a series of progressively worse dirt roads that were soon no better than dusty tracks across a rocky, sage-covered, high plains plateau. Mules and a covered wagon would have been more suited for the job. I was working on spec and hoped the money from this story would at least cover the damage to the car. I'd spent the last hour kicking myself for turning down the insurance to save a few dollars.

"It was fine," I said.

He walked away and I followed at a safe distance. The hot sun and stiff wind were rapidly drying the mud on his body. It fell in clumps to the ground and raised swirling clouds of dust. Beneath the dirt were arms and legs that looked like lengths of steel cable. Picture Charlie Brown's buddy Pig-Pen; grown-up, slimmed-down—and ripped from head to toe.

As he led me toward the odd-looking structure that was his home, we passed an outdoor wood furnace. I'd seen them before in upstate New York. Pipes above the burn chamber carried water that was heated and then flowed underground to the house. Most systems efficiently provided heat and hot water. One of the drawbacks was the large supply of wood that was needed. Near the furnace a pile of firewood for the following winter had been started. Next to that were three uncut logs, a bow saw, and a wood maul.

I looked at the barren land surrounding us. There wasn't a tree in sight.

"Where do you get your wood?" I asked.

He raised an arm and pointed to the southeast. The distant mountainside was a patchwork of green and brown. At the time I thought it was at least a couple of miles away. Later I learned it was almost six. Guessing distance in Wyoming is an exercise for fools. You either know the distance ... or you don't.

"Bahk beetle," was all he said.

I'd been told he was a man of few words. The court transcripts had been evidence of that. I wondered if the time I spent here would be a complete waste.

Everyone else involved with the whole sordid affair had been interviewed; the Loyal Few, the Disillusioned Many, the Righteous Prosecutor, the Unbelievers ... the Traitor.

The story was written. I was certain I'd uncovered the truth. But my editor had said, "No sale, not without Cowboy Joe's side of the story." That was the only name by which the world knew him; a simple moniker for a simple but mysterious runner.

I had to pull something from this man who had uttered a total of seventy-three words for public consumption during his months of celebrity. That's why I was standing in front of this weird conglomeration of medieval construction and 21st century technology.

While he pulled a wet sponge from a galvanized bucket and worked on removing the dirt that hadn't already flaked off, I studied the structure that would be my home for the next two weeks.

A sod roof topped stone walls eighteen inches thick. Leather hinges and wooden latches held a thick door in place. Set in the walls were the most modern, energy-efficient windows available. Planted in the roof was a series of solar panels that provided electricity during the handful of days during the year that the wind didn't blow. Hanging from the eaves was a satellite dish that was his only link to the outside world.

The outside world ... from Cowboy Joe's home, you would not believe it existed. To the east, the peaks of the Snowies dominated the view from north to south and held no trace of civilization. In the west, the prairie stretched to another distant range. Rumor held that a tiny, tumbleweed town was down their somewhere. The naked eye could not confirm it.

From where I stood, the world looked timeless. A band of Indians could have come galloping across the valley below me; I would not have been surprised.

Cowboy Joe cleared his throat. I turned to find him standing at the open front door, still naked although it was hard to tell the difference. His skin was bronzed to a tone not much removed from the color of the mud. Steel gray hair hung to his shoulders and framed a face that was defiant in every way. The sun-darkened skin was fine-lined but ageless, glowing with health like polished leather. Piercing blue eyes and a jutting chin told me that I would earn every word that I teased from between those tight, wind-cracked lips.

"Quite a place you've got here," I said. "Did you build it yourself?"

He appeared to be considering whether to spare a syllable to answer, but he just nodded and then ushered me in. Like the exterior, what I saw was a fascinating combination of old and new. In places, the rough stone was bare; in others, the hides of pronghorn antelopes had been stitched together and hung like tapestries.

His home consisted of a single, square room, oriented so that the corners matched the compass. The setting sun angled through the southwest windows and gave the rough interior an orange glow.

To the right, in the north corner, was a plain desk of weathered pine planks. On it was all the latest technology. Ergonomic keyboard, oversize monitor and more; it all looked top of the line. I was jealous. His equipment made my office in New York look out of date. There was even a wireless modem mounted on the ceiling.

Cabinets and a refrigerator separated the desk area from the sink and a kitchen counter that reached to the east corner. Along the wall opposite the office/kitchen was the sleeping area.

In the south corner, an old canvas cot was crowded about by an antique dresser, a floor lamp and rocking chair, a World War I army footlocker, and hand-made tables loaded with books. The west corner was bare except for a small table, a sleeping pad, and a pile of blankets. That he'd cleared the space for my arrival was evident by the worn spots on the wood floor that matched the base of the lamp and the rockers of the chair.

Between the blankets and the cot was a closet-shaped hanging of more antelope hides that looked new. He pulled back one corner to reveal a toilet and I breathed a sigh of relief. I might have to sleep on the floor, but at least I wouldn't be stumbling around the prairie in the middle of the night, looking for an outhouse.

In the center of the room was a long, aspen trestle table that had aged to a golden yellow. It served as work bench, dining area, and training table. One end was covered with a drop cloth which protected the table from some muddy pieces of cracked water pipe, a hack saw, a piece of new pipe cut to match the old, and some connectors. Scraps of hides and leather strings were strewn about. Various running clothes, shoes, a hydration pack, and a sweat-stained Rockies baseball cap were piled on the far end.

I dropped my oversize duffle next to the pile of blankets.

"So, when do we get started?"

Taking the new well pipe from the table he headed for the door, tossing some precious words over his shoulder as he left.

"We'll run when ahm done."

My gut told me two weeks wasn't going to be near long enough to get Cowboy Joe's side of the story.

CHAPTER TWO

Never Trust a Writer

When chasing a story, a journalist rarely fails to push against whatever ethical boundaries he or she hasn't already destroyed. Being left alone in the home of the object of my investigation wasn't an opportunity I was going to let slip away.

I set my laptop bag on the small table in my sleeping area and made a beeline for his computer. Through the window I could see Cowboy Joe bending over in the trench, well pipe in hand.

His computer screen was blank, but came to life when I bumped his wireless mouse.

On the screen was the website that had played a significant role in Cowboy Joe's "coming out." It is called "Dailymile," The Profile page showing was for "runnercowboyjoe." Since I'd spent the last nine months trying to transform myself into a runner, I'd heard of the website. It was a place for athletes of all kinds to post and track their training while receiving and making comments on the training of people they had "friended" on the site.

According to a button on the left of the page, Cowboy Joe had 973 friends. That was surprising enough, but what shocked and amused me was his latest post that was at the top of the page.

For the Twitter age it was about average, but for Cowboy Joe it was downright chatty, gabby even. I could possibly go as far as verbose.

"Felt like I always do on this run but couldn't go as far as I wanted 'cause that damn NY writer fella is showin' up tomorrow and I have to clear out a corner so he'll have a place to lay on the floor. And I gotta dig up the !#@&!' well pipe and fix it so I can get the water running. He won't want to take a crap out on the prairie like I've been doin' the last week.

"Need to find a way of gettin' rid of that guy. Whatta ya'll think of me runnin' him up to Wilson Ridge and makin' him haul a log or two down?"

There were eighty-seven comments to his post.

"Crazy miles, Joe" and "You rock!" are good examples of most of them.

Then there was: "Hell, yeah. Run that guy into the ground. He'll be out of your hair tomorrow."

And "Maybe he'll have a heart attack. Oh, but then you'd have to haul him out with the logs ... or leave him for the coyotes."

Still another suggested "Leave his gloves behind, he'll be so blistered, he won't be able to write a word."

Cowboy Joe had responded, "Hey, I like that idea!"

At least now I knew what he had planned for the "writer fella." He was in for a surprise.

I clicked on the 'Edit Profile' and found the listed name for the account was Joe Franklin.

All my previous research and interviews hadn't turned up his real name. Bobby Sorvik had insisted this was it. Sorvik was the guy who'd broken his vow of silence and gotten the ball of controversy rolling. After weeks of chasing a wild goose, I'd come to hate Sorvik; I didn't know Cowboy Joe's real name, but I was certain it wasn't Joe Franklin. Now it looked like I was being fed the same red herring that Sorvik had taken.

To my surprise, I checked the security settings for his computer and found that there were none. He had a good virus protection suite, but that was all. If Joe was hiding anything, I doubted that I would find it on the computer.

Returning to his Profile Page, I put the computer to sleep and rushed over to his sleeping area.

A name, I just needed a name. If I could find his wallet, I'd be golden. Driver's license, credit card, social security card, even a library card would do the job. On the dresser was an empty crystal tumbler. Behind it was a violin. Its base rested on a scrap of red velvet and its delicate neck lay on a pile of old books.

I quickly searched the dresser drawers without finding out anything interesting except that he was a briefs man, not boxer. The faded green footlocker was full of his running stuff; a variety of shoes, hats, gaiters, and hydration packs for long runs; a hip belt for shorter ones, even headlamps for nighttime running.

As I was closing the footlocker, I saw faded letters inside the top that spelled out the name Franklin Wetherill. Of course I didn't know it then, but that name would come to haunt me. Then? Well, then I thought it was probably the name of the World War I soldier who'd once owned the footlocker. I continued my search, knowing my time was running short.

Besides a warren of dust bunnies, there was nothing under his cot. When I stood up my eyes were drawn to a small shelf high in the corner to the right of the bed. On it was a small box. In the box were items of men's jewelry. A pocket watch, cuff links, a money clip, and a tie tack. The cuff links and tie tack had the initials FW engraved on them.

On the inside cover of the elegant watch was the inscription *Franklin, my Dearest.* In strong, Garamond type, the name Franklin J. Wetherill was etched into the money clip.

I'd only been there ten minutes and the clues to a story much stranger than the one I had come for were in the palm of my hand. Except for Cowboy Joe's real name, I thought I had all the facts and, as a journalist, I was confident they told the whole story.

CHAPTER THREE

Who Was That Guy?

O n Friday, June 18, 2010, a wiry man arrived at the starting line of the Bighorn Trail 100, an endurance race in north-central Wyoming. Of the more than one hundred fifty starters, not one recalled speaking to him. The handful of ultrarunners who remembered seeing him gave widely disparate descriptions.

"That guy looked as old as the mountains," one of them said. "I swear he was the oldest person I've ever seen running one of these."

"Vibrant, vital ... like a young stallion," said another, "you could just sense the energy waiting to be unleashed."

"He was munching on granola from a cloth bag that was tied to his hydration pack when I saw him," Jon Burgess was quoted as saying. "That hydration backpack was huge, like he was carrying enough water for the whole race."

That was the first clue to what would become Joe's downfall—the water.

At the line he was wearing the number assigned to Karen Kuehne, a Dailymile friend who'd registered solely so that Cowboy Joe could race anonymously. And race he did.

The bugle sounded and he took off like he was running a 5k, not 100 miles. Bighorn veterans shook their heads and chuckled, certain they would see him soon. They didn't. His lead grew ever larger as the hours passed. When the sun set and evening settled over the mountains it became even harder for race officials to track the speedy, unknown runner who would flash into and out of the aid stations with only a penlight to break the darkness. If the last station at Lower Sheep Camp hadn't called in a warning, the finish area in Dayton, Wyoming would have been unmanned when he came through before three o'clock in the morning.

Breaking the record on a wild and rugged course by more than four hours raised many eyebrows and, long hair or not, when Joe came across the finish line bare-chested, it was obvious he wasn't Karen Kuehne. But race officials never got the chance to question him. He hardly slowed as he passed through the chute and disappeared into the night.

Although every aid station verified that "Karen" had checked in and out, the race director was not able to verify his identity and it was obvious the mysterious runner had not been properly registered.

"Of course we voided his finish," Cheryl Sinclair said, "We didn't know who he was or where he came from. And he just took off. What else could we do?"

Then the first rumors started.

Karen Kuehne was Anton Krupicka in disguise; or one of those Tarahumara Indians.

Kyle Petrie, one of the volunteers at Dry Fork Ridge, claimed he saw Cowboy Joe the next morning when Petrie was heading home to Casper. Joe looked exactly as he had during the race and he was running along a dirt road that paralleled Interstate 25. Seventy-five miles south of Dayton.

He also said that Joe hadn't refilled his water supply at Dry Fork, or eaten anything but what he pulled from that cloth bag. Other aid stations verified that he did nothing more than check in and out.

As the week went by, he was spotted in various places, always on foot, always headed south.

CHAPTER FOUR

The Coming Out Party

"The morning mist was still clinging to the aspen trees in the shadow of the mountain when he came rolling down the trail. At first, he seemed to be made of air, a tendril of vapor reaching out toward me, a natural extension of the forest."

Wendy Tynan is a self-proclaimed ultra groupie-poet. During my research, the outgoing strawberry blond was valuable for giving this running phenomenon context within the extreme sport of ultrarunning. On that memorable Saturday, the 26th of June, she was manning the aid station halfway around the 5.8-mile loop in the Medicine Bow National Forest on which the 24 hours of Laramie was run.

"Joe had flow," Tynan once told me, in a reverential tone. "He flowed through the landscape like a rushing river. You can sit along a riverbank watching the water and it never slows down, doesn't look different from one hour to the next. Cowboy Joe ran like that; he was a force of nature."

Bighorn was a point-to-point race that never gave anyone more than a fleeting glimpse of that force. The loop course at Laramie gave the running community a closer look at the man registered as "Cowboy Joe."

Before nightfall, he had lapped all of the runners, most more than once.

Never the shy, retiring type, Tynan took it upon herself to find out more about this running superman. After seven o'clock, when pacers were allowed, she noticed that Joe didn't have one and asked the race director if she could run some laps with him. They gave her a pacer number and, when he came around on the next lap, she fell in alongside.

"From the moment my inadequate stride brought me next to him, I knew our time together would be short."

A conversation with Tynan is like talking with a slam poet, every line a performance.

"He was like a locomotive with too much momentum; I was a lowly hobo who could never hop *this* train. It was all I could do to stay close for one lap."

I could imagine her frustration with such an unresponsive audience.

"My words were like drops of water on a raging fire. No evidence of their effect could I see. The eerie stones of Vedauwoo talk to me more than did this running monolith. And yet I sensed no resentment of my presence. It was if I was just another element in the cosmos through which he was traveling."

Air. Water. Fire. Earth.

In her overblown, emo fashion, Tynan presented the man in a way that resonated.

On a flat, fast road course at sea level in New York City in 1989, Rae Clark set the American one hundred-mile record with a time of twelve hours, twelve minutes and nineteen seconds, with a crew aiding him for the entire event.

Twenty-one years later, on a hilly trail more than eight thousand feet above sea level, an unknown, unaided runner calling himself Cowboy Joe ran his second one hundred mile race in a week.

To the cheers of "Go, Joe, go!" he finished that race in exactly twelve hours.

And then, as if he was a breath of Wyoming wind, he blew off into the night.

CHAPTER FIVE

The Big Switch

Aglance out the window showed him crawling out of the hole. I set the jewelry box back on its shelf and rushed to my duffle bag. I could hear the sound of water sloshing from the galvanized bucket just outside.

When he came through the door, I was changed and lacing up my Merrill Trail Gloves, ready to run.

Joe reached the table and grabbed a pair of running shorts. As he stepped into them, he glanced toward me ... then he yanked up the shorts in a hurry.

"Uh ... uh ... uh ... uh."

If they had been words, this would have constituted a speech for Cowboy Joe. After a long pause, he spit it out.

"Yer a woman!"

I smiled as innocently as I could.

"Well thanks for noticing!"

Early in my journalism career I'd spent a few months as a sports reporter for the Washington Post and learned that it was often helpful to disguise my gender when I was covering a story. Otherwise, whatever macho athlete I was interviewing tried to tailor his responses in a totally unsuitable manner.

My hair was comfortably short and I usually wore jeans, a loose fitting shirt and a baseball cap. Whether I was running or working, I was often thankful for being "less endowed" than many of my friends. And I'd long ago grown accustomed to the face I saw in the mirror in the morning. Strong and full of character was my loving mother's description.

I was comfortable in my skin and I'm woman enough to get whatever story I'm chasing, which is all I care about.

He shook his head as if denying what his eyes were seeing.

"But Dylan's no woman's name!"

"My mother would choose to disagree, since that's how she tagged me." His reaction was what I expected. Since my publisher was paying him good money for his side of the story, I also figured he'd get over it.

"This isn't a problem, is it?"

His inner struggle didn't last long. He gave one vigorous shake of his head.

"Not for me, it ain't." Turning away, he continued dressing. "Just ... they ain't never been a woman up here, that's all."

While I wondered how long he'd lived up here alone, I put on my hydration belt, went to the kitchen sink and turned the handle. After hissing and spitting for a moment, the tap produced a flow of rusty brown fluid that I wasn't about to put in my water bottle.

"No way am I drinking this," I said.

Clad only in shorts and shoes, Joe walked up and, from a distance, looked over my shoulder. He waited for me to move far out of the way before stepping up and turning the water on harder, staring at it as if he could will the sediment away.

After a minute, he slapped the handle closed with a disgusted snort and turned toward me. I could tell he was considering his options and then he grabbed the bottle from my hand. He yanked on the refrigerator door and opened the nozzle on a five-gallon plastic container that took up half of the top shelf.

Here it was ... the miracle water. The secret of his strength, some claimed; snake oil, said others. Just water, the chemical analysis had revealed.

When my bottle was half-filled with water so clear it sparkled, he passed it back to me.

I considered the long, hot run ahead and looked doubtfully at the five ounces of water he'd given me.

"Is this going to be enough?"

"More than enough," he replied.

Then he put his mouth under the nozzle, took a long swallow and went out the door.

CHAPTER SIX

Blood From a Stone

The well worn single-track rose through dusty green sage and bleached tumbleweed straight across the windblown high prairie toward the distant mountainside.

I was running comfortably behind Cowboy Joe, glad for all of the long loops around Central Park that had comprised the bulk of my training. Although the sun was hot, the strong wind was cool and pushed firmly at our backs.

Then the trail steepened and soon I was drawing long, gasping breaths, desperate for oxygen. Topping a ridge to find even more challenging climbs ahead, I grabbed for my bottle and took advantage of the short downhill to draw a long swallow.

The crisp, invigorating fluid hit the back of my throat like an elixir from the gods. When we reached the bottom of the small slope and started up again, I was refreshed and ready.

Although my lungs were still working hard, I found some breath for talking.

"How far up?" I hoped that short, simple questions might get him to open up.

He held his opened right hand out where I could see it.

"Five miles?" I asked.

A nod was all I got.

My eyes drifted down from the dark gray of his head to his broad shoulders. The muscles moved smoothly, rhythmically, beneath his sun-darkened skin. Each stride was quick and confident, lightly touching the surface of the rocky trail.

"How old are you?" I asked, half expecting him to start flashing fingers at me again.

"Old," was his efficient reply.

But that wasn't the body of an old man running in front of me. There was an unprofessional part of me that wanted to run her hands over that strong back. I slapped her down and considered another question.

"Do you run up here often?" When he just nodded, I resolved to avoid any more yes or no questions.

"Where were you born?"

I waited for an answer as we topped another ridge. In front of us was a wide meadow that was still spotted with wildflowers. Beyond the meadow was our destination; a climb toward the forested mountainside.

An answer didn't seem to be forthcoming and I doubted if my lungs would provide enough wind for conversation once we hit that next steep slope.

"You know my publisher is paying you for your story. That means I need answers to my questions." I didn't spend twenty years in the newspaper business without learning to play hardball when I need to.

It looked like the muscles in his neck tensed and, for certain, the pace increased.

"New York," he finally answered.

At last, a fact worthy of note. I'd thought I'd noted the faint echoes of a New York accent underneath that western twang.

"City?" Oops, another yes or no question.

He nodded.

"You?"

That he had voiced a question surprised me ... and gave me hope.

"I was born in Kansas, but my parents moved to Maine when I was just a baby. I moved to New York City five years ago."

There, I thought. *That's how you answer a question.*

We were nearing the end of the meadow and I threw caution to the stiff wind.

"Is your name Franklin Wetherill?"

His stride faltered. Then it strengthened and he accelerated toward the mountainside.

There had been no answer, but the shocked face he revealed when he glanced back told me the name meant something to him.

CHAPTER SEVEN

Human After All

Hitting the slope, he pumped his arms and drove his knees into quick, short steps. I fell behind rapidly as we passed through a multitude of stumps that sprinkled the lower half of the slope.

He was soon out of sight and I continued up the trail alone.

It was probably how his competition had felt at the Tahoe Rim 100, Cowboy Joe's third 100-mile race. Three weeks after "the Laramie miracle," Tahoe was the first event where Joe had to face the running community without the cover of anonymity.

Scott Callahan, one of the best, and most liked, of America's ultrarunners told this story about his encounter with Cowboy Joe.

"He had this inner-focus going on that created a bubble around him … it made you give him space, ya know, like he was one of those Greek gods or something? But he was standing there at the starting line with that monster hydro-pack on his back. I just had to know.

" 'It's my water,' he said. Like I didn't know that.

"But I asked him, 'why carry so much weight? Haven't you ever heard of refills?'

" 'It's *my* water,' he said again, 'they don't have *my* water at the aid-stations.'

"I figured he had 80-proof in there, ya know? Cause you had to be a drunk to want to carry that much liquid to the starting line of a 100-mile race.

"So I asked for a swig—no one's ever accused *me* of being shy.

"It was water; but I'd never say *just* water. It tasted like something from the Garden of Eden or something. Pure. Man, it tasted … holy. When that race started, I felt like I had the power of God in me."

Callahan destroyed the course record at Tahoe by more than an hour … and was a distant second place.

Cowboy Joe and Scott Callahan ran together for thirty miles. When they hit the steep climb to Bull Wheel, Joe dropped Callahan like a stone.

And now I was experiencing those same "he can't be human" thoughts.

After a time I reached a stand of trees. My lungs burned and I was close to collapsing when I spotted him up ahead, sawing on a fallen log. Near him on the ground was a coil of rope, a hammer, a plastic jar of large nails, and the oiled-canvas bag from which they had been dumped. The heavy bag rippled in the strong wind, held in place by the hammer and nails.

Around us was a brown forest; Ponderosa pines killed by a beetle no bigger than a grain of rice.

I slumped against a nearby tree and took another swig from my bottle, wondering at its pure taste and the soul-deep refreshment it brought.

The saw cut through the log and a portion rolled away. Joe took a long piece of rope and used two of the long nails to secure it to the log. He pulled it toward the trail and left it next to one already rigged in the same manner. It was then that I realized that the wide dirt path all the way back to his stone hut was the result of hundreds of these logs being dragged off the mountain.

After I got my breath back, I stepped away from the tree and was about to ask what I could do to help when a loud crack was heard above the wind.

"Heads up!" Joe said.

I looked around, and then up toward the sound of breaking branches.

Like a barbed club swung by a giant bent on mayhem, a huge Ponderosa pine was plummeting toward my head.

Even if I hadn't frozen in place, there was no time for the "get the hell out of the way" message to pass from my brain to my muscles. It was a "life flashing before my eyes" moment. What I saw was long stretches of loneliness broken by camera shots of hard-earned rewards too brief to remember.

The shove to my back was like getting hit by a cannonball. I flew from under the falling tree and rolled clear to look back at a swirl of dust, pine needles, and bark.

When it settled, Cowboy Joe was there amid the bristling pine branches. He twisted his arm as he tried to get a look at the long cut that stretched from his shoulder to his elbow.

I couldn't tell if the scowl on his face was from pain or from the aggravation of having had to save the "writer-fella" from getting crushed.

"Let me take a look at that," I said as I walked back up the slope and around the fallen pine tree.

"It's nothin'… a scratch." Joe clenched his teeth and shoved his way through the branches. After stuffing his tools and supplies back into the canvas bag, he turned uphill and hung it on the branch of a tree.

I've never seen a man like Joe who didn't try to hide his feelings from a woman, or who would admit to needing help … ever.

"Blood is dripping off your elbow." I blocked his path when he turned back around. "You can't even see the cut. Stop being silly and let me examine your arm."

When a glare didn't move me, he tried to barge past. I put my hand on his chest.

"Pleas—" The word froze on my tongue just as fast as his body had stiffened at my touch.

Like a pillar of stone, he stood rigid, his eyes tightly shut.

I stepped around him and looked at the arm. It was just a long scratch, except for a three inch gash near his elbow that was oozing blood. Unclipping my bottle, I sprayed water on his shoulder and let it run down the wound. My running shirt was sacrificed to gently wipe away the dirt and blood. Then I folded it into a narrow strip and tied it over the gash.

"There, that should take care of it until we get back."

When I looked up Joe had opened his eyes and was staring at my white sports bra.

Then his eyes met mine.

"I may be old," he said. Something more than anger was in his voice. "But I'm still a man."

He looked down at his chest where my hand had left a print in the sweat and dirt.

"Ought not to be touchin' me like that."

∽

CHAPTER EIGHT

Down From the Mountain

"I can do it, damn it!"

With an unladylike grunt, I heaved against the rope and edged the log over the top of the short ridge. Joe's hut was now in sight on the prairie below and no marathon finish line had ever looked so good.

At the start, Joe had suggested hauling it down would be too difficult for me.

Although "leave it" were the only words that actually parted his lips, the implication was clear; I was a woman and not up to the task.

When he stepped into the loop of rope and started jogging down the trail, I did the same.

After hauling his own log down, he'd run back and tried to take my burden.

My quads were aching, I was hot and thirsty, and there were rope burns on my hands and waist, but I was not going to take his help, especially not with the end in sight. I took the last swig of water. It vanquished my thirst and stiffened my spine enough to finish the job.

"Go bandage that arm properly," I ordered. "I'll be along shortly."

"Muleheaded woman," he muttered, shaking his head. But down the trail he went.

I followed, dragging the log behind.

My stubborn insistence to go that last mile allowed me to prove to myself that there was within me a well of strength and toughness that had gone untapped for the first forty-one years of my life.

The pain and exhaustion I experienced were the price I paid for that discovery.

After a sponge bath and change of clothes, I had to do some bandaging of my own. But Joe's Dailymile friend was wrong. Even though my hands were a blistered pulp, it didn't keep me from working on my story.

That evening, Cowboy Joe made an obvious effort to keep his distance.

While I sat at the aspen table with my laptop and Googled Franklin J Wetherill, Joe, with a freshly-bandaged arm, began hanging blankets from the ceiling around my sleeping area. He'd changed into a buckskin shirt and jeans. It was as though he had dressed up for me.

For the first time, I saw his hair clean and combed. The vibrant dark gray was swept back into a loose ponytail; it made him look somehow regal and natural, like the rugged mountains visible through the window behind him.

Not for the first time, I fought stirrings that threatened to derail my concentration.

"You don't have to do that," I said, about the privacy screen he was erecting.

"Not doing it for you," was his gruff reply.

Shrugging my shoulders, I turned back to the screen.

The usual universe of useless hits showed on the screen. I started working my way through the 61,300 results for Wetherill.

Pay dirt was reached only after I was becoming bleary-eyed.

"Vanished— The Golden Boy of Wall Street ... Franklin Joseph Wetherill." Among a host of seemingly unrelated tidbits—and without any indication of the time-frame—the link referenced a magazine piece from *The New Yorker*. It was a tantalizing clue.

I had to get my hands on that article.

A clink on the table brought my head out of the computer and I realized that the sun had set. The ability to concentrate on one thing to the exclusion of others has always been one of my talents ... or faults, depending on your point of view. The few men I'd allowed in my life had concluded that it was definitely a fault; mainly because that concentration was rarely on them.

My mouth was watering before I realized that the scent of a sweet, roasted meat had permeated the room. Next to my computer was a plate holding a slab of dark meat, several paddle-shaped pieces of what looked like a grilled green vegetable, and a serving of something that looked like grits.

A chair scraped on the floor and I watched Joe sit at his computer in the corner with his own plate. Although a conversation over dinner may have furthered my own interests, I closed my computer, set the plate on top of it, and dug in.

The meat had a sagey, strong flavor while the vegetable tasted like tart green beans; the grits were smooth and filling. I was hungry enough that I devoured it all without a question about origins.

"Now that I've been a good girl and eaten all my dinner, how about telling me what it was?"

He turned away from his computer and the gleam of good humor that I'd seen in the ditch was there again.

"Pronghorn, cactus, and quinoa. Hope it suits ya, since it'll be ninety percent of the diet while you're here."

I almost missed the answer while I focused on counting the words. Nineteen! It amounted to a Cowboy Joe filibuster. Maybe this was my chance.

"Well ... it was delicious. Isn't it funny ... how running hard can make food taste so much better? Where do you get it?"

He pointed out the window and I worried that he was clamming up again. My shoulders must have visibly slumped, because his smile grew larger.

"Out there," he said. "I bow hunt every couple weeks. There's more Pronghorn in Wyoming than people. And the cactus? Well," he nodded out the window, "the variety we got at this altitude stays close to the ground ... because of this wind that never stops. If you step off the trail out there, you'll find it most everywhere, except in the field of quinoa I have down below."

It may have been the wind outside that I heard, but it sounded like ice breaking to me. And I noticed that the more he spoke, the less he used that folksy, western drawl.

"Since you're feeling so talkative, why don't you come over?" I gestured to the spot across the table from me.

"I won't bite." I watched his good humor begin to fade and pushed a little harder. "Don't worry, I'll only ask friendly questions tonight. We'll save the hard ones for when you've gotten to know me better."

Inside, I cringed at the flirtatious tone in my voice. It wasn't needed and I wasn't sure why it was there.

There was a resigned look on his face and it showed his years more clearly. He walked over and plopped down.

I moved the plate aside and my notepad took its place. While deciding on that important first question, I babbled.

"I don't know why, but I wasn't expecting this place to be so different from New York. And it isn't just that it's open and less crowded. I think it's more basic than that. The air here is so much fresher, and yet it challenges you … all the time. I know it's the same sun I saw in New York, but here it feels so close. It never lets you forget it's there; it's brutal at times.

"And everything is so dry. Back home in Maine, it sometimes felt like you couldn't take two steps without stepping in a creek or a pond or a lake. This land is so different. It's like I'm on another planet."

My chatter had succeeded in getting Joe to relax, so I asked an easy question.

"Why did you move here?"

He looked at the table for a time, considering his answer.

"I had tuberculosis." Joe kept his eyes focused on the table and spoke as if he was summoning up memories from long ago. "Used to go to Estes Park every summer; the air in New York was so dirty. My doctor was the one sent me west to the mountains … he said it would prolong my life."

His laughter … it was soft, almost rueful at first. Then it burst out in a sharp, bitter bark.

"Boy, oh boy. He sure had that right."

Joe pushed away from the table and went to the refrigerator. He filled two glasses with water from the jug.

With a deliberateness that seemed to challenge my vow to avoid the hard questions, he set the crystalline liquid in front of me. His eyes were locked on mine as he took a long swallow from his glass. Then he returned to his seat.

I took a drink and closed my eyes, savoring the crisp, cold bite of the water as it swept down my throat.

"It's just water." I said. "All the tests confirmed it. It isn't some magical elixir."

My vow was intact; it wasn't a question.

"Never said it was."

He leaned back in his chair and rested the glass on his lean stomach.

"Callahan, Elliot, Jensen ... they all believed. They *paid* you because they believed it was *more* than water." Again, it was a statement, not a question.

"Never said it wasn't."

There was a sparkle in his eyes and it wasn't a reflection from the glittering water. He was teasing me; trying to get me to ask the hard questions.

"But wh—" I caught myself on the edge. Not yet.

Besides my vow, I wanted to wait before I asked the hard ones because I wanted to learn Cowboy Joe's true identity first.

"Will you take me there?"

"The spring?" He smiled and took another drink. "Maybe ... we'll see if you can handle it."

Twice he'd guided small groups of ultrarunners to the hidden spring. Callahan was the one who'd pushed Joe to part with some of the water. They couldn't take any technology; no watch, no GPS.

They were blindfolded for parts of the rugged forty-eight mile run and still he only agreed after they'd signed confidentiality agreements that said what they could and could not do with the water they collected.

They could not have it tested. Could not sell it. Could not talk about where they got the water ... it was a long list.

They could drink it themselves was the one "could" on the list. And they paid good money for that privilege.

Only Sorvik had broken his vow. He'd come down from the mountain and shattered his left kneecap in a cycling accident the next week. Unable to run, he lost his Nike sponsorship. Cowboy Joe's water became a financial instrument.

CHAPTER NINE

Running Dreams

I wanted to get the conversation back to safe ground. And the story he had started to tell had grabbed my attention. The "holy" water had pulled it away. Now, I wanted to hear the rest.

"When did you move out here to stay?"

His face darkened, the smile was gone. At the time I wasn't sure why; I only knew that it wasn't as safe a question as I had thought.

"One summer, I realized how much I loved the mountains and dreaded the thought of returning to New York. I made plans to live in Estes Park full time."

The glass was set on the table and he folded his hands in his lap. With his head bowed, he continued. "Then something happened and I decided to come here instead ..."

"What happened?"

His chin was on his chest and this time I was sure he'd clammed up. So I pushed.

"C'mon, Joe. This is the kind of stuff I need to know; that you're being paid ..."

Joe jumped up and slapped his hand on the table.

"I don't want to talk about it!"

Then he stormed out the door and into the night.

Stunned, I sat for a few minutes and replayed the scene in my head. What happened to Joe in Estes Park was a pivotal occurrence in his life and might have bearing on the story I was writing.

I opened my computer, pulled up my e-mail and prepared a message to Lenny, my research assistant. It basically said, "Get me that New Yorker article or your ass is grass!"

Lenny required a specific type of motivation; no carrot—all stick.

Then I dealt with my inbox, checked the latest online news and spent some time surfing for Estes Park history.

Before long the day hit me over the head like a sledgehammer. I looked at my watch. It was one a.m. in New York, where I had started this long day.

I pushed away from the table, stumbled through the makeshift privacy panels and burrowed into the pile of blankets; in moments I was fast asleep.

How I came to be chasing Joe up the mountain while I was dressed like some 1920's Flapper was a mystery. But I knew I had to catch him or something terrible would happen.

I stumbled on a rock and looked down to see a solid floor beneath my feet. Joe was gone. I was still running, but my feet weren't the only source of movement. The train I was on was hurtling through low hills. Dashing forward from car to car, I started yelling "Stop the train! Stop the train!"

As I passed a window, I saw a platform flash by; the Stratton, Colorado sign was flapping in the draft of the racing locomotive.

After a long run, I reached the front. The engine compartment was empty and I had a clear view ahead.

Far in the distance was Joe, standing barefoot in his jeans and buckskin shirt. The rawhide tassels on the sleeves bounced wildly as he waved his arms over his head.

Then I noticed the deep chasm that separated the two of us.

There was no bridge. It had been swept away by a flash flood. The fear that rushed through me was as powerful as any torrent.

A jarring thump resounded through the soles of my feet and then the train was in the air.

I stared in horror as the raging waters below came closer and closer.

Then the thump repeated as I relived the fall, over and over again.

Finally, there was no thump, the train fell into the dark, raging water and I jerked awake.

After I untangled myself from the blanket pile, I rubbed my eyes and looked outside. Joe was standing next to a pile of split firewood, wiping sweat from his forehead. He was back in what I was certain was his normal summer attire; dirty running shorts and those tattered "work" shoes, a pair of Nikes that had outlived their useful mileage.

As if he could sense my eyes on his lean body, he turned toward the window and waved.

I waved back and stepped away from the window. Then I noticed, on the small wooden table, a white enameled-metal bowl of water, with a washcloth folded neatly over the rim. On a plate next to the bowl was a bar of soap surrounded by a variety of wildflower petals.

They brought a smile to my face.

Was this Joe's idea of an apology for storming out last night? Who would have guessed he could be so considerate?

I was about to wash the sleep from my eyes when the front door was opened and then slammed shut.

Joe's gruff voice floated over the blanket-curtain.

"Don't bother cleanin' up just yet. Git yer runnin' duds on. We're late gettin' started."

So much for considerate. And it sounded like the "cowboy" was back.

"What are we late for?" I called as I headed for my gear.

"Yer mornin' run." I couldn't see his face, but the sadistic glee in his voice was not well hidden. "You wanna gander at the spring, doncha?"

"Forizzle!" I thought to balance his western drawl with some ghetto slang. In a snap, I was in my shorts and tech top. I grabbed my shoes and headed out.

"Come again?" Joe said as I came through the curtains. While we'd been talking, Joe had gotten into his running shoes and slung a hydration pack onto his back. My water bottles were filled and on the table next to my belt.

"Yes, of course." I said, with an exaggerated, upper-crust accent as I sat at the table and put on my shoes. "I would like to view the source of your water."

Thrown off track, he shook his head. But his wicked grin quickly returned.

"Well, fer that ta happen, we gotta git you trained up."

He headed out the door. "From what I seen yesterday, that's gonna take a while."

Disappointed, I strapped on my belt, grabbed my bottles and chased him toward the mountains.

"What about breakfast?"

A chunk of some type of homemade granola bar was pulled from the canvas bag tied to his waist.

"This'll have ta do," he said as he passed it back. "Next time don' stay s'long in the sack."

The granola forestalled my hunger pangs enough to focus on the run, which was a nightmare and a fairy tale all rolled into one.

Twisting and rocky, the trail was the most technical I'd ever run. In places, I was scrambling on all fours up scree slopes that threatened to shift and send me tumbling down the mountain with every move I made. Then there was a steep, knee-destroying descent into a narrow cut that immediately began climbing again. Each step was an invitation for an ankle sprain.

I felt like I'd been running for hours before we reached a trail that could be considered runnable. It wound up switchbacks through the tree line and climbed to a secluded alpine meadow where the fairy-tale portion of the run began.

Greeting my arrival were wide fields of riotous color painted on a green backdrop bordered by glittering snowfields. Gurgling rivulets of melted snow turned into gushing streams and then plummeted over rock cliffs.

The water spray from the falls rose on the sun-warmed breeze and hosted a shimmering rainbow that faded in and out like a playful ghost wearing a cloak of many colors.

Above our heads, the frosted peaks carved geometric perfection from a canvas of flawless sapphire.

While Joe used the friendly terrain to increase his stride and loosen his muscles, I puttered along, in awe of my surroundings.

I had to relive the nightmare portion on our return journey, and it took time to add the right perspective to the experience. But, for the rest of my life, my soul will be lifted by the dreamlike memories of that first magical morning.

CHAPTER TEN

Quarrel For Another Day

Although I was tired and hurting for much of that run, the nightmare–fairy tale kept me from thinking about how far we'd come until the end was in sight.

Then it hit me.

My brain went through the calculation and then repeated it when the number made no sense. I'd arrived at the number thirty-seven ... thirty-seven miles! It just wasn't possible.

Joe ran on, as strong as ever, while I wobbled back on legs that had turned to jelly because of a number in my head.

I walked the last hundred meters so I could catch my breath. I wanted to have enough wind to blast Joe's doors off. For the time being, the fairy tale was forgotten. Never had I been so exhausted. He'd run my legs into an aching pulp.

"You are one sadistic bastard!" I said as I stumbled through the door and fell into a chair. "I'm probably crippled because of your insanity!" Dizziness cut my diatribe short. Even that little bit of anger took my breath away.

"Quit whinin'," Joe said as he approached me with a glass in his hand. "You just ran forty mountain miles in seven hours, how'd you think you'd feel?"

"I didn't *know* I was going to be tortured for seven hours, you maniac!"

"Oh, shut up!" He slapped the glass next to me on the table. It held a yellowish-green concoction that looked more like something that would come out of my stomach, not go into it. Then he went to the sink and shut off the tap.

For the first time I noticed the hose that stretched from the sink, across the floor and under the curtains. I don't know how I'd gotten past it without tripping.

Joe grabbed a crossbow and a handful of quarrels from a shelf by the door. He jammed the short arrows in the pouch at his waist. His jaw was set and he growled his next words.

"Goin' after dinner." He pointed at the glass. "Drink that and then git in the tub."

Once again he stormed out the door.

I was pretty steamed that he was escaping and I didn't have the leg strength to chase him and continue my harangue. The glass was in my hand and most of its contents down my throat before I was even aware of what I was doing.

My rising temperature was the first clue that something powerful was in the drink. Beads of sweat began popping out on my forehead and followed the salty tracks of their many predecessors from the long run.

The pain in my legs dulled slightly, enough for me to push out of the chair and stumble through the curtains.

In the corner made by the hanging blankets was a big galvanized tub. It was filled with ice and water. Next to it was a stool with a towel folded on top.

At the time, I was too tired to think about the effort Joe had gone through to relieve my pain.

Since the temperature of my skin was nearing that of the sun, I quickly stripped and stepped into the tub, expecting my body to melt the ice and turn the water to steam.

The tub was just large enough for me sit with my legs extended and tall enough for the water to reach my shoulders. I dipped my face forward and let some of the heat leach out.

Forty miles? Was that what Joe had said?

In all of his races, no one had been able to stay with Joe forty miles. All the big names in ultrarunning had shown up at Leadville that year, drawn by the rumors about Cowboy Joe.

Through the cool night air, they'd all gone after Cowboy Joe; Callahan, Dean Jensen, Neal Elliott, a half-dozen others. When Joe cruised through the first aid station at May Queen without stopping, they'd all grabbed what food and water they could and chased after him.

As the sun was rising, they held on to Joe as he coasted over Sugarloaf Pass. At twenty-three and one-half miles they reached Fish Hatchery and the pack dropped their first two pretenders.

Then they headed out into the bright morning sun and the heat rising off the blacktop of Route 300.

"None of us believed he could keep that pace," said Jensen, "but none of us wanted to take the chance of letting him go. When we turned onto Halfmoon Road, I was right on Cowboy Joe's shoulder."

"I glanced back at the faces of the guys behind us. They looked like it was a 5k we were running. Huffing and puffing. You could see the strain on their faces and we still had seventy-five miles to go. It was just plain crazy."

"Joe didn't stop at the Halfmoon II aid station either and two more dropped there."

"I told myself there was no way he'd skip Twin Lakes, thirty-nine and one-half miles without even breaking stride? No way! Not with a 3500-foot climb to Hope Pass staring him in the face. But he did … at Twin Lakes he dropped the rest of us."

"After Leadville, Scott, Neil and I would not be denied. We were going to find out his secret no matter what it cost."

I wasn't naïve. I knew that Joe hadn't been racing me, but still …

A different warmth developed inside me. Despite all the long miles I had logged training for this assignment, I'd never really felt like an accomplished runner; not really believed I was capable of such a feat. Forty miles!

With a smile on my face, I folded the towel into a pillow, leaned my head back and fell asleep.

CHAPTER ELEVEN

Flying Too Far

I awoke to the sound of rattling silverware and my own rumbling stomach. The water sloshed in the tub as I got my feet under me.

Before I realized it I was standing, amazed at how little I hurt. There were aches and twinges throughout my body, but I could move ... and without wincing. I'd been in more pain after the New York Marathon than I was now.

"Good thing you didn't drown, fallin' asleep in a tub of water like that."

I unrolled my ad-libbed pillow and wrapped it around me, then I wondered how to get out of the tub without getting water on the floor. That's when I saw that a new towel had been placed on the stool and a bath mat was on the floor by the tub.

A shocked squeak escaped before I could clamp my hand over my mouth.

"Didn't see a thing." Joe's voice floated above the curtains. The soft chuckle that followed made me blush.

While I dressed, the scent of food magnified my stomach rumblings and made me forget my embarrassment.

"What's for dinner?"

"Baked prairie turkey with chokecherry dressing, quinoa and gravy," There was a pause. "And green beans ... canned, sorry. Some things just don't grow so well up here."

"That sounds like a Thanksgiving feast to me."

"It is." He chuckled, louder than before. "I'm giving thanks that you managed to survive our run today, despite all that whining you did."

"Funny," I called. "By the way, I know you're pulling my leg with that prairie turkey crap."

I slipped on my Crocs and stepped through the curtain.

Joe had his back to me, pulling something from the oven.

"Okay, you got me. That's just what I call jackrabbit." He turned and walked toward the table. "They get pretty darn big out ..."

Halfway across the room he looked my way. His jaw dropped and he stood there in the middle of the room, looking very domestic in a faded-blue cook's apron, holding the black roasting pan between two green oven mitts.

"... here," he finished with a gulp. Then he set the pan on a hot pad next to the rest of the food.

"You look nice," he said. I was certain his neck grew a shade redder.

I brushed my hands across my light-yellow tulip skirt. It and the lacy white top I was wearing had been packed "just in case" there was a chance for a night on the town. My straight figure didn't have much in the way of curves, but what I had, the skirt managed to accentuate. I don't know what possessed me to wear it that night.

I could say that it was the aggressive reporter in me, working any angle to get my story. But I think that would be a lie.

Dinner was a quiet affair. I'd already seen that most ultrarunners regard eating as part of their training and consume a prodigious number of calories, leaving little time for conversation during a meal. As we both crammed in helping after helping of rabbit and quinoa, I realized I was learning from a master.

Despite the lack of words, it felt as though communication was taking place on some level. When our carbohydrate and protein stores had been replenished, we pushed away from the table satisfied with more than just the meal.

A connection had been made, I was sure. He was letting his guard down, beginning to trust me.

Joe went to his computer and tapped some keys.

Haunting, soft tones filled the room. It was as if someone had captured the rustle of a morning breeze through the pines, or the wind through the hoodoos in a desert canyon. Once corralled, those sounds were formed into notes ... and those notes made into a music so natural, the entire piece could have arisen whole from the bosom of the earth.

I closed my eyes, entranced. I imagined Joe asking me to dance with him to those slow, captivating sounds.

"What is that instrument?"

"Native American plains flute. Joseph Fire Crow playing." From a distance, his voice wove through the sounds and I opened my eyes.

There would be no dance.

With an open book in hand, Joe had settled into the rocker in the corner below the box with the items belonging to Franklin Wetherill.

My mental train jumped back on track and I remembered why I was here. I slipped into my own corner behind the curtains, plumped the blankets into the shape of a beanbag chair and settled in with my computer.

Lenny would have some results for me by now, I was sure.

Not.

His e-mail created mysteries instead of solving them.

Hey, Dylan!

Don't pull the plug on me, please! I'm doing the best I can. So far I've found eleven copies of the New Yorker magazine that should have the article in it. Yes, I did say "should." In each one, the article you're looking for has been neatly cut out. Got a line on another copy that I was told is intact, but you aren't going to like my expense report. I've got to fly to Toronto to track it down.

If you're reading this after nine p.m. eastern time, then I'm already in the air. I wish I understood why some article from 1929 is so important to you.

I'll e-mail when I know something,
Lenny

My head fell back and I stared at the ceiling, mentally cursing my luck and the money Lenny was wasting—1929! How did I get sucked into that dead-end? I thought about the article that had been redacted from so many copies and let my imagination run free. Maybe the search wouldn't be a complete waste. A novelist was what I always wanted to be and the mystery of Franklin Wetherill seemed like a perfect hook. And, somehow, it was connected to Joe.

I cast about for some other angle to explore when a snapshot from my dream the previous night popped into my head. Stratton, Colorado.

On a hunch, I added "train wreck." when I Googled it. "Stratton, Colorado train wreck."

Sweet! For once, the hit that I wanted was right on top. Wikipedia, you are awesome! It was there under "List of rail accidents, 1900–1949."

Despite being almost buried in blankets, the date and what followed made me shiver. I had no idea what was going on.

"July 18, 1929—Flash flood waters sweep away the Chicago, Rock Island & Pacific Railroad bridge at Stratton, wrecking a passing Rock Island passenger train. Ten bodies are recovered after floodwaters recede."

A particularly ghostly air came whispering from Joe's speakers. It took me back to my run through the doomed dream-train. Silk brocade curtains, richly upholstered benches and flickering lights beneath Tiffany lampshades flashed by the corners of my open eyes.

I was startled enough to slap my computer closed and lay it aside.

My heart raced until new, soothing tones wafted across the room and reached my ears.

Confusion still reigned in my mind, but another exhausting day had rendered me unable to work this through. Slowly, I let thoughts of this dream fade and the music lulled me to sleep.

After a time, I fell into a different dream; one I had often. Though asleep, a part of me groaned at having to live through this fantasy again; I already knew how it would end.

I was running across an indistinct landscape. If I ran perfectly, my arms and legs working in harmony, my heart believing it was possible, I could take longer and longer strides, amazingly long strides. With enough effort ...

I could fly!

It was hard and, eventually, I came back to earth. Still, those moments in the air felt so real. Pure. Sublime.

But my dream-self knew it was dreaming and that wonderful feeling wouldn't last, no matter how hard I tried to hold on. Soon each stride came with an agonizing, bone-deep exhaustion until it was like running in slow motion.

And then, when I was at my lowest point, I realized I was being chased by a dark shadow. I couldn't see it, couldn't turn around because the air was thick, viscous; restricting every movement. Only a dream, but still …

Ahead I saw something sparkle in the hazy air. If I could reach it, I knew I'd be saved.

I struggled desperately to move my legs, but it was hard, they hurt so much. And the shadow came closer. Every cell in my body experienced the desperation … each cell was paralyzed by the exhaustion I felt.

A cramp in my right calf wrenched me from the dream. One torture rescuing me from another.

Sweat was pouring down my face, the pain was that bad. A strangled cry escaped my lips as I tried to reach the bulging knot of muscle.

There was a loud rip, the curtain was swept aside and Joe was there. He flipped me on my stomach and grabbed my calf. For a moment the pain flared and I held my breath. Then his thumbs found the release point and pressed hard.

The pain ceased its escalating attack, staged a brief holding action, and then leaked away like air from a popped balloon.

"Ahhhhh!" My lungs added the matching sound effects when I was able to breathe again.

My tense muscles began to relax and I felt his hands start to pull away.

"No, please!" I begged. "Keep going."

Something more than pain was being massaged away and I didn't want him to stop until it was gone.

His fingers erased even the memory of the pain from my right calf and I had him do the left. When the calves were done, I tugged my wrinkled yellow skirt up further and had his magic hands massage my hamstrings …

Then I removed the skirt and top so my glutes and back could receive that same glorious treatment.

I don't know at what point his clothes came off, but when I rolled over, there were places that yearned for more than the touch of his hands.

And there was no going back.

CHAPTER TWELVE

Off the Deep End

"Get dressed," he said. "Time to run."

When he'd delivered that line I was still catching my breath after the frantic activities that had followed his massage. They weren't the most romantic words I'd heard from a lover, but at least he wasn't running out the door again.

Well, as a matter of fact he was, but this time I was expected to go with him.

The morning had not yet broken, only bent a little; enough that the path beneath my racing feet was a tenuous guide through an obscure landscape climbing toward a high, distant pass visible only as shadows against a sky of darkest blue.

Subtle, at first, was the growing brightness in the sky. On the trail above me, Joe slowly changed from a shadow to a silhouette and then to a man with form and features. This mimicked the transformation that had already taken place in my mind.

"We've got to push," he called back to me, "faster!"

I'd thought I *was* pushing. Six fast, uphill miles had already passed beneath us. Every muscle ached and my calf was twitchy, although I thought it would hold. Driving my arms harder, I reached deep inside with more confidence than I had ever had in my life.

I considered the forty miles yesterday, one for each year of my life ... and this morning with Joe. They'd demonstrated that my life had not started that long, downhill battle which inevitably ends in defeat. It was still rising toward victories that filled me with sweet anticipation, though I could not know what form they would take.

"Hurry!"

Joe was standing at the top of the pass, facing east; his hands extended toward the heavens as if awaiting a blessing from above.

I reached his side and saw the eastern horizon aglow; the sun about to begin its rise above the far mountains.

"Reach up, face the sun and close your eyes."

Joe sounded like a priest, a prophet in the wilderness.

"Use your mind to see the sun coming up ... feel it rising within your soul."

A rose luster lit the inside of my eyelids as the rays of the sun broke free of the horizon and hit my face. I stretched higher, every muscle straining to reach ...

I don't know what it was ... a sense of a door opening, a connection made ... something gentle, but powerful. It wasn't a thing I could see, or test, or prove. But, at that moment, it was real to me.

Through the soles of my feet, the mountain seemed to drain the aches from my body. Energy flowed from the sky through my upraised hands and renewed me.

"This awakening world is a new gift that God gives us every day. Accepting it imbues us with a power that sustains."

Somehow, it did not seem strange that Joe had transformed into this runner-philosopher who stood beside me. At that moment I realized that, all along, I'd been sensing a depth, a gravitas to Joe that was lightly hidden underneath his quiet and rough-hewn manner.

At that moment I felt in tune with the world.

"Open your eyes."

I did what he asked and the brilliant light overloaded my senses. Quickly shutting my eyes, I turned my head away. But for a split-second, while I was connected to that power flowing into me, before my sight was overwhelmed, I saw something miraculous.

It wasn't the sun or the mountains and it wasn't the blue sky or the blazing red clouds. Or maybe it was all of them. It wasn't my intellect that recognized the features, for there were none.

Yet, in that brief moment, my heart and soul leapt at what I saw ...

The face of God.

Our run off the mountain that morning was serene. I felt as though I was in the process of being remolded into a new person and welcomed the metamorphosis.

The sun rises every morning on a new day; a gift beyond reckoning that I had rarely taken full advantage of and never truly appreciated. Every day could start like this one, I thought; if only in my heart. I swore that it would.

When we got back, Joe told me he had to run into town for some supplies.

"How far is it?" I asked.

"Not far. Sixteen miles, give or take."

"There and back?"

Joe shook his head. "There. Sixteen back."

I couldn't believe it. We'd just finished a fast thirteen miles and he was all set to go out for another thirty-two; the last sixteen of that with a full backpack.

"Why don't I drive?"

"Nah," he said. "It'd take too long. That car would be an hour gittin' to the highway, then forty-five minutes to town. I can make like a crow, beat the car by fifteen minutes."

"But…"

"Besides, it'll be a good warm-up for our run this evening."

"What am I going to do while you're gone?" I almost choked on the words and felt silly for sounding like some love-starved teenager. Our encounter that morning had been physical only, I told myself. I was *not* going to fall for the guy.

"Cross-training." Joe pointed out the window at the jumbled pile of firewood. "Git all that wood stacked over by the furnace."

"That won't take very long."

He paused and looked around the room. Then he gathered his hair in a pony-tail and put on his cap.

"Ain't you supposta be a writer?" Joe slipped on his empty pack and looked pointedly at my computer.

"Well then … write."

And, once again, he ran out the door.

The wood was stacked and I was standing by the table staring at my computer with a glass of his refreshing water in my hand. I couldn't understand my reticence.

Sure, this was the first time I'd slept with a person I was writing about, but I was a professional. I'd keep digging and get the story done.

When I finally forced myself to log on, I found that Lenny had come through. Three JPEGs were attached to his e-mail.

An insistent part of me wanted to turn away from the computer, forget the article. What bearing could it possibly have anyway? But a good reporter can't help but smell a story and, even if it wasn't connected to Joe, Wetherill's smelled like a winner.

The first picture was of the New Yorker magazine cover from November 30, 1929. On it was an art-deco drawing of a platform crowded with people waiting for an arriving subway car. The platform looked like the one from my dream, the one with the Stratton, Colorado sign. Silly, I know. Train stations all look the same and this was a *subway* platform.

Second was the first page of the article.

Vanished: The Golden Boy of Wall Street … Franklin Joseph Wetherill
By E. B. White
In the wilds of Northern Colorado, a mystery arises that confounds police and provides Wall Street a welcome diversion from recent woes.

Franklin Joseph Wetherill, the Golden Boy who beat the Market, has disappeared in the mountains north of Steamboat Springs, Colorado. The precise date and location of this vanishment is in dispute, as sightings of the recently reclusive millionaire have been frequent, and frequently unfounded, in recent weeks.

Steamboat Springs Chief Constable Vernon Simpson gave the following statement via telegraph:
WETHERILL FRANKLIN JOSEPH MISSING FEARED DEAD IN REMOTE MOUNTAINS OF PARK RANGE NEAR COLORADO WYOMING BORDER STOP WEATHER CLOSING IN AND SEARCH ABANDONED STOP LOCATION OF WETHERILL FORTUNE UNKNOWN STOP FOUL PLAY IS SUSPECTED AT THIS TIME END.

On orders from his doctor, Wetherill has been summering in Colorado for the past several years. This would have been Wetherill's first winter in the Rocky Mountain state.

A denizen of New York City until this summer past, Wetherill had been exhibiting erratic behavior since the tragic deaths of his wife, Clara and young son, Joseph, in the horrific Rock Island train accident near Stratton, Colorado on July 18 of this year.

Following the accident, Wetherill became reclusive and his position as Chairman of Wetherill Industries was called into question, as was his seat on the New York Stock Exchange.

On the morning of Thursday, October 24, 1929, Wetherill arrived unannounced at the Exchange, looking more a wild-eyed mountain man than a scion of New York society. Within an hour of the opening bell he had liquidated his entire investment portfolio, which had an estimated value above five million dollars. Some observers believe this event triggered the staggering market-wide losses whose ramifications are still being felt on Wall Street and around the country.

The World War I veteran was born in Hicksville, New York on July 1, 1888.

I clicked on the final file, expecting more of the article.

What opened on my screen was a photograph of Franklin Joseph Wetherill.

The portrait showed a well-dressed, intense man with strong cheek-bones, a high forehead, and shiny slicked-back hair. His skin was pale and unwrinkled.

Without a doubt, there were differences; this man looked sickly, he didn't have long hair or weathered skin. But the face in the picture was the spitting image of Cowboy Joe. And he was wearing the tie-tack from Joe's jewelry box.

CHAPTER THIRTEEN

The Grapes of Wrath

I felt like a snake, a turncoat, a two-timing Delilah without the guts to even face her Sampson. But Joe would not be back for at least two hours and I didn't know when I would have another chance.

With a touch that would make even the most proficient cat-burglar proud, I began to systematically search every inch of Joe's cabin, determined to learn his true identity. Did Wetherill survive? Was Joe his grandson? Great-grandson?

If it wasn't for his incredible ultrarunning success, I might believe that Joe was as old as sixty. But no sixty-year-old could do what Joe had done.

My first finds didn't help with the identity, but they were of interest. They were copies of the contracts Joe had signed with the eight ultrarunners who'd received his water.

The first four were dated August 29, 2010, a week after Leadville. This was the group that Callahan had led to Joe's door. Like me, the contract had committed them to spending two weeks with Joe. From what Neal Elliott had told me, they went through the same wringer into which I was still being pulled. Elliot put it this way:

"He had us running up and down mountains, dragging trees, hauling rocks for two frigging weeks! Said it was 'to see if you are worthy'.

"The kicker was when he gave us these empty five-gallon containers and we had to run twenty-four miles to fill 'em. And then we had to turn around and haul those heavy suckers all the way back.

"Everyone always wants to know where to find that spring. Couldn't tell you and wouldn't if I could. He stuck those blindfolds on us three times during that run, I guess whenever there was some landmark coming up that we'd recognize.

"Good thing, since that rat Sorvik would've sold that, too. Selling his water to *60 Minutes* was a stupid thing to do. It was hilarious when Anderson Cooper showed up at Joe's hut with those TV cameras and Joe just ran off into the mountains without saying a single word."

"After the four of us who had gotten Joe's water crushed the course record at Bear, I figured it made all the stuff Joe put us through worth it. I don't care what those tests say ... it was the water."

Sorvik and *60 Minutes*, the only two nails Joe's coffin needed.

Leadville had turned Cowboy Joe into an instant legend, a celebrity. At his next race, the Wasatch Front 100 Endurance Run, both ESPN and NBC Sports attempted to get on-air interviews with Joe, to no avail. He was like a ghost, with an uncanny skill for avoiding their cameras. They soon were calling him the Wasatch Sasquatch because of this elusive ability.

The Wasatch course had a total of over 26,000 feet of climbing. Sorvik and a few others tried to do what Callahan and his friends had done at Leadville, but with even less success. Joe left Sorvik behind at the Bountiful B aid station after only twenty-four miles. It was a point-to-point course and they never saw him again.

Joe's record-breaking performance at Wasatch was unbelievable ... and some people didn't. In this age when heroes in every sport are consistently pulled from their pedestals by the accusation of using performance-enhancing drugs, the perception of cheating alone was enough.

After the race, officials asked Joe to voluntarily submit to blood and urine tests.

"People were asking questions," said a Wasatch race director, "and we felt we had to do something to assure the integrity of the race ... and the sport."

Joe refused.

During the summer, a camera crew from *60 Minutes* had filmed footage of Western States, Badwater, and the Vermont 100 in preparation for a human-interest piece about the fast-growing sport of ultra-marathoning.

Wasatch was their first look at Joe and it was supposed to be the last film-ing before production of the segment began.

Joe's refusal raised eyebrows and changed the *60 Minutes* segment from a fluff piece into an investigation. Their interest fell first on the homemade granola that Joe used during races. Through some undisclosed method, they obtained a sample of the granola.

When that test did not turn up any banned or unusual substances, they shifted their attention to his water. Getting some of that turned out to be much harder until Sorvik's injury and subsequent financial need came into play.

By then, both Callahan's and Sorvik's group had paid out a total of $40,000 for the two-week session that ended with their receiving the promised five gallons. Another group was scheduled and there were even rumors that Cowboy Joe was going to market his miracle water.

The extensive tests that *60 Minutes* performed on the water and their resulting exposé on Cowboy Joe created a firestorm in the running com-munity. Although none of the tests on either the granola or the water had turned up anything incriminating, Cooper did a masterful job of convict-ing Joe for his refusal to be tested at Wasatch and portraying him as a hustler and con-artist. The piece called for drug-testing in what had always been a friendly, open, and completely unregulated sport.

Sorvik's suit for fraud was filed the day after the *60 Minutes* segment aired. Although the suit was eventually dropped, it helped drive Joe back into the wilderness.

And that's where my story stood.

I carefully slipped those folded contracts back inside Joe's copy of Steinbeck's *The Grapes of Wrath* where I'd found them. Then I noticed the handwriting on the inside of the front cover.

Franklin J. Wetherill, 1939.

Ten years after the Wall Street "Golden Boy" had disappeared.

The faded dustcover showed the back of a slump-shouldered man in a brown shirt and overalls. Beyond his battered Model T a line of wagons and cars were crossing a dusty valley toward mountains of shaded blue that offered the promise of a better tomorrow.

It was a first edition.

Books are a passion for me and I knew this one was probably worth $15,000.

I worked my way around the room studying his collection of books and their inscriptions.

Some Came Running—*Franklin J. Wetherill, 1957*

A Wrinkle in Time—*Franklin J. Wetherill, 1962*

Wetherill would have been seventy-four years old in 1962. It was improbable, but he could have fathered Cowboy Joe that late in life. Little did I know I was about to step from the improbable into the bizarre.

The next book I picked up was *Roots: The Saga of an American Family*. It also had the handwritten inscription—*Franklin J. Wetherill, 1976*. I moved on.

The Color Purple—*Franklin J. Wetherill, 1982*

The Pillars of the Earth—*Franklin J. Wetherill, 1989*

Besides living to a ripe old age, Wetherill had maintained an active mind and an eclectic taste in books.

The Girl Who Loved Tom Gordon—*Franklin J. Wetherill, 1999*

If Wetherill was really Joe's father, he had lived to an incredible 111 years old. I was amazed!

Amazed, but not yet finished. I picked up another familiar title.

The Da Vinci Code – *Franklin J. Wetherill, 2005*. It seemed impossible!

Then I looked at Joe's rocker in the corner. On the seat was the book that Joe had been reading last night.

The Wise Man's Fear. It looked brand new.

With trembling hands I picked it up and opened the front cover.

Franklin J. Wetherill, 2011

CHAPTER FOURTEEN

All In

Reporters are like poker players and politicians in at least one way; they are good at not letting their true feelings show on their faces. I was holding five jacks and they were grinning back like loons. It was probably a winning hand except for the fact that it was also an impossible hand. I wasn't sure what to do with it.

It was ridiculous that I had even started to consider the possibility that this man was 123 years old. What I was dying to find out was why he had written that name and those dates inside all those books.

But it would require a few days for me to get my head around this latest clue. In the meantime, there were questions I could ask that would fill gaps in the story I'd written.

Earlier that day we had pulled another couple logs off the mountain, then cut, split and stacked the wood. I'd had an easy day of it and for once wasn't struggling to keep my eyes open. Less than thirty miles running ... yes, I was downright peppy.

I savored the last bite of Joe's antelope & quinoa stew and pushed my plate away.

"Why'd you sell the water, Joe?" With a room full of first editions that were possibly worth hundreds of thousands of dollars, I was sure it wasn't for the money.

For once he didn't scowl or even hesitate.

"Wasn't tryin' ta sell it. I thought ta scare those fellas off." He shook his head and chuckled. "There was a day when five thousand was a fortune.

They're just runners. I figured they'd be on the nut. Those guys had to be crazy to pay that kind of money for a little bit of water."

"On the nut?" I asked, "What does that mean?" His language seemed antiquated.

"Pinched. Busted ... flat?"

My puzzled look was fading too slow for Joe.

"You know ... poor."

"Ok. So you tried to scare them off and it didn't work. But then you did it again ..."

"Yeah, well. I've been alone for a long time. I guess those ultras got me used to people again. When Scott and his crew showed up here, I found I liked having some folks around, other voices on the trail."

The simmering hiss of locusts in the prairie filled the silence that followed.

"It's one of the reasons I agreed to this arrangement with you."

Evening had crept in and was sucking the light out of the room. What remained lit the silver streaks on Joe's inclined head, while the rest remained in shadow.

In the dusky room, I relaxed; my poker face was no longer needed.

"Why didn't you take the blood test? What were you using?"

Silver lines shimmered and bobbed as his head shot up. I was glad I couldn't see the hurt in his face.

"I wasn't takin' nothin'! Never! There's reasons why I don't want to take no blood test and they're my reasons. I don't have to explain myself to nobody."

"But you should have defended yourself ... said you were clean and denied the charges."

"I may be isolated out here, but I do have the Internet. I seen how the media works nowadays. No matter what I said, they'd cut it up and use it however they saw fit. I wasn't gonna give them any words to work with."

"But your running ... all those races, the records; you left it all behind."

"I still have the running. As much as I want; when and where and how-ever long I want to go. I never cared about the races ... or winning. I just wanted to see what I could do out there."

"Was it the water? Is that what made Callahan and the others improve so fast?"

Joe's laughter filled the night-veiled room and drowned out the locusts. The clap of his hand on the table echoed around the room as he fought to control his mirth.

"Those fellas, they were nice enough, except for that Bobby. But you'd think their college educations would have provided a small touch of common sense."

"I brought them up here; worked their tails off for two weeks. Nothin' here ta do except run, eat, and read. Then I sold them on the belief that they were gonna run faster. And they did."

"So it wasn't the water?"

"Didn't say that."

"Joe!" I felt like throwing my glass of that water in his face, the teasing rascal.

"Honey, you're gonna have to decide that for yourself."

I had a lot to think about and many decisions to make in the days ahead. But they wouldn't be made tonight.

Sitting there in the dark, I sipped some of the water and savored the clean bite of it washing down my throat. I hadn't felt this good in years.

Sure, I was tired from the work and sore in places; but it was a pleasing soreness, one that provided evidence of the work I'd done and the improvement that work would bring.

Then I remembered how Joe's hands had worked that soreness out of my body this morning ... and the deeper pleasure that had replaced the pain.

I stood up and walked around the table behind Joe's chair. My heart was pounding in my ears, adding a bass rumble to the sibilant murmur coming through the windows.

That beat quickened when I laid my hands on the warm steel sinews of his shoulders.

"Joe," I said. "I owe you a massage."

CHAPTER FIFTEEN

Believe It or Not

With an effort, I put off thinking about the mystery of Franklin Wetherill and enjoyed the days that followed as one rolled into the other.

We ran to the sunrise every morning; ran again before lunch; completed the day with a run in the evening. We ate what the land provided and Joe continually demonstrated a talent for making it taste good.

During the lulls between running and eating, we cut wood or worked on a senseless stone wall Joe was building in the middle of the prairie. From the looks of it, Joe had been hauling rocks down from the mountains for years.

"Why a wall all the way out here?" I asked.

"Cause it's there," was his preposterous reply.

"Joe!" I screamed in frustration, "It's *there* because you're building it *there*!"

He smiled brightly. "That's right!"

There was some mystical nonsense mixed in with the solid, common-sense way Joe lived his hard, isolated existence. His approach to life was a hodgepodge of the logical and the arcane.

For ten minutes at a time, twice a day, he would perform a series of five exercises. He seemed to hold himself in an almost spiritual state while spinning, flexing, or arching in a precise manner.

When I asked about it, he told me:

"It's just something I picked up when I was traveling around as a young man."

He often meditated before dinner while lying head down on his thatched roof and he fasted one day a week, drinking only the water from his spring.

I think now he was trying to give me a glimpse of something important, something magical; to share a part of himself that he had never shared before.

The pretense of moving slowly from massage to sex was dropped after that first day. Joe discovered I was willing ... more than willing. After that, it seemed as if he was making up for lost time.

It's amazing how good the snow beside those high mountain meadows can feel to a naked body after a long, hot summer run.

Joe opened up more each day. He talked about his love of books and shared his knowledge of the mountains and prairie. I learned about adventures he'd had through the years with bears and mountain lions, avalanches and lightning storms.

There were hours of conversation and I learned that there was not a fraudulent bone in Joe's body.

I also learned that no man had ever really listened to me the way Joe did.

One evening he asked me, "Why aren't you doing what you want to do?"

The question came out of the blue and left me floundering for words.

"I ... uh ...what do you mean?" I asked weakly.

"You have an imagination that makes your eyes sparkle when you're using it. And you have a way with words that doesn't really fit a journalist."

He leaned toward me across the table.

"I wonder why you aren't writing the Great American Novel instead of chasing around dead-end stories like this one."

The way his eyes met mine, I felt like I'd been invisible my whole life and a person was seeing me for the first time. The glib lie that I was happy with my life and career died in my throat.

"I will someday. Maybe not a great novel, but hopefully a book people will want to read and enjoy."

"Steinbeck gave me a line somethin' like that. Know what I told him?"

John Steinbeck had worked odd jobs while living in New York in the mid-1920s. Franklin Wetherill had been living in New York during the same period. And then disappeared in 1929 less than one hundred miles south of where we were sitting.

Franklin J. Wetherill, 1939
Franklin J. Wetherill, 2011

His unguarded statement had set my mind vibrating like a tuning fork struck against a rock-hard, and totally implausible, reality. The phenomenon must have caused a noticeable shaking of my head that Joe took for a "no."

"A week has seven days in it, I told him ... none of 'em are named 'Someday'."

After a moment of silence, Joe noticed my shock and realized that the name Steinbeck had caused it.

I didn't have time to determine whether it was amusement or fear I saw in his eyes because he closed them and pulled away from the table. Then he covered his face with his hands and just sat there, silent.

"Joe," I said when I had recovered my wits, "you can't expect me to believe that you knew John Steinbeck."

Then it hit me.

The old picture that looked so much like Joe, the engraved jewelry, the footlocker, the inscriptions in the books ... even my dreams seemed to confirm what my mind was telling me was impossible. My mind might have carried the day and found plausible explanations for all of the evidence. But it would not have mattered because something deeper had already decided.

I did believe.

It was like Newton getting beaned by the apple.

Only my apple was 123 years old and weighed 160 pounds.

CHAPTER SIXTEEN

Life in the Storm

Thunderstorms develop rapidly in the high plains. This one had formed and raced over Joe's little stone cabin with impressive speed and awe-inspiring power. The temperature dropped twenty degrees in only a few minutes and a sudden wind drove the cool damp air through the room.

Billowing curtains snapped as Joe and I rushed toward the western windows. As quick as the wind arose, it just as quickly subsided before we got all of them closed.

The front had pushed up against the mountain range in the east and stalled.

There were a handful of fat raindrops that soaked quickly into the thirsty ground, followed by a few minutes of hail that pinged off every hard surface.

Only when the drumbeat of hail ceased did I hear the low growling that was coming from beyond the windows. Looking out I saw the prairie landscape in ghostly white flashes as the rapid strobe of lightning made the shadow of the house appear and vanish in abrupt, uneven pulses. The steady, deep rumbling was the unbroken thunder-song of the storm.

I crossed the room and opened the front door on a panoramic view of a clash of titans.

When I took a step into the dark and looked up, what I saw was beyond the technological wizardry of any movie-maker, more powerful than the armaments of any nation.

Behind me, the western horizon had cleared and the sun, though already set, sent a wave of blood orange splashing across a massive bank of roiling gray clouds that were struggling mightily to tear down the mountains using an electric onslaught that lit the sky.

For an hour I watched the awesome display. Sometimes the jagged streaks of white would flash across the face of the clouds in brilliant strokes that followed one after the other across the sky. Then the lightning would return in the background and create a throbbing glow behind the clouds, revealing their anguished attempt to clear the lofty peaks.

"So much energy, so much ... life," Joe was in the doorway, watching the light show over my shoulder.

"Looking at this," I replied, "I could almost believe the earth is a living organism."

"Almost?" Joe said. He sounded hurt ... disappointed; as if I'd missed something important he'd been trying to teach me.

"After all those sunrise mornings when you felt that energy flowing through you ... how can you not *know* it's true?"

Since I'd arrived almost two weeks earlier, I had seen so many amazing sights, felt so many powerful emotions, and gone through such a physical and mental transformation that it changed how I looked at myself and my life.

And I had uncovered mysteries that bewildered me. There was no more room in my head for another. As the sky devolved into a whirling vortex of light and dark before me, I felt overwhelmed. I couldn't find the words to explain this to Joe.

"I just need a little more time," I said, "time to think all this through. How can it be? How can you be that old?"

Turning my back on the storm, I spun around to face him.

"I need to know wh—"

The doorway was empty.

CHAPTER SEVENTEEN

Tempest Tossed

I can't clearly express all that I was feeling when I saw Joe at the top of the pass.

Relief was part of it.

I'd turned around to confront him the previous night and found him gone. Not in the doorway and not in the cabin. How he got by me was just another mystery for which I didn't have an answer. A minor one compared to the others facing me. After waiting hours for his return, I'd finally fallen asleep.

Disappointment was another part.

The time remaining for us was short, and I had missed my last chance to greet the sunrise and feel that mystical energy flow through me. I'd awoken to an empty cabin and the sky beginning to brighten. A note on the table had sent me out the door in a race against the rising sun.

When the rays of that sun revealed Joe's body in dark outline as he reached for the sky, I was still on the slope far below.

There was a healthy dose of anticipation in what I felt that morning.

We would be running to his mysterious, hidden spring that day. The source of the water that, despite the negative tests, a few still believed was imbued with some extraordinary quality. I'd been revived and invigorated by just a swallow, but that wasn't what interested me the most.

Was the water the reason for Joe's incredibly long and healthy life?

Sadness was in the mix, too.

After our long run to the spring and back, I would be packing up. Before sunrise the next day, I would be on my way to Denver and the flight home. At that point, I was just becoming aware of the fact that I did not want to go.

Finally, there was anger. Joe owed me answers and I'd gotten very few. The ones I *had* received only generated more questions.

When I reached the pass, Joe was already gearing up. He'd brought everything that we would need for the journey to the spring.

"It'll be faster if we leave from here," he said. It was apparent that he didn't want to give me a chance to explain or apologize. "Even so, we'll be all day gettin' there and back."

He handed me an empty five-gallon container with custom backpack straps attached. The one he had on looked twice as big. I shuddered to think how heavy it would feel when it was full of water.

I shrugged it on and turned to find that Joe was already headed off the ridge, angling away from the trail that would have returned us to his cabin. The steep mountainside was draped in morning shadow as I gave chase and all my concentration was needed to keep from tumbling down the rocky slope.

And so it wasn't until we were deep in the mountains that I'd gathered my thoughts enough to consider talking to Joe about the previous night.

But, before I could decide on whether to start with a question or an apology, Joe began to speak. Though I was running behind him on the trail, his voice was strong and clear, as if the mountain itself amplified his words and brought them to my ears.

I had no way to record those words, but the facts of his story are so gripping, I could never forget them. Here is my poor attempt to fashion them into a narrative structure. But only Joe's voice, echoing from the dramatic mountain landscape where they were first delivered to me, could ever do these words justice.

"I was born in Italy, in a small mountain village called Campodimele. My parents were Giuseppe and Rosa Addona; I was given my father's name. Two years after my birth, we left Italy from the port of Naples on the *Neustria*, bound for New York.

"It was a crossing plagued by storms and disease. My mother was lost at sea, swept overboard by a rogue wave. My father died of dysentery in the ship's dispensary as we were docking at Ellis Island. I arrived in America orphaned and alone.

"It was a cool, clammy evening and dense fog surrounded Ellis and the thousands of anxious immigrants awaiting the start of their new life.

"Manhattan was a mass of ghostly tendrils in the glowing mist across the mouth of the Hudson. Above it all, the dome of the Pulitzer Building was a beacon, the newly crowned tallest building in New York.

"November 29, 1890, had been a miserable day for Joseph Wetherill. He'd spent a tense afternoon and most of a combative evening dealing with labor issues at his company's construction facility on the island.

"As he was walking along a street of mud on wood planking that served as a sidewalk, what weighed heaviest on his mind was his wife, Adaline. A week earlier she'd suffered her third miscarriage and doctors had performed a tubal ligation in order to prevent further pregnancies. They were both approaching forty years of age and had no children ... no heirs.

"When I escaped from the morgue where they had taken my father, I was probably confused and scared out of my wits. Who knows what I was thinking? I certainly have no memory of the moment I met Joseph Wetherill.

"He once told me that, when I raced out of that alley, I looked like a miniature Oyster Burns, barreling for home plate. When I tripped and landed face first in the street, I completed the charade and splashed mud all over his new English Grain Creedmors.

"Name and age was the only information immigration officials had been able to get out of the frightened little orphan. Many immigration officials Americanized names as a matter of course, so they told the man who pulled me out of the mud that my name was Joseph. It seemed like fate.

"Joseph Wetherill had money, influence, and the power to circumvent rules when he chose. I was adopted the next day as Franklin Joseph Wetherill."

Though the sun was climbing higher in the sky, Joe had kept us in the shade of the mountains as he wound through a succession of canyons, each narrower and deeper than the one before.

He hadn't blindfolded me yet, but I'd been so captivated by his story that I had run along without paying any attention to where I was going. My brain was bubbling with questions but Joe didn't pause long enough.

"Before long, all memory of my Italian roots faded. By the time I was four years old, Joseph and Adaline were the only Mom and Dad I could remember.

"It wasn't until I graduated from Fordham in 1911 that my father told me about my birth parents. That fall I began a trip around the world, pushed out the door by my father. 'To discover yourself,' he said. I was gone for two years.

"In Campodimele, I found long-lost relatives with whom I had little in common except blood. Some of them were over one hundred years old and it was then that I discovered that Campodimele is also called the 'Villaggio per Sempre Giovane'—the Forever Young Village.

"After a time, I moved on, traveling wherever my internal compass would point; Africa, China, India, Siam, Japan. I was like an iron filing and the old places of the earth were the lodestones that drew me forward in my journey.

"Along the slopes of Mount Catherine in Egypt was a group of people who still held to the ancient practice of purification through fasting. Three days a month they would abstain from all food, drinking only water and lotus tea. During a time when the average life span was fifty years, these folks often doubled that.

"When I continued further east, I found another community where longevity was common. It was a Tibetan lamasery, high in the Himalayan Mountains. In a stone temple among the icy spires lived a group of spry, active monks who claimed to have the secret for life without end. They believed in spinning wheels of energy that affect the aging of our bodies and they taught me five yoga exercises that they said would keep those wheels spinning properly forever.

"I was in Japan when news of Hiram Bingham's discovery of Machu Picchu in the Andes led me to Peru. There I found myself less enthralled by the 15th century ruins than I was by the village of active centenarians living nearby. They attributed their long life to the ancient grain quinoa that was a staple of their diet.

"It might sound as though I spent those two years of globe-trotting obsessed with finding the fountain of youth, but it isn't true. I'm just telling you the parts you need to hear. You have to remember that when I left, I was only twenty-three years old. For certain I had my share of hare-brained adventure and foolish excess. I was still of an age when I thought death couldn't touch me.

"Boy, was I wrong."

CHAPTER EIGHTEEN

Joe's Story, Part Two

Joe and I worked our way silently through rocky switchbacks on our way toward the crest of a knife-like ridge. The sun had cleared the mountaintops and there was no shade in sight. Only the katabatic wind flowing out of higher, snow-covered crevasses provided some relief.

I guessed that we'd been on the run for three hours or more. Even considering how slow the going had been through the narrow canyons, I was sure we would be nearing the spring soon.

Despite my fatigue, I was anxious for Joe to continue his story.

"How did death touch you, Joe?" I asked.

"Hush!" he replied, "not here. Death is close enough without talking about it."

We crossed the sharp ridge and began angling down a long, loose talus pile that led into a bleak, gray box canyon. The talus looked like jagged teeth and the walls of the canyon held a yawning gap, dark and close. The mountain was waiting for one false move so that it could chew us up and swallow.

Every step sent pieces of scree chittering down the slope. It sounded like the devil was impatiently tapping his fingernails on a stone altar as he waited for the sacrificial offering.

Joe was right. I held my breath many times during that scramble down, as death stayed near.

When I reached the bottom safely, I looked back and wondered if we could make it up again carrying the weight of the water from the spring. Then I gazed down the arid space enclosed between the high gray walls.

The sun was nearing its zenith but the eastern wall leaned sharply to the west, leaving that side of the narrow canyon in shadow.

I spotted Joe on his hands and knees at the far end. He'd removed the water container from his back and was pushing it along. As he crawled into the shade by the canyon wall, he remained visible for a moment before disappearing into the solid rock like a ghost slipping through a closed door.

Rushing to the spot where he had vanished, I found a waist-high cut in the granite, hidden by the contours of the rock face, just a darker shade of gray in a wall of shadows. It was only a crack at the top, but widened enough toward the bottom that a person could squeeze in.

"Come on in," Joe called. Though his voice seemed to come from a great distance, his disembodied hand reached out of the rock and beckoned.

I knelt and peered into the stygian triangle. His hand vanished into the inky void and I could hear scuffling sounds as he moved deeper into the hole.

"This isn't quite what I had bargained for, Joe," I said. I don't care much for pitch dark or tight spaces. Putting the two together made me more than a little nervous.

"It widens a little beyond the opening," He sounded closer, now that I was level with the gap in the rock wall. "We don't have too far to go, just follow the sound of my voice."

Pushing my own container before me, I crawled into the bosom of the earth.

As I shuffled along, the passage did widen like Joe said. But the light from the outside world faded and the darkness pressed down, arresting my attempts to move forward.

"Listen," Joe had stopped, too.

Although his voice was near, I could not see him. Then I realized that I could no longer even see my hand on the floor beneath my face. I looked back at the speck of light so far behind me.

"I'm not sure I can do this." I forced the words from between my clenched teeth.

"Just listen," he repeated. "It's the sound of the spring."

I held my breath and could just make out a faint, watery bubbling. It was like a language that I couldn't quite understand and it came from the direction in which we were crawling.

"I won't lie to you and say we're almost there," Joe said. "But you can hear it and, if you stay with me, you'll get to see it."

"All the others came this way?" I asked.

"Yep. 'Course all those fellas had blindfolds on. They didn't know where the heck they were goin'."

Joe laughed and the sound rang through the tunnel. "I suppose some of them mighta chickened out if they'd had to face their fear like you're doin'."

The idea of working so hard and not reaching my ultimate goal was difficult to swallow and Joe's laughter had tempered the effect of the oppressive dark.

I shoved the container forward and hit Joe's feet.

"Good girl," he said in response and began to move forward again.

Soon he renewed his story.

"My two-year excursion around the world had shown me how resilient and long-lasting life could be. During 1917 and 1918, in France and Italy, I learned how fragile it was and how quickly it could be taken away.

"I'd returned to the States in the fall of 1913 and joined my adoptive-father's business. Once the United States entered World War I, I enlisted and was on the first ship that landed at Bordeaux.

"In the trenches, there were so many ways one's life could be stolen; sniper's bullet, exploding shells, chlorine gas, trench foot. Even a thing as simple as an infected cut from the jagged top of a ration can was often deadly.

"I saw friends and enemies alike swept away by all of these, but the Spanish Flu was the killer that struck the closest. After the Armistice on November 11, 1918, I returned home in time for the funeral of my parents; brought down by a virus that killed far more people than all the wars of the 20th century combined.

"A stoicism that I'd developed during the war served me well as I threw myself into the work of Wetherill Industries. For five years I was blind to everything except that which would make the company more successful.

"Clara Mellette saved me from becoming a 1920's Scrooge. We were married in 1924 and in 1925 New York's population became the highest in the world. My son, Joseph Addona Wetherill, was the most beautiful addition to that total in March of that year.

"In those years, almost every man in America thought and felt like I did. More and better was the ticket. The economy was growing by leaps and bounds and the sky was the only limit."

There was a moment of silence and my container knocked against Joe once more.

"Let's take a break," Joe said.

I was wrapped up in his story and about to protest when I realized that my sore knees and tight back were screaming for relief.

"Use your hands to find a spot on the wall that isn't too rough and sit back for a few minutes."

It was eerie how I'd grown accustomed to this utter darkness. My mind had accepted that I was blind and allowed me to function with the resources I had at hand. Each breath he took and movement he made was clear to my ears and brought an image to my mind. As the bubbling sound of the spring grew stronger, the scent of the air had also grown sweeter, more moist.

When I had found a comfortable spot, Joe resumed his story.

"It was in '27 that I developed a cough and started to lose my appetite. Tuberculosis, my doctor said. I was shocked. When my coughs began to bring up blood, he started sending me to the mountains to avoid the dirty air. For the next two years I recovered enough during the summer to survive another year.

"In the spring of 1929, when my handkerchiefs were again being stained red and I didn't have the strength to walk my son to the park, I decided that this was not how I wanted to live. I was not even forty years old and I had no intention of surrendering my life without a fight.

"I left for Estes Park and ordered construction of a new, permanent home for my family in the mountains. While the majestic structure of stone and stucco was assembled on a ridge above Estes Lake, my mind searched back to my days after college; to the places and people I had found throughout the world.

"Their location among the mountains of the world was one common thread, one that I had now incorporated into my life. But I began to apply their other secrets to my life as well. My recovery was swift and soon I was an active part of the construction crew.

"Driving the workers hard and sparing no expense, the home was set for completion on July 19. On July 7, I sent for Clara and Joe."

CHAPTER NINETEEN

The Water of Life

The silence that followed was complete. My breath was caught in my chest and my heartstrings tightened. In my mind I could already see the train plunging into the rain-swollen gorge. I was prepared for heartache and tears. Joe's ... and my own.

But something changed at that moment. I sensed the darkness become a comforting blanket. It felt as though we had been pulled together and cradled in arms so strong that the approaching sorrow would only touch our hearts, not overwhelm them. Truly, the earth was holding us close.

His voice continued in a whisper, but the words were clear and controlled, as was the sorrow.

"My wife and child never made it to Estes Park.

"The darkness around us now is like the sun upon the mountain on a cloudless day compared to the black pit of despair into which I fell. Thoughts of a long life ... any life ... became torture to me. I wanted my life to be over as quickly as possible, but there was always some part of me that thwarted my many attempts to end it."

I wasn't surprised. That elemental strength that I sensed in Joe would abhor the thought of suicide. He gave a small sigh and I could feel the stirring of air in the passage.

When he went on with the story, his voice was stronger.

"Memory of those days is mercifully weak. Frustrated by my inability to take my own life, I contrived a plan to get help. Man's inhumanity to man is well known and can usually be relied on, especially when large sums of money are involved.

"Dissolving all my assets resulted in a substantial amount of cash. As I returned through Denver to Estes Park, I took steps to make a certain element of Denver society aware of all those millions I was dragging around with me.

"As I had planned, my journey into the mountains was watched from a distance by a shadowy crew of rough-looking characters. I was disappointed when they hadn't struck while we were making our way along the river in Big Thompson Canyon. It seemed a logical place to dump my body.

"I continued generally north and west on whatever old mining roads I could find, driving my Stanley 740 Roadster through snow that piled higher as my pursuers and I wound deeper into the mountains.

"This was the beauty of my scheme. Either I would die at the hands of the criminals that were behind me, or I would succumb to the brutal elements that waited ahead.

"I drove for hours until the road finally ended, then I pushed ahead on foot with the duffel bags of money slung over my shoulders. As night came creeping in, snow began to fall. I struggled on, blind in the whiteout and happy in the knowledge that my death was fast approaching.

"But it wasn't meant to be. You know … best laid plans and all that.

"I awoke, groggy and exhausted, in a small cave. Water was bubbling from a fissure in the rough wall to my left and flowing into a deep crystal pool. Reflected in the surface of the pool was the dim light from a crack in the rock above my ahead. On my right were the ashes of a fire; a seared portrait of Ulysses Grant revealed the source of the fuel. The full duffel under my head let me know that at least I hadn't burned up all the money.

"I don't know how long I'd been asleep, but my muscles ached and my throat was parched and dry. Leaning forward, I put my face to the pool and drank. The water was like nothing I'd ever tasted. One sip left me refreshed and gave me the strength to get to my feet.

"Two passages led out of the cave. The one on my right was short and dark. In the weak light from the crack, I could see where I'd dragged the duffels into the cave. That is how I'd entered. From the taller passage on the left came a feeble glow.

"Walking toward that faint light, I soon came to another entrance. It was high above an isolated valley deep in the mountains. Sunrise was approaching. Above my head, the mountain in whose depths I had slept was revealed by a brilliance that descended the cliffs in a cascade that drove the shadows away.

"As the sun pierced the horizon, I reached up toward the light, closed my eyes and felt its warmth move down my arms and across my body. The soul-crushing weariness that had held me for months drained away and all thought of death evaporated in the radiant sunshine."

While Joe spoke, the scene came easily to my mind; I'd welcomed the sunrise at his side so many times during the past two weeks.

"Let's go see the spring," Joe began to move down the passage once again.

My stiff muscles complained, but I followed without hesitation, no longer afraid of the total darkness. As the bubbling sound grew louder, Joe finished his story.

"That duffel full of money allowed me to lead a simple, isolated, and anonymous existence for decades. I learned to fend for myself and live off the land, or rather, live *with* the land. My time was spent trekking through the mountains, listening to the wind, communing with the earth.

The runs into town were rare ... and short. Few people would recognize me from one visit to the next and there was no name to attach to my face. I was always a stranger.

Changes were slow to reach that little town, but as they did, I incorporated them into my life where it was practical. Sometimes I was even ahead of my time. The Jacobs Wind Turbine I put up in 1931 was the first in Wyoming.

Books were the only medium through which I learned what was going on in the world beyond the high plains. I was thankful that the owner of the general store was an avid reader. World War II, the civil rights movement, the moon landing; they were all just obscure events whose impact I knew only by inference in the literature I read."

We turned a corner and the dark was no longer complete. Ahead of me I could see the faint outline of the soles of Joe's shoes.

"Didn't you ever stop to wonder why you weren't getting any older?" I asked.

"My existence was timeless, so I'm not sure when I realized that my body wasn't getting older. By then I was using all of the so-called 'secrets' of long life that I'd learned in places like Tibet, Egypt, and Peru. And I added a couple of my own; the water from the spring, the sunrise greeting."

"Don't you know what is keeping you young?"

"No," was Joe's simple reply. "Is it genetics? The five rites? Quinoa? Fasting? Is the spring I found the Fountain of Youth? Could it be the power of the earth that touches me so frequently?"

He stopped and leaned against the wall. The light had grown strong enough for me to see his face. For the first time, I recognized the hard-won wisdom in his gentle smile.

"Imagine that your life is in balance. You hold in your arms a selection of items that help you keep that balance, that harmony. Would you drop one of those items by the wayside simply for the sake of knowing which one is the key? If they are not a burden, why would you even consider it?"

His smile broadened because he saw from the fervently reverent expression on my face that my attention was no longer on him or his question. It was, instead, on the vision that was revealed to me when he'd moved to the side of the passage.

A gesture from Joe sent me crawling eagerly past him and into the cave alone.

The sun at high noon was casting its rays through the narrow crack in the ceiling. Streams of light cavorted and caromed through the room, inspired by the rippled surface of the crystal pool and brushed lightly with the hues of a prism.

Joe had brought me through the tunnel when the spring was at its most magical.

He stood behind me and put his hands on my shoulders.

"Listen," he said. "Do you hear that?"

Wind pushed down through the high, narrow crevasse. Soft tones ebbed and flowed through the room, singing a duet with the sparkling water as it murmured and trickled from the rock. The colorful light danced around the room in rhythm with the haunting music.

"I can hear, Joe." My voice was barely above a whisper.

What I was hearing shook me to the core. The message was simple, and yet, so much was wrapped up in those three words. They scared me.

Joe wrapped his arms around me. I could feel his smile against my neck.

"What is it saying?" He already knew, I'm sure. He just wanted to hear the words from my mouth.

At first, I couldn't respond. Those three words would take away so much of what I had made of my life. They would change everything. I didn't know what to say. But years of training had taught me what to do.

I lied.

"I don't know," I said.

CHAPTER TWENTY

All Dreams Must End

I watched with painful regret as a sliver of dawn crept up to touch the horizon and betray the distant mountains which had hidden so well under the moonless sky. A multitude of stars twinkled and called "look how magical we are" in an effort to distract me and delay my leaving.

But my packed duffel was already in the rental car. For forty years I've lived with the comforts, responsibilities, and expectations of a fast-paced modern society. These two weeks have provided a glimpse of a different way of living; a wide abyss separates the two. How do you just step from one life to another? I haven't found a way across that chasm.

If I was staying, Joe and I would be preparing to leave for our run to greet the sunrise. He has asked me to stay in a dozen different ways; none of them required words.

Joe told me once that spoken language is overrated. I believe he's right. So often what comes out of our mouths doesn't reflect what is in our hearts. Sometimes it is even true of what is written on a page.

Humans have come to rely too heavily on words for communication.

In the dark, a woman may lay her hand upon a man's face to read the emotions written on it. A lover without voice to speak may draw a bow across the strings of a violin and express his devotion more clearly than any other sound.

This reliance on words is leaving us deaf and blind to the other forms of connection we have with the world.

The myriad ways in which communication can take place in nature is astounding and goes far beyond words.

Have you ever stood on a mountaintop on a cloudy day and watched a patch of sunshine glide across the far green hills in the valley below? Or sat along a rocky brook and listened to the water as it babbled, gurgled, and splashed among stones worn smooth by eons of babbling and splashing? Have you knelt in the crashing waves of the ocean and felt their irresistible power? Walked among an aspen grove and heard the quaking of its leaves? Have you ever had your face touched by a refreshing breeze on a hot day?

Joe showed me that the earth is a living organism, the beating heart of nature; vastly intelligent and adaptable in its own way. It speaks to us all the time. For thousands of years, man understood the earth when it spoke, when it revealed itself in the natural world. But the knowledge gained led to hubris; man began to listen only to himself and lost the ability to hear or understand the wisdom of the earth.

One man has recovered that ability. It is revealed in how lightly he lives upon the earth. It shows in the elemental force of his running. The years prove it in how slowly they wear on him, like water over solid rock.

Words on a page are not able to pass on the wisdom Joe has attained; they cannot confer that capacity to understand the language of the earth. You must first be in a place where the beauty and voice of the earth can be experienced; a place where it has not been dug up or destroyed by the ceaseless manipulation of mankind.

And then you must have the heart to listen.

DENVER NEWS POST
July 21, 2011
New York writer presumed dead in car accident
A wrecked Nissan Sentra that had been rented by New York writer
Dylan LeClair was recovered yesterday afternoon from the rain-swollen
waters of an unnamed ravine west of Stratton, Colorado. Sheriff August
Kenton from Carson County stated that LeClair became disoriented dur-
ing a severe thunderstorm and crashed through the railing of the Interstate
70 bridge. Search and rescue officials believe that her body was swept
away by...

From: submissions@pspublishing.net
To: runnercowboyjoe@gmail.com
Dear Mr. Joe,
Although this work of Dylan's is not the investigative reporting piece
we were expecting, our fiction editor has expressed an interest in publish-
ing it. Our legal department has informed me that this is within our rights,
since we had, prior to her death, contracted with her for the manuscript.
Thank you for forwarding it.
Sincerely,
Elise Feagler
Submissions Editor

Epilogue

Joe leaned against the rock wall and studied the solitary figure as it crossed the prairie toward his cabin. Though turning red, the sun was still bright as it hung between the clouds and the western horizon; but dust and tumbleweeds, driven by the approaching thunderstorm, obscured his view.

He wasn't sure if he was ready to welcome another outsider. The ache he'd acquired as a result of his last visitor would be a long time fading. Although his body was still strong and his eyes keen, he felt the burden of his loneliness more acutely than he had since the loss of his wife and son eighty-two years before.

The temptation to run off into the mountains and hide was strong. But the lightning would start soon and, here against the house, he was out of the stinging wind. So he moved to the doorway and waited as the sun touched the mountains, painting the prairie a delicate rose that softened the turbulent gray of the thickening clouds.

There was a bandana tied across the runner's face to guard against the dust; hat and sunglasses lessened the sun's last glare. Driving strongly across the final yards, the lean figure stopped in front of Joe, and, for a moment, stared into the man's startled eyes as the first drops of rain started to fall.

"Who are you and why are you here?" Joe said, with an uncertain frown on his face.

Dylan had anticipated this moment from the instant she'd started the long run from Stratton after watching her car plunge off the highway. Starting a new life with Joe meant erasing her old one.

"I'm here because I did understand. When we were at the spring ... the voice in the wind and the water." A rumble of thunder accompanied her words. She lifted her hands and face toward the clouds. "Even now I can hear the words."

The frown was transformed as the sunglasses and bandana came off.

"What the earth was telling me that day ...

"Stay with him." Dylan stepped under the eave and into his arms as the hail came. They both heard applause in its rising clamor.

About The Author

Michael Selmer was born and raised in Maryland. He and his wife, Kathleen, moved to Wyoming in 2010. In his leisure time, he runs and reads, both to excess. He has run numerous marathons, including Boston and, in August of 2010, completed the one hundred mile Race Across the Sky in Leadville, Colorado.

The Author's working life has been a smorgasbord of careers and occupations: UPS driver, mall cop, maintenance man, cabinetmaker, woodturner, master electrician, business owner, and more. All his life, he dreamed of being a writer. Writing was something he dabbled with in the little spare time he had while he and his wife raised their four children. With the children grown and bringing along families of their own, the urge grew to take that leap of faith into a writing career.

In January 2011, the stars aligned and circumstances finally allowed Selmer to pursue his passion. The result was like the bursting of a dam- the 125,000 word rough draft for his debut novel *Harvest of the Heart* poured onto the page in just seven weeks. With the help of Bill Thompson, who has worked with such authors as Stephen King, Peter Straub and John Grisham, Selmer honed his craft and his manuscript.

Released in December, 2011, *Harvest of the Heart*—the first book of *The Elsa Chronicles*—has received excellent reviews, setting the stage for his short story collection, *Running Scared*. Next up is *Avenging Angel*, the sequel to *Harvest of the Heart*, scheduled for release in the fall of 2012.

For more information about Michael Selmer,
visit his website-www.Michael-Selmer.com.